Lucky Chica

ALSO BY BERTA PLATAS

* * * * * * * *

Cinderella Lopez

Friday Night Chicas

Lucky Chica

* * * * * * * * * *

BERTA PLATAS

 St. Martin's Griffin 🐾 New York

LUCKY CHICA. Copyright © 2008 by Berta Platas. All rights reserved. Printed in the United States of America. For information, address St. Martin's Press, 175 Fifth Avenue, New York, N.Y. 10010.

www.stmartins.com

Book design by Susan Yang

Library of Congress Cataloging-in-Publication Data

Platas, Berta.
   Lucky chica / Berta Platas.—1st ed.
     p. cm.
   ISBN-13: 978-0-312-34174-9
   ISBN-10: 0-312-34174-1
   1. Lottery winners—Fiction.   2. Hispanic American women—Fiction.
  3. Life change events—Fiction.   4. Self-realization—Fiction.   I. Title.
   PS3616.L38 L83 2009
   813'.6—dc22

2008030151

First Edition: January 2009

10 9 8 7 6 5 4 3 2 1

ACKNOWLEDGMENTS

Much gratitude to my long-suffering and always supportive editor, Nichole Argyres, and her fab assistant, Kylah McNeill. I love you guys. And I wish to thank the helpful folks at the Georgia Lottery Commission for their assistance in understanding how to claim a big lottery prize. May we all get to experience it first-hand one day, though not all at one time, or we'll end up with seventeen bucks apiece, like in the film *Bruce Almighty*.

Lucky Chica

CHAPTER ONE

* * * * * *

Won the lottery? Don't quit your job!
Plan before you stop that steady paycheck.
—*The Instant Millionaire's Guide to Everything*

Rosie Caballero rushed up the stairs of her apartment building, her heels echoing against the worn concrete risers, a tattered dog leash loose at her side. At its other end Tootie bunny-hopped up, poodle dreads bouncing, no doubt eager to get out of the cold that made her arthritic joints ache.

The little dog was probably nostalgic for the days when she'd been carried up and down the stairs by Rosie's mother.

Tough, Rosie thought. Tough on the dog and tough on her. Mami was gone and the two of them had to pull their own weight. She glanced at her watch.

Only fifteen minutes until Lana unlocked the front door at Cartwright Office Supply, and the knowledge made the key shake in Rosie's anxious fingers. If she was late to work it would be the third time this week and she would catch hell *and* get a letter in her file, so of course the decrepit lock was stuck.

Rosie jiggled the key, pulled on the door, then tugged up on the knob until she heard the click of the tumblers, a trick her father had shown her when she was just starting high school and was given a key of her own.

Before then her mother had been there to greet her after school, but at fourteen Rosie was considered old enough to stay by herself for a couple of hours in the late afternoon, and Mami had gotten a job with *los chinos,* what all of their Spanish-speaking neighbors called the Chinese-run dry cleaners' that had been a fixture on Buford Highway long before the rest of Asia and Latin America had discovered its cheap rents. The perfect place to start a business, a family, and a new life in America.

It had worked for her grandparents and their children, who had come in the mid-sixties and had become Americans as soon as possible, although they'd never let Rosie or her cousin Cheeto forget that they were from Cuba.

The minute Rosie unsnapped the dog's leash, Tootie ran inside, headed straight to the old bed pillow by the couch, and flopped over onto it, giving a good impression of a doggie faint. Rosie tossed the leash toward the dinette table, then glanced around at the empty apartment to make sure everything was as it should be. Too quiet, like the rest of her life.

She pictured her mother standing at the kitchen counter, chopping peppers in quick, precise strokes of the sharp knife, like the professional cook she'd always wanted to be, the smell of simmering onions and spices strong enough to make passing neighbors swoon from hunger.

"Like your Abuela taught me, when I was little in Ciego de Ávila," Mami would say, so that Rosie would remember, or maybe because she feared that she would forget her own birthplace.

Now Mami would never get old enough to forget, Rosie thought. She kissed two fingers and touched them to the beautiful couple in her parents' wedding picture on the wall, careful not to touch the funeral card that was tucked into the frame.

Anamaría Suárez and José Antonio Caballero. Rosie had never read the back of the card, refused to. She'd stared at it blindly on the day it had been tucked into her nerveless fingers, just before they'd left for the church, and she'd put it in the wedding frame. Maybe it was superstitious not to remove it, but everyone had their little *manías*, as her Abuela always said.

Rosie pulled the door closed and rushed back down the stairs and across the faded, crumbling, age-pocked asphalt parking lot.

It hadn't looked this bad when her parents were alive.

Of course back then they considered the apartment a temporary stop on the road to home ownership. Papi had just been promoted to line manager at the General Motors plant and she and Mami had been busy planning her college wardrobe.

They'd been four weeks away from closing on their house, a sixty-year-old bungalow in Decatur, on the train line. Rosie would be able to get to Georgia State University in fifteen minutes, giving her time to have a part-time job at Cartwright Office Supply, too, even though Mami and Papi had objected, saying that she needed to concentrate on her schoolwork.

She stopped worrying about schoolwork the night a truck driver ran a red light while her parents' Subaru was in the intersection, killing Papi and seriously hurting her mother. Everyone had said that he'd died instantly, that it had been merciful.

Mami had lived another two weeks, although the doctors said that she was not really alive. At last Abuela had consented to have the machines disconnected, and Mami's breathing grew harsh, then wispy, then stopped.

The coma had eaten up all of Rosie's college money. Rosie had promised God that she didn't need college if she could have her mom, and then Mami had died anyway.

The only thing she had left of her parents was the apartment and the little rituals that she'd shared with them. Eating black beans and rice on Friday nights, getting her nails done with Mami at Mirta's apartment downstairs, walking Tootie in the mornings and buying lottery tickets with Papi.

After, she'd gotten a job and although she hated it, she endured it, remembering the times Mami had come home from the dry cleaners', her face burned and hair frizzy from the steam.

"*Nena*, they can take your dignity, but your heart is inside. No one can see it. No one can touch it, unless you let them." Mami had winked at her, a hint of the sassy girl she'd once been. "*Los chinos* work just as hard. They are not mean, it's just hard work."

Rosie heard her mother's voice repeat those words often, in her memory, and she used it to shield herself from pain. When the other girls at work all went to lunch together and didn't invite her, when her boss Lana yelled at her because she'd gotten some detail of a spreadsheet wrong, or passed a phone call to the wrong person, Mami's voice soothed and armored her.

She was going to need that strength this morning, because she was not going to postpone checking her weekly lottery ticket, especially after last night, when a five-dollar bill had magically blown onto her shoe just as she'd thought she'd hit the lowest point ever.

The sun had just topped the trees now, and their silhouetted branches were dotted with buds that would soon swell. Spring in Atlanta was lush and beautiful, but today's harsh wind made it seem far away.

She hunched her shoulders against the unusually bitter March cold and hurried along the uneven dirt path that bordered Buford Highway. The city's big push to build sidewalks hadn't reached here yet. On the opposite curb was her destination, Mr. Kim's bodega, open for business and already busy.

She waited to cross the street, picturing Mami beside her, holding her hand, making her feel safe, just as she'd done when she was a little girl. It had been two years since the accident, but sometimes it felt as if it had happened yesterday. Or worse, that it would happen tomorrow, and she wouldn't be able to stop it.

Rosie glanced at her watch. Eight twenty-five. Lana, her clock-watching boss at Cartwright Office Supply, would be standing in the reception area at eight thirty sharp, arms crossed over her skinny chest and eyes shifting from her wristwatch to the front door.

Lana's bad temper was legendary. Rosie would have to slink in, smile an apology, and slide into her chair. She had extra reason to suck up to Lana.

Today was payday, and Rosie was so broke that yesterday she hadn't thought she'd have enough money to pay for Tootie's dog food. Luckily, when she got off the number-30 bus in her little dance dress on her way home last night, a sudden gust had slapped a damp five-dollar bill around her ankle. It was a sign from God, she'd thought, and she'd raced into Mr. Kim's to buy a lottery ticket two minutes before the ten thirty P.M. cutoff.

Afterward she'd regretted it, although she had enough left to get a couple more cans of discount dog food.

That she could afford to give Tootie a meager supper didn't offer her any consolation or make her feel better about the night's events. Her crush Rick had ditched her long before their date had ended, as if she'd been a casual pickup at the dance club and not someone he'd known for months.

She'd had a crush on Rick ever since she met him at the diner where her cousin Cheeto hung out with his landscaping coworkers. He always paid attention to her, looking right into her eyes when they talked. He was thrilling, five years older, already working at a job that paid a lot of money. A catch, she'd been told, although Cheeto warned her that he was a player. He couldn't be. He was handsome and classy, and very different from the other men she knew. Not rough like most of the other guys in the area. He was no mega-hot star Brad Merritt, either, but who could complain about that?

Cheeto laughed at her movie star obsession, but then, he laughed at everything, and Rosie had been the one smiling when Rick had finally asked her out. She'd totally forgotten her Brad Merritt craziness as she prepared for the date. Mami's friend Mirta had lent her a nice dress, and her high-heeled sandals from Payless were only three years old, and she'd coaxed her straight hair into a cute updo with Mirta's help.

Rick's eyes had been wide with surprise when she opened the door, and she'd felt confident that this would be a date to remember as she'd followed him down to his car. Two hours later, he'd spotted his old girlfriend, Nieves, on the dance floor, and he'd ditched Rosie. He'd turned away from her as if he didn't even know her, and when she'd followed him to ask why, he'd glared at her and told her to take the bus home.

She'd been too humiliated to tell anyone. She'd whispered Mami's words as she waited for the bus. More of her typical bad luck—get what you want, and lose it anyway.

She knew she should wait until noon to check her ticket, when she walked to Tower Liquors to cash her check as usual, then rush to el Value—the Big Value Supermarket—to pay her utility bills so that her power and phone wouldn't get cut off. She'd have just enough left to pay her overdue rent, and if she ate some meals at Abuela's house, she could make it to next week's paycheck.

She hesitated, stepping aside for a woman pushing a stroller over the rough ground to pass her, her baby bundled up in blankets. Rosie pulled her old quilted nylon coat closer to ward off the wind. What would it hurt to check it now? She was already late for work.

Music blasted through the bodega's glass door and front window, weird for this early in the morning. She knew the inside would be warm and steamy with the smell of nuked burritos, the favorite breakfast food of hurried workers, but usually Mr. Kim played the news.

Her mouth watered at the thought of a hot burrito, limp from the microwave and leaking orange grease, but until she cashed her check at lunchtime she had no money. She'd grab a cup of coffee at work and put extra creamer and sugar into it.

She pulled the little paper lottery square from her pocket

and held it up to compare it to the winning numbers Mr. Kim had posted in his window.

This morning, Mr. Kim's big block letters read: 14-23-03-16-7 MEGA BALL 5. Below he'd scrawled, $600 MILLION! Six hundred million dollars, a ridiculous amount. Enough for six hundred people to be millionaires. The ticket fluttered in the wind and she grasped it more tightly and compared the numbers to Mr. Kim's impromptu poster.

It was a match.

She stared at it for a second, then checked the number again and again, holding the ticket with fingers that no longer trembled just from the cold.

"Let it be real," she whispered. Her shaking fingers smoothed the crumpled MegaBucks lottery ticket and held it higher. Had her eyesight gone blurry?

She glanced around. The neon signs of the liquor store on the opposite corner, dim now in daylight, were in sharp focus. So was the check-cashing store and the *botánica* next to it, the vacant discount shoe store and the cars pushed against the white crosswalk, edging forward, waiting for the light to change. There was nothing wrong with her eyesight.

Her heart beat faster and her fingers trembled. She blinked and focused on the numbers in front of her again, holding the crumpled slip next to the posted winning numbers. She wasn't seeing things. *Dios mío,* it was true. Her mind raced with all of the ways her life would change. She wouldn't ever have to skip paying a bill, or sigh over clothes she couldn't afford.

She could tell Lana that she'd never answer the phone for her again. And her grandmother wouldn't have to be a hotel maid, and her cousin Cheeto could give up landscaping, working outdoors in all kinds of weather. She had to tell them. Joy turned to paranoia, and she snatched the ticket back down and looked around quickly.

None of the bored drivers in the city-bound morning logjam seemed to be looking at her.

Life seemed normal. Next door, a small knot of guys huddled together in the parking lot of the gas station, waiting for day jobs. On the opposite corner, Dog the crack dealer was lurking, sipping from a fast-food coffee cup, seemingly impervious to the chill wind. No one looked at her or the lottery ticket in her hand.

She hitched her tote bag higher on her shoulder and stuck her head in the bodega's door, and was immediately hit with the scent of spicy meat and corn tortillas from the corner microwave, and the blare of trumpet-heavy salsa. Mr. Kim was dancing with his wife, hands in the air. The narrow aisles of the store were crowded with well-wishers. Of course, she thought, the store that sold the ticket would receive a cash bonus.

"Mr. Kim, may I use your pen?" Rosie's voice had a little quaver, but not bad.

"What? I can't hear you. Come in. The burritos are on me this morning." Mr. Kim twirled his wife. "I sold the winning ticket, Rosie. Jenny and I are rich!"

Jenny Kim waved at her, grinning, still dancing her Charleston/salsa boogie.

"Congratulations." Rosie reached around the register for the blue ballpoint next to the "give a penny" tray. She turned the ticket over and signed the back, then tossed the pen onto the counter.

Her hand trembled as she refolded the ticket and shoved it back into her pocket, anxious to get away. She had to tell her grandmother and her cousin.

"Hey, that's the Fox News truck," someone behind her called out.

A camera crew? She pictured waves of people chasing her for her ticket and shuddered. She had to get out of here. She backed out of the door and pushed it closed before Mr. Kim could remember that he'd sold her a ticket late last night.

Should she go to work? Lana would yell at her, a good incentive to call in sick, but at the moment she was still broke, and she couldn't just abandon her job, especially on payday.

She'd work until lunch, collect her paycheck, then go to cash it and stop by Abuela's afterward to tell her the good news. This wasn't the kind of news you could tell someone over the phone.

It was her grandmother's day off from her hotel housekeeping job, and by noon her little apartment would be filled with her canasta buddies, but she could pull her aside to tell her she could quit her job. No more pushing the laundry cart, not ever again.

Rosie hurried down the street, the ticket seeming to burn in her pants pocket, her mind awhirl with plans. *Sign, redeem, and disappear.* That's the advice she'd heard in every TV interview she'd ever seen with lottery winners.

She needed a financial planner. And she needed to keep her mouth shut. Despite the cold, she felt sweaty, almost feverish. She glanced at her Timex. Eight forty. If she'd hung around the front of Kim's bodega a moment longer Dog would've thought that she was a competitor.

Doubt struck her. What if she'd imagined it? The light had changed, stopping traffic. She hurried across to the Quik Mart on the opposite corner. They sold lottery tickets, too. She'd double-check the numbers, just in case Mr. Kim had written them down wrong.

At the Quik Mart, she grabbed a preprinted lottery slip from the pile on the counter next to a display of the latest tabloid magazines. Brad Merritt, her favorite movie star, grinned at her from the cover, more luck. She knew everything about Brad, and it seemed he was smiling right at her.

"Hey, Rosie, heading to work?" Jorge Canoso's easy smile met her from above, where he was stocking the overhead cigarette rack. He climbed down from the ladder.

Darn. Jorge *would* be working today. She'd gone out with him occasionally, mostly because he looked like Jake Gyllenhaal, if she'd had a few drinks and squinted.

"What can I get for you?" Jorge asked.

She opened her mouth, and then quickly shut it again. She'd almost started to tell him. Instead, she snatched the tabloid with Brad on the cover and dropped it on the counter. "Just this."

The magazine flopped open to a story titled, "Won the Lottery? Ten Things You Should Do from *The Instant Millionaire's Guide to Everything*!"

She slapped her hand down on it, closed it, and smiled at him.

Jorge rang up her purchase, and she paid him with coins she'd dug out of the couch the night before, then shoved the magazine into her tote and ran around to the side of the building, away from the bustle of people pumping gas and buying coffee.

She glanced at the slip. No surprise. The MegaBucks numbers matched hers. She inhaled shakily and leaned against the red-brick wall.

As of this morning, she, Rosa Maria Caballero, was worth six hundred million dollars. Now what did she do?

CHAPTER TWO
* * * * * *

Sign that ticket, and don't tell anyone!
—*The Instant Millionaire's Guide to Everything*

There were three things Rosie wanted to do now that she was richer than anyone she knew:

1. Quit her job and tell Lana Cartwright and her brown-nosing Cartwright Office Supply employees that her days of being treated like a low-class intruder were over.
2. Shop at Tiffany's. Just the sound of the store's name was enough to make her heart beat faster. Her fingers, neck, and ears felt naked, but she'd soon make them sparkle. No more flea-market jewelry for Rosie Caballero.
3. Make Rick regret that he'd ditched her for Nieves. What should have been special had turned into one of the worst nights of her life.

She had no idea what to do next, except get to the office as fast as she could, then face the scolding awaiting her. She'd already been warned about her tardiness. Lana was probably drawing up Rosie's termination papers for job abandonment. She felt the old twinge of panic, even though she'd never again have to rush into the office, coat off and purse in her hand so that she could pitch them under her desk and look as if she'd gotten there earlier.

She'd only been working at Cartwright for a month when her parents had been hit by the truck that killed her father and put Mami in a coma. Lana's piggy eyes had narrowed when she'd asked if she could leave early to relieve her grandmother at her mom's bedside. She'd acted as if Rosie wanted to leave early to hang out with her girlfriends, instead of to sit by her mother, listening to her gasping breath as the ventilator pushed air through her dying lungs.

Despite the doctors, Rosie was sure that her mother would wake up, if only to say good-bye. Lana looked at her disapprovingly and said, "Do what you have to do." Which turned out to mean "I won't forget what a slacker you are."

Rosie imagined stepping out of a stretch limo and walking into the office wearing furs and diamonds, and not the little rings and earrings her boss flaunted as if they were the crown jewels. Rosie would wear real carats, and lots of them.

She laughed, a strangled chortle that made a passing woman walk a little faster. Rosie stepped carefully around her, not wanting to pitch into traffic and become a hood ornament before claiming her prize.

At the corner, she waited impatiently for the light to change, thinking how ironic it was that she was sitting on millions, yet she was on foot, her rent and utilities were overdue, and she was in danger of losing her job.

She had a quick image of going to the Cash Advance store to get a fast 50 percent interest loan against six hundred million.

Not likely, and she'd have nothing until she claimed her winnings at the lottery office downtown. She needed this paycheck, or she'd be living under the bridge at Jimmy Carter Boulevard, a homeless multimillionaire.

Storm clouds followed her as she hurried up Buford Highway. The coming rain meant that Cheeto was probably at Harold's Diner up the street. Landscapers usually got rainy days off, with no pay, of course. She walked faster, feeling lighter on her feet. Cheeto's landscaping days were over. She couldn't wait to tell him, but first she had to get to the office.

Cartwright Office Supply occupied a squat gray concrete building with offices in the front and a warehouse in back that was filled mostly with the photocopy paper that was their bread and butter.

The dark-tinted glass hid the interior. Rosie hurried up the short sidewalk and pushed open the jingling door. No hope of sneaking in.

As expected, Lana stood under the wall clock that read nine o'clock. She looked at her watch, then pinned Rosie to the floor with a glare, pivoted on her short heel, and stomped back to her office.

Rosie took off her coat, carefully transferring the ticket and the winning-number slip to her wallet, then stashing it in her tote bag under the desk as she turned to hang up her coat.

Lana reappeared, followed by one of her toadies, a bland girl with limp, mousy hair and a malicious smile.

"Rosa, follow me. Pat will answer phones."

Pat kept her eyes on the phone, as if it needed to be watched closely.

Rosie calmly picked up the tote and shouldered it as she stood.

"You won't need that," Lana said.

"I don't want to leave it."

Pat stiffened and narrowed her eyes.

Rosie smiled at her. The ticket was already changing her life. Yesterday she would have been shaking and fighting tears, wondering if she'd ever get another job that paid as well as this one.

Lana's office was crowded with knickknacks, presents from vendors, but her desk was uncluttered, empty except for a personnel folder lined up in the middle, tagged with the colored stickers that corresponded with the first two letters of the employee's last name. This one was marked "CA." Caballero. Rosie's heart thumped despite her previous calm.

"Sit, Rosa." Lana waited until she was seated, tote bag on her lap like a shield.

"I'm sure this does not come as a surprise. You've been warned in writing about your tardiness, and today you appear half an hour late."

Rosie started to speak but Lana held up a hand. "Not yet." She launched into a speech about the team, company values, and blah, blah, blah. Rosie felt numb. She just wanted her paycheck.

"Am I boring you, Rosa?" Lana's sharp voice made her realize that she was nodding off.

"Am I fired?"

Lana's eyes widened. She looked down at the folder. "Well . . ."

Rosie stood up. "Then I quit." She held the tote bag like a baby as she walked out, followed by a sputtering Lana.

"You can't quit and decide to come back here, you know. If you leave, it's for good."

Rosie smiled at Pat, whose eyes were wide. "Move aside, Mousy. I still quit, Lana. I've had enough of you and your micromanaging ways." She grabbed her coat from its hook and pushed past Lana and into the March morning. The air seemed crisp and fresh, full of possibilities. Then she remembered she hadn't gotten her paycheck.

CHAPTER THREE

* * * * * *

Choose a financial advisor, and make sure
he or she is reputable. Don't let yourself be cheated!
—*The Instant Millionaire's Guide to Everything*

Rosie debated going back for the check, but kept walking. No use
spoiling a good exit, and Cheeto was getting paid today, too.
His check could tide them over until they claimed their prize.
Who cared if they cut off her phone? Tomorrow she'd buy a
fancy little cell phone, and one of those silvery cockroach-
looking things to put in her ear.

The bored drivers caught in traffic watched her stride by,
revitalized by her confrontation with Lana.

Little do you know, she mentally told the drivers, *I am your
dream come true, the person who hit it big.* She might have to
share the prize with someone who'd picked the same numbers,
but it was so much money that she didn't care.

She'd laughed whenever she heard lottery winners say that
they'd never stop working. Who were they kidding? As of today, Cartwright's Queen of Micromanagement was out one receptionist.

She'd need an honest attorney, but how could she know whom
to trust? The telephone directory didn't list them according to
integrity. Maybe the lottery people could recommend someone,

or Abuela might know. Rosie's grandmother worked in a fancy downtown hotel, and she knew a lot about how rich people lived. She stored away every little fact she overheard. Abuela could probably write a book about how to be rich.

Rosie imagined what Cheeto would say about her news. He'd always dreamed of being his own boss. He could do that now. They could all do anything they wanted.

She stopped in front of the battered metal-sided trailer that was Harold's Diner. She'd tell Cheeto first, if he was here, and they could tell Abuela together.

The windows were less grimy than usual, and between the heads of the occupants of the booths that lined the diner's front wall, she could see Cheeto at the counter, waving wildly, talking with his hands, as usual. The guy next to him shoveled food into his mouth, while the cook listened, a spatula in his hand. Rosie took a deep breath, and with her hand protectively shielding the ticket in her pocket, she climbed the three steps and walked in.

Harold's was always packed at mealtimes. The tinkling of the bell on the door went unheard in the loud mix of conversations and CNN blaring the morning news from a TV high up in a corner. The wind slammed the door closed behind her, pushing her.

She stumbled in, then recovered her footing and crossed the cracked linoleum toward the counter, where Cheeto was now slouched over a plate of eggs and bacon, listening to the craggy, skinny guy next to him. Some of his coworkers were sitting in a nearby booth, but Cheeto hated booths, hated feeling shut in.

"A Corvette, that's what I'll buy. No, make that two. Chicks really love 'em." The skinny man leaned closer and grinned. He was missing several teeth. He thought a Corvette would increase his chances with women? Pathetic. Major dentistry might make that happen. Might. He did remind her, however, that now she could afford to get her teeth whitened.

"Good timing, Rosie. Want to help out for an hour?" Fred the fry cook's thick Eastern European accent made him sound like Bela Lugosi. He was cleaning off a table, which meant they were really shorthanded.

"Not today." Not ever. She'd worked at the diner off and on for extra cash, but she'd never have to again.

Cheeto turned to face her, surprised. His round face, floppy brown curls, and big brown eyes made him look like a cute little boy. To her, he was an annoying younger brother. His many girlfriends described him differently.

His parents had died when he was little, and their grandmother had raised him. Abuela had begged Rosie to move in with them when Mami had finally died, but Rosie had refused. The tiny apartment held cherished memories of her parents. They'd dreamed of owning a house, of Rosie going to college, of retiring to the beach, and none of those dreams had come true.

"Why aren't you at work?" Cheeto tapped his heavy white china coffee cup, a signal to Fred for a refill.

"I decided to take the rest of the day off." Rosie dropped her canvas tote bag on the floor next to an empty stool.

"At nine in the morning?" Cheeto frowned and grabbed her elbow to pull her close. "Did you get fired?" His whisper was loud enough that Fred turned around to look.

Rosie pulled loose, embarrassed. "No, but something big happened. I'll tell you later."

"You can work for me, Rosie," Fred called. "I'll make room in the schedule for you."

"Thanks, Fred, but I'm cool. Really."

"Is it Rick? I heard he's back with Nieves." Cheeto's brows twisted and he clenched his fists. "I never liked that guy."

Rosie's stomach ached. Word had spread fast about Rick and Nieves. She wondered if last night's pathetic escape from the club was now part of the story.

"Is this your girlfriend, Cheeto? She's hot." The Corvette guy's eyes were on her, doing a mental clothes peel.

"She's my cousin, Grant, and you'd better back off."

"You threatening me, little boy?" Grant the Corvette guy stood up menacingly, skinny lips flattened to a straight line.

"Take it outside," Fred warned. He turned back to his grill. "Sheesh. It's only breakfast time."

"Yeah, dude. Calm down," Cheeto said. "Now what I want is a loaded H2 Hummer with a matching Mini Cooper as a spare in the back."

Corvette guy stared at him for a second, then grunted. "All size, no style." He sat down again.

Rosie didn't know if he was talking about the Hummer or Cheeto. She plucked the biscuit from Cheeto's plate and bit into it.

"We're deciding what cars we'll get when we win the lottery." Cheeto took a swig of coffee.

Her face muscles twitched from the effort to keep her secret. "Be careful what you wish for."

"Yeah. Grant here wants two Corvettes. I want a Hummer. What about you, Rosita?"

She gave him the evil glare. She hated being called Rosita. "I'm getting a nice big Mercedes sedan."

"Old-school," Cheeto scoffed. "But a good choice for you, since you'll need a driver. Or you can learn to drive." He faked fear. "Watch out, Atlanta. Rosie's on the road."

"Can I talk to you outside?" If she didn't tell him the news she'd die, right here on Fred's grimy black and white tiles.

"I think she's hinting that she needs a ride home," Grant the Corvette guy said.

"Sure. Soon as I get my Hummer." Cheeto grinned, a disarming dental display that made women melt. It didn't work on this crowd, and Rosie was immune from repeated exposure.

She rolled her eyes. *"Pendejo,"* she muttered.

"Such language. Shame on you. I'm telling Abuela."

"Right. This is her day off. Interrupt her canasta game and she'll cut you out of her will." Of course, she'd totally forgive Rosie for *her* interruption, as soon as she heard the news.

He laughed. "Oh yeah, I'll never get that set of Kmart dishes and the collection of creepy glass clowns."

Thunder made the windows vibrate.

"Looks like that storm's finally here." Fred ambled up from the fry baskets and aimed the duct-tape-mended remote control at the TV high in the retro diner's corner. CNN disappeared, replaced by the Weather Channel.

"Look at that." Fred pointed with a sauce-stained finger. The weather map showed Atlanta in the middle of a brilliant yellow streak dotted in dangerous reds and purples. "The front's moving through fast, but it looks hellacious. Guess you boys won't be working."

Rosie watched, dismayed. Even if Cheeto gave her a ride to Abuela's, she'd get soaked, and she'd just straightened her hair yesterday. Twenty minutes of styling down the drain.

"What about you, Fred? What kind of car would you get?" Cheeto picked at his nails with the twisted edge of a paper napkin, a habit that made Rosie grit her teeth.

Cheeto's nickname wasn't some funny Latino *apodo*. It came from his love of a certain brand of crunchy cheese-flavored snacks. As a kid his fingers were always coated with cheesy orange residue, and eventually, everyone forgot that his real name was Enrique.

Now the cheesy powder only accumulated under his fingernails, not that it was much of an improvement. She still found him gross, just like a little kid.

"I don't need a car," Fred said. "This lottery fever is ridiculous. The MegaBucks lottery hits six hundred million dollars and the entire city of Atlanta goes insane. I'm tired of hearing about it."

"I agree," Rosie said. "Buying a ticket is one thing, but spending grocery money on a game of chance? *Pura locura*. Totally nuts." Especially since she knew who held a winning ticket.

Cheeto reached up, snatched the remote control from Fred, and quickly turned the TV back to the news. The cook threw his hands up and stomped off, muttering in Bosnian.

"Listen to this one, guys." Herb Sanchez, a fellow landscaper, had come to stand next to her. He read out loud, stabbing each word with a finger as big and red as a chorizo. "Won the Lottery? Ten Things You Should Do from *The Instant Millionaire's Guide to Everything*!"

Rosie glanced down at her tote bag, which gaped open at her feet. The tabloid was gone. "You went into my bag!"

"What is that, the *Star*?" Cheeto laughed.

Rosie snatched the tabloid from the counter, leaving Herb pointing to the stained Formica. "Leave my stuff alone."

"Wait till I'm rich, baby," Herb said. "You'll be sorry you were so mean to me."

She leaned back. Herb needed a mint.

"Yeah, me too." Grant the Corvette guy clapped a hand on Herb's shoulder. Herb glared at him. The hand pulled away.

She leaned close to her cousin. "I've got something really important to tell you. Privately."

"Ooh, *privately*, Cheeto." Herb Sanchez laughed.

Rosie rolled her eyes and stuffed the magazine back into her tote. She looked around to make sure she had everything, grabbed her jacket, and waved at Cheeto. "Ready to go?"

Cheeto pretended to look scared. "*¿Con el tiempo de madre? I don't want to drive in that big storm. We'd better stay here.*"

"We have enough time for you to take me to Abuela's house since you're not working any more today." *Your landscaping days are over.* Too bad her cousin couldn't read her mind.

"Whatever. The guys were headed over to Dave and Buster's by the mall to shoot pool. Go on without me, bros. I'll join up with you later." Cheeto grabbed her by the coat collar and started to drag her toward the door. "Come on, cookie. I can't wait to find out what's so damn important."

"You are such a jerk." She wrestled free of her obnoxious cousin and straightened her jacket. It was hard to act mature with him around.

Maybe she wouldn't tell him at all. It would serve him right to shovel manure and plant flowers at apartment complexes while she and Abuela lived in a mansion with servants. That wouldn't work, of course. Their soft-hearted grandmother would give him anything he wanted.

"What's so important that you ditched work?"

"I'll tell you when we get to Abuela's house."

Cheeto snorted. "They were right. It's just an excuse for a ride."

As usual, he drove his truck as if NASCAR scouts were watching him from every street corner. Okay, so Rosie knew there was no such thing as NASCAR scouts, but he *was* on a first-name basis with all the local cops. He skidded to a stop in front of Abuela's apartment building.

"Aren't you coming up?"

"Nope. I'm going to catch up with my friends. We're in the middle of a big landscaping job in Buckhead and we'll be back at it tomorrow, pouring cement and laying railroad ties. I don't know when I'll get another day off. But just to show you what a great cousin you have, I'll take you to work in the morning. We're coming right by your apartment around seven. I'll be in the big truck, but there's room for you in back."

"I'm not going to work tomorrow."

He frowned. "That bitch fired you. I knew it." He slapped the steering wheel. "You need any money? I know you're good for it."

She looked at him in silence. "I was thinking how immature you are, and here you're offering me money and rides to work." She dug in her pocket. "I didn't get fired." She pulled out the folded ticket, her signature visible on the back. "I won the lottery."

Cheeto stared at the ticket in her hand. "You're shitting me. This is a MegaBucks ticket. You get four numbers? That's probably worth something." He sat straighter, excited. "Four and the big ball, that's more than a thousand bucks for sure."

"All the numbers, *primo*. All of them. I double- and triple-checked it." She took a deep breath, but it didn't stop her shaking. His excitement had brought back the thrill, and she was jumpy all over again. "It's why I left work early."

Cheeto's blank gaze was aimed at the raindrops running down the windshield; his mouth was slack, but gears were spinning behind his eyes. He gulped. "The news said a single ticket won."

"A single ticket?" She threw her arms around him and let out a yell. "I hadn't heard. I thought maybe there would be more than one winner. We don't have to share. We won the whole thing!" She released him and held out the ticket, along with the winning-numbers slip she'd picked up at Jorge's Quik Mart.

He took them, fingers trembling, eyes wide.

"Rosie," he whispered. "You're rich."

"*We're* rich," she corrected. "And Abuela. That's why I wanted you to bring me here. It wasn't safe to tell you at the diner."

She tugged the two slips from his fingers and put them deep into her coat pocket. "We have to tell Abuela. Ready?"

"Ready?" He whooped, opened the truck door, and started dancing in the rain. Rosie laughed and joined him. They jumped into puddles, yelling and splashing.

Their grandmother appeared on her tiny, plant-filled balcony.

"Rosie, Cheeto! *¿Están locos?*" She frowned, hands on her

hips. "What are you two doing? You're acting like a couple of babies. Rosie, I called your office. What's going on? Come in right now before someone calls the police." She and her frown disappeared inside.

Water dripped into Rosie's eyes. "My shoes are ruined. I'd better buy new ones." She giggled.

"Get a million pairs. Hell, get six million." He pointed at his beloved old pickup. "Look—my truck has a dent in it. Oops. Better get a new one." He threw his head back and laughed, drinking down the rain.

She shivered. Water had dripped inside her coat. She was ready for Abuela's warm apartment. "Race you to the door."

They ran up the small concrete steps outside and then thundered up the interior stairs to their grandmother's second-floor apartment.

"Wait till you hear our news." Cheeto's voice reverberated from the concrete walls.

"You need to sit down to hear this, Abuela." Rosie pulled at her freezing-wet pants legs, trying to get them away from her skin.

Abuela stood in her doorway, face grim and arms loaded with folded towels. "I know your news. You got fired, and you are going to tell me why, but not until you've dried off."

"I didn't get fired—"

Her grandmother paid her no heed. "Take your coats and shoes off right here, then go straight to the bathroom. Rosita, take a shower first. My robe is on the hook behind the door.

"Enrique, go to my bedroom and put on your *abuelo*'s robe until she's finished."

"But Abue, we have something huge to tell you," Cheeto said. He hadn't complained when Abuela called him by his real name, a sure sign he was excited.

"Later, later." Abuela pushed him down the hall.

Rosie rushed through her shower, afraid Cheeto would tell their grandmother the news before she got there.

"*Mucho mejor*," Abuela said when Rosie entered the living room wrapped in a velour robe. "Much better. I thought something awful had happened to you. I called and called your office, *niña*. Different people kept answering the phone."

She wished she could have been a fly on Cartwright Office Supply's wall. The employees were probably all buzzing about how she'd quit. Or maybe Lana said she'd been fired. "I left work. Something great's happened, Abuelita." She threw her arms around her grandmother and kissed her.

Cheeto glared at her from the hallway. "You didn't tell her, did you? Is there any hot water for me?" He made signals with his chin, eyes wide. *Don't tell her.*

She shook her head. "When we're all together. And there's plenty of hot water. I took a quick one."

"I don't know what the two of you were thinking. Behaving like little children, and then coming up here all wet and leaving poodles on my floor."

"Puddles. A poodle is what Tootie is." Another thing for Rosie to add to her to-do list—what to do for her old dog, Tootie, who had once been her mother's beloved companion. Doggie spa treatments, gourmet food. From now on Tootie would live better than Paris Hilton's dog.

Abuela sighed. "Yes, yes. Puddle. Forty years you'd think I'd learn better English. *Imposible.*"

"So why were you calling me at work?" Rosie kissed her grandmother's soft cheek.

"To invite you to dinner. My friends are bringing potluck and there will be more than enough for you. After our card game we're going to eat, then play some more. Let me tell you, they are not happy with you at your office. I could tell in that Lana's voice when she told me you didn't work there anymore."

Abuela folded her hands over her stomach, her signal for "you may commence with the excuses."

Thunder crashed overhead, and the lights flickered.

Abuela gasped and crossed herself.

Cheeto appeared dressed in oversized khakis and a guayabera that hung on him. Their grandfather had been a big guy. He'd been dead for fifteen years and Abuela still kept some of his clothes. Cheeto waved a flashlight around, and then set it on Abuela's dining room table. "Just in case."

Abuela clasped her hands together. "So, the big news. The one that requires both of you here, and neither of you at work." She pursed her lips, waiting for the worst.

"Sit down, make yourself comfortable." Rosie sat at the dinette table, and Cheeto sprawled on the love seat that served as a sofa in the tiny room.

Abuela parked her gnarled fists on her ample hips. "I don't have to sit down. What do you want me to know? Is it drugs? I don't want to hear about drugs."

"Not drugs. Did you see that a single ticket won the Mega-Bucks lottery?"

"Yes. Which just goes to show that we shouldn't gamble. All that money wasted. How much did you spend, *m'ija*? Ten dollars? That's what you spent the last time."

Rosie tried to interrupt, but Abuela was on a roll.

"Ten dollars wasted, you know? You could have bought a chicken and some vegetables and made a nice dinner. Food for several days. Or even dog food for your poor *perrita*, that little dog that your Mami loved so much, may she rest in peace." She crossed herself again.

Cheeto had both hands over his mouth. Suppressed laughter squeezed tears out of his eyes.

"One dollar." Rosie almost shouted the words. She'd jumped up and now loomed over Abuela. "And it wasn't wasted, because I won. I won—"

"You don't have to shout. I am not deaf. And—"

"—I won the lottery." Rosie felt deflated. She turned away and sat down hard on the dinette chair. This wasn't the way she'd pictured it.

She heard a thump behind her.

"*Caray*," Cheeto yelled and leaped over the coffee table. Glass clown figurines went flying.

Their grandmother had fainted and was stretched out on the floor.

"Abue!" Rosie looked around wildly. "Smelling salts. When I fainted at Mass once they woke me up with them."

"Salt?" Cheeto was useless. He was patting Abuela's hand as if that would wake her up.

She didn't have time to find smelling salts, if Abuela even had some. She ran to the fridge and got an ice cube. Holding it gingerly, she dabbed it against her grandmother's throat. Two dabs into her improvised treatment, the cube squirted from between her fingers and slipped into the neckline of her grandmother's cotton top.

Abuela sat straight up, yelling. Rosie had a second to think that she looked just like the Cryptkeeper coming out of its coffin before she tugged at the back of her grandmother's blouse and let the ice cube slide to the floor. The old lady gasped, relieved.

"Are you okay? I'm so sorry," Rosie cried, her arms around her grandmother's cushiony shoulders. "I was trying to wake you up."

"With ice? Cheeto, what are you doing?" She pulled her hand out of his. "*Gracias,* both of you, but you almost gave me a heart attack."

"I tried to help." Cheeto sounded wounded.

Abuela flapped her arms dismissively. "I'm glad neither of you decided to go into medicine."

"You made a joke. You must be okay." Rosie got to her feet and offered her grandmother a hand. "Didn't I tell you to sit down?"

Abuela leaned on them, and they helped her stand up. She grinned. "Is it true? You won the lottery?"

"Yes, it's true. I couldn't call you—"

"How much? Can you pay your student loan? Or maybe buy a little *carrito*? Maybe a used Honda. I hear they're reliable."

Cheeto jumped up and spread his arms wide. "*La gorda,* Abuela. The MegaBucks."

Abuela's rumpled face sagged. Her mouth opened, then snapped shut. "You won," she whispered. She flapped her hands, excited again. "*Dios mío*. How much, how much?"

"Six hundred million. After taxes, I think it'll be about three hundred million."

The screaming stopped, replaced by an open-mouthed stare. "*Madre de Dios.*"

They heard another thump. It was Cheeto's backside landing on the dining room chair again. "Three hundred million. It just hit me how much that is."

She hadn't really stopped to think about it until now. Her knees felt rubbery, and she felt behind her for the love seat, then dropped into it.

"Who else knows?" Abuela reached over the coffee table, littered with toppled figurines, and grabbed Rosie's hand. "Who have you told?"

"No one else," Rosie said. "Just the two of you. We have to redeem the ticket at the lottery office downtown."

"What time do they close?"

"Five, but Abuela, we don't have to go today. It's better to wait a few days and decide what to do."

"Decide?" Cheeto was up again, dancing around the living room. "What's to decide? We're going to act like millionaires. Big cars, great clothes, every cable channel, season tickets to the Braves, and trips to Vegas for the boxing."

"Pick up the *payasos* you knocked over, Cheeto. They're Murano glass." Abuela got up and sat at the dinette table.

"By next week, I'll have servants to pick up all the *payasos* I knock over." He picked up the heavy glass clown figurine and put it back on the coffee table.

"I'll have a servant just to tell the other servants to pick up *my* stuff." Rosie helped set the table straight.

Abuela threw her arms up. "I'll be in a big enough house that I won't have to listen to the two of you order your servants around." She surveyed her apartment. "Actually, I want to stay here."

"You can't be serious, Abuela. We can get a huge house. We can get three huge houses." No more miserable apartment. Rosie didn't think her grin could get any bigger.

"On the beach," Cheeto added. "I want to live near the surf."

"We have to plan," Rosie said.

"Claro que sí," Abuela said. "And meanwhile I'll make us *un cafecito.*"

They huddled around the little dinette table and planned their next step surrounded by the aroma of brewing Cuban coffee.

"The best thing," Abuela said, pouring the thick black coffee into tiny porcelain cups, "is that now Rosie will be able to find a good husband. Someone decent, not like that Rick person."

Old ladies had big ears.

Cheeto dumped a hill of sugar into his tiny coffee cup. "For three hundred million dollars, she could buy one."

"Buy a boyfriend? That's interesting." Now Rosie had to worry if men were interested in her for her money. A first.

"So what happens now?" Cheeto's eyes were bright, and he squeezed his hands together like he did at ballgames when the Braves were behind and at bat with the bases loaded.

Rosie thought. "Now I go home and pack only the stuff I want to keep. I don't think I want to go back to stay in my apartment." The good times she'd shared with her parents made the little rooms precious to her after they'd died, but it had been years ago. She was twenty-four now. A giggle erupted as she thought of how much she could afford.

"You can move in here with me," Abuela said quickly.

Cheeto rolled his eyes. "Give me a break. You aren't really thinking of staying in this dump, are you? We can live large now."

Abuela's eyebrows rose in indignation. "Dump? I belong to the neighborhood watch. There are no gangs here, like over at Rosie's—you'll pardon me for pointing that out, cariño—and all of my friends live here."

Her cousin shrugged. "I'm just saying. I want to live in a huge mansion, so you'll have an extra bedroom. At least I don't have to worry about whether you can pay the rent by yourself."

"So you are packing up today and tonight," Abuela said, turning her back to Cheeto and addressing Rosie. "What happens tomorrow?"

"Tomorrow we go early to the lottery office downtown and claim the prize." Rosie bit her lip. "Actually, the advice the experts give is to find a financial advisor and hide for a long time, then come forward when everyone's forgotten about it, but I can't wait."

Abuela grunted. "Especially since you have no job."

"Do you think you could go back to changing sheets and cleaning toilets at the hotel, knowing that you have three hundred million dollars?"

Her grandmother gasped and put a hand to her throat. "Every time you say how much, I am amazed again. What if it's not true?"

Rosie thought of the ticket in her pocket and suddenly was afraid to pull it out. "Then I'm out of work and have no place to live. I'll move in with you and find another job. Fred said I could help at the diner. I can do that until something else comes along." Her heart thudded as she spoke, because she wanted the money so much. But it was true, she thought. She'd double-checked.

Abuela opened her arms, and Rosie went to sit next to her on the love seat, to be enveloped in her grandmother's love.

"Tomorrow we claim our prize." She kissed Rosie's forehead. "Go pack your things, *nena*. My friends will be here soon for the canasta game."

"You can't tell them," Rosie said, pulling away from Abuela. "We can't tell anyone until we've claimed the money."

"Why? Because someone might steal the ticket?" Cheeto's grin faded as he considered the possibility.

"I signed the back of it, so I don't know if anyone else can claim it now, but they might hurt us to get it." Rosie shrugged. "I'm not sure, though."

"Then why wait?" Cheeto stood up. "Let's go. We'll claim it right now."

"But the financial advisor—"

"I agree," Abuela said. "We can do it now."

"Then what? Just go downtown to the lottery office, claim the ticket, and come back home?" Rosie shook her head. "We need a plan for afterwards. For instance, we shouldn't come back here for a few days. I read a great article in the *Star* that says lottery winners should stay in a hotel."

"The La Quinta by I-285 is nice," Cheeto offered.

"La Quinta?" Abuela looked offended. "We'll stay at the Ritz. Either downtown, or in Buckhead."

"That sounds expensive." Rosie stopped talking and laughed. "Did you hear what I just said? I almost forgot."

"So call the Ritz and make reservations," Abuela said. "And we'll take a cab from downtown, because we don't all fit in Cheeto's truck."

"And it would be so stupid to get on the bus with the giant Styrofoam check." Cheeto grinned.

Rosie laughed. "I'm going to frame that giant Styrofoam check and hang it in my new living room where I'll see it every day."

Abuela stood and picked up the coffee cups. Rosie hurried to help her. "So what'll it be, Rosie, downtown or Buckhead? If we're downtown, we'll be close to the lottery office."

"The Ritz in Buckhead," Rosie answered. "Brad Merritt stays there when he's in town, and it's right next door to Phipps Plaza."

Cheeto shrugged. "So?"

"Excuse me? Tiffany's is at Phipps. I'm going to get some diamonds." She was sure her eyes were sparkling as brightly as the diamonds she would soon buy.

"What I'm going to get is some sleep. All of you go home." Abuela pointed at the door. "Rosie, think about what you want to keep from your apartment."

Cheeto got up. "Come on, *prima*, I'll drive you home."

What to keep? It hadn't occurred to Rosie that she'd have to choose.

CHAPTER FOUR

* * * * *

Once you have hired your financial advisor or
legal team, disappear. Don't talk to the press.
—*The Instant Millionaire's Guide to Everything*

From Blue Collar to Blue Chip—Meet the Caballeros
—*Star* magazine

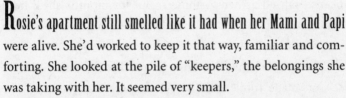

Rosie's apartment still smelled like it had when her Mami and Papi
were alive. She'd worked to keep it that way, familiar and comforting. She looked at the pile of "keepers," the belongings she
was taking with her. It seemed very small.

She'd been poking around the small rooms, half packing
and half reminiscing, since Cheeto had dropped her off at six
o'clock and gone to his own place to pack. The *Star* was open to
the article about lottery winners. It seemed essential that she
find a copy of the "instant millionaire" book. She didn't want
to make any mistakes.

She'd called the Ritz and made the reservation using Abuela's
Visa card, which was only used for very special occasions.

Abuela had also called a lawyer friend of hers, who agreed to
meet them at lottery headquarters at noon the next day.

It gave Rosie a thrill to think about her new, luxurious life,
although until the ticket was turned in, she was broke.

Maybe she would keep the place as a reminder of what her life had been like. The Rosa Caballero Poverty Museum, complete with *cucarachas* and worn linoleum. Ironic that she'd be leaving now that she could afford the rent, with no more hiding from the landlord.

Tootie crawled out from under the bed and wagged her stumpy tail. Her long poodle hair was straggly and matted in places, hanging in yellowed dreadlocks. Rosie bit her lip. Poor pup. It was time for a day at the doggie spa.

Her old high school friend Milagros sometimes clipped her, after making Rosie triple swear not to tell any of her beauty parlor clients that she'd done a dog. She could lose her license as well as her customers. But for months she'd been too busy to fit her in, so Rosie had tried to groom her, with scary results.

The poodle bangs that Rosie had hacked off with manicure scissors made Tootie look like she was wearing a bad wig. The red toenail polish on her claws that Rosie thought would spiff her up made her look like a worn-out doggie streetwalker.

Rosie snapped on her leash. "Come on, old girl." She carried Tootie down the stairs and then waited while the dog sniffed around and did her business by the bushes in the back. Although Rosie felt self-conscious, as if there was a big "lottery winner" sign over her head, no one paid them any attention.

Back upstairs, Tootie stared pointedly at the refrigerator.

"You'll eat when I eat." She refused to feel guilty about the bean dinner she was going to serve them. The absolute last bean dinner, ever.

Tootie gave her wounded puppy-dog eyes, then dropped her

snout and sniffed, as if to say that it was mean to yell at geriatric poodles.

Rosie ignored her and warmed up leftover black beans and rice. Before it grew too hot she spooned some into Tootie's bowl.

The old dog hurried over, stiff-legged, examined the contents of the bowl, then looked sad again.

"Hey, I'm eating that, too. We're millionaires with no cash." She ate her beans and rice, then washed up and turned on the TV, aware that everything was a "last." Last meal in this apartment. Last time she'd reheat beans and wonder what she'd eat the next day.

At ten, Rosie skipped her usual shower and headed to bed, dropping clothes as she went, one of the advantages of living alone. Tootie barked at a noise on the street.

"Shut that dog up," Mrs. Garcia yelled from downstairs, her voice muffled through the hallway and the carpeted floor. She seemed to lie in wait for any dog noise. *Last time Mrs. Garcia raised hell over nothing.*

"Bark louder, Tootie. Heck, I'll bark with you." She stomped down the hall, and barked along with Tootie, to the accompaniment of Mrs. Garcia's broom handle pounding into the ceiling of the apartment below. She would not miss Mrs. Garcia. Maybe Mrs. Garcia wouldn't miss her, either.

She got ready to sleep, enjoying the scent of yellow Dial soap in the bathroom. Like Mami's perfume and Papi's pipe, it was one of the smells that had defined her life. Beans cooking, *sofrito* simmering, hot milk at night and brewed coffee in the morning. Pine-Sol on cleaning days and Tide for her clothes. She surrounded herself with the tastes and scents of her childhood, as if changing brands would make her parents fade away. That was something she could keep, no matter how grand her new life would be.

At eleven thirty, when she was usually asleep, she drank hot *café con leche* in front of her little TV set and studied the hip, clingy dresses on Jay Leno's guest stars, evaluating how they'd look on her. Tomorrow she'd be able to buy a better TV, a huge wall-mounted plasma screen, and all the premium channels. She'd never again have to arrange the crappy rabbit ears until she had a decent picture.

Tootie tried to hop onto the sofa. She made it on the third try and settled onto a soft cushion next to her. After Leno, a movie started. Rosie couldn't believe it. Brad Merritt's *Desperado's Journey*. This really was her lucky day.

Of course, she'd seen every one of his films several times. She could order all of his DVDs, and download all of his movies. She needed an iPhone so that she could have Brad at her fingertips, 24/7.

No work tomorrow. She smiled and stretched, watching the opening credits. Brad lifting his head to reveal those astonishing eyes. She was loving life already.

At midnight, she couldn't fight off sleep any more. The cab would be here at eleven, and she wanted to savor her last night on her worn sheets and lumpy mattress.

The telephone woke her up the next morning. She lifted her head from the pillow and squinted at the pre-digital wood-toned clock radio. Its little dangling number paddles told her it was eight thirty in the morning. Bill collectors showed no mercy. She fumbled for the phone.

"Rosa Caballero?" The angry voice sounded familiar.

"Yes, this is Rosa."

"This is Lana Cartwright."

Panicked, she sat straight up, until she remembered the lottery ticket. Warmth filled her chest. She never had to work for her again.

"Are you there?"

"Um, yes. I am." She wanted to yell, "I'm rich!" into the phone, but instead bit her lip, resisting temptation. No one must know yet.

"You need to come in to sign your termination papers. Company policy says that I can't release your paycheck until you do." Lana's voice was crisp and unyielding, like the woman herself.

"Lana, I—"

The line went dead.

"—don't need your money." Rosie stared at the phone for a second, then hung the receiver on its hook again. On second thought, she did need the money. She'd earned it.

She picked up the receiver again, but there was no dial tone. Her phone had just been disconnected. She laughed. Lana would think she'd been the one to hang up. Oops. Yesterday's tragedy was today's joke.

Tootie came out of the bedroom, yawning.

"Well, Toots, they say that one of the first things to do when you win the lottery is disconnect your phone. We're doing great so far."

She dressed in jeans and a T-shirt, took Tootie for a walk,

then finished cleaning her apartment. She found herself staring at the neatly folded piles of worn panties and cheap bras. She put everything in plastic grocery store sacks on the dinette table.

She glanced at her watch. Ten thirty. Time to get ready at last. She was so antsy she was ready to jog down the road toward the lottery office and let the taxi carrying Cheeto and Abuela catch up with her.

Wild thoughts of what awaited her spun through her head while she changed into her only suit and put her jeans, T-shirt, and tennis shoes into a grocery bag for later. The taxi didn't honk until just after eleven, causing her three whole minutes of anxiety, until she realized that since she had the ticket, they couldn't go without her. She put on her old coat. Its days were numbered. As soon as she could, she'd get a beautiful new one. Maybe a fur coat, full length.

"You be good, Tootie. I'll be back later to get you."

Tootie wagged her stumpy tail, then realized the outing wouldn't include her and she laid down on her old pillow.

Rosie locked the door behind her and went down the cracked concrete steps.

Abuela waved from the taxi. She had her coat on her lap, and was dressed in a pleated red dress printed with a design of giant white flowers with a crocheted lace collar pinned at her throat. She'd removed the dress's blocky shoulder pads back in the nineties, and the sleeves drooped strangely, making her look like a giant strawberry.

Cheeto wore black pleated slacks and a banana yellow spandex shirt, his clubbing outfit.

"What's with the lawyer gear?" he asked, opening the cab door for her.

She looked down at her good dark blue suit from JCPenney. "I'll have you know this is normal business attire. It's very classy."

"If you say so. I call it boring."

"I want them to take us seriously." Which was going to be tough, the way the rest of her family was dressed. She got into the taxi and tugged her skirt back down her thighs. She'd gained a little weight since the last time she'd worn it. "Where's Gloria?"

"I didn't tell her." Cheeto grinned.

"You didn't tell your girlfriend?"

"She'd want to marry me. It's not that kind of relationship."

"Right. And it's going to stay a big secret? You're nuts." She kissed her grandmother. "*¿Lista?*"

"*Claro que sí.*" Her eyes took in Rosie's outfit and widened. "Why did you shorten your skirt?"

"I didn't."

"It wasn't that short in August at Carmita Otero's funeral."

Rosie clenched her teeth. That had been fifteen pounds ago. She added a personal trainer to her mental list. Plasma TV, personal trainer, mink coat, Tootie's doggie spa.

Abuela patted her knee. "You look better in bright colors, anyway."

"That's what I told her," Cheeto said.

"You guys are bright enough for all of us," Rosie retorted.

Their grandmother ignored them. "Guess what? I called the hotel and resigned."

"That's great. Just what you've always wanted." Rosie hugged her grandmother, not an easy thing to do while squeezed in the backseat of a taxi. "I'm almost free. Lana called this morning and said I had to sign some papers." She laughed. "She says she's holding my check."

Abuela snorted. "Let her keep it."

Rosie shook her head. "Oh, no. That's money that I worked hard for. I'm going to get it."

"I quit, too," Cheeto said. "Max took it well. He said if I ever wanted to come back, my job is waiting for me."

"You didn't tell him why you quit, I hope. You're not supposed to tell anyone, remember?" Rosie didn't trust him.

"Are you nuts?" Cheeto laughed nervously.

Rosie watched him exchange glances with Abuela. Whatever. In a few hours they'd have their money.

As the cab pulled onto Buford Highway and headed toward the perimeter highway, a car honked behind them. They ignored it until the vehicle pulled up alongside and honked again.

"You know them?" the cabbie asked.

It was a big red truck with the Max Arnold Landscaping logo on the side. The truck's bed was full of landscapers, waving rakes and hooting at them. Herb Sanchez was driving, his white grin wide in his dark face.

Rosie turned to Cheeto. "You did tell them. You didn't tell your girlfriend but you told everyone at work."

Cheeto's grin faded. "I didn't think it would hurt. Look how happy they are for us."

A second truck joined the first, and soon they were the lead car in a parade of cheering landscapers.

The cabbie laughed. "You guys win the lottery or something?"

He glanced at them in the rearview mirror when they didn't answer. "Holy cow, did you?"

"Yes, we did," Rosie said. Why not? Everyone else seemed to know.

He picked up speed, as if they were being chased.

"You're going to have to throw your friends a big *fiesta*." Abuela took a little pad and pencil from her oversized purse. She licked the pencil lead. "*Lechón*, of course, and a nice salad."

Rosie slouched down in the seat. She wanted to disappear. Is this how they'd start their lives as millionaires? With a barbecue? It was so Beverly Hillbillies.

"Beer," Cheeto added. "And a giant cake."

She saw herself stepping out onto the golf course behind her new mansion. As her rich neighbors came up to greet her, truckloads of landscapers would swing by, trenching the beautiful grass and hooting at her, yelling in Spanish. She would serve beer and cake and her guests would offer to repair the lawn in their free time, at a big discount, while Cheeto ate cheese crunchies on the front lawn.

Her eyes opened. She would not be mortified by a daydream. She lifted her head again, but the trucks had peeled off. Cheeto was waving at them through the back windshield. Abuela was still making party notes.

The rest of the ride downtown was uneventful—until they swung onto Williams Street and the Inforum. The street in front of the building that housed the lottery offices was choked with TV camera trucks with impossibly long antennas sticking out of their tops. Each vehicle bore the call letters of a local TV station; CNN and Fox News were there, too.

Several well-groomed people were finishing up their noon on-site broadcasts.

"I can't go through," the cab driver said. "Can I let you out here?"

"Yeah, right here is good," Cheeto said.

"No, wait." Rosie stared at the unexpected crowd. "Those news trucks are here because of us. Why else would they be in front of the lottery building?"

"Because it's not just the lottery building, *tonta*. It's probably the FBI or something. Come on." Cheeto opened the other door and helped Abuela get out.

"Hey, I've got an idea for a restaurant." The cabbie was scribbling on a sheet of paper. He tore it off the pad. "Give me a call."

Cheeto tucked it into a pocket and paid the fare.

"Look at that. How exciting." Abuela shaded her eyes with her hand. "That girl with the blond hair? That's the one from Channel Five. I love her."

"You never watch Channel Five. You watch Univision." Rosie reapplied her Maybelline lipstick in the cab's side mirror.

"Yes, but they have the prettiest weather pictures, and I understand those. But where's Univision and Telemundo?" She looked disappointed.

"I wonder if there's another door?" Rosie didn't like the look of the crowd in front of the Inforum. Every time she'd seen an interview with lottery winners they always looked like slack-jawed idiots. She was sure it was because camera people made them look that way when they took them by surprise.

"I'm not going in a back door," Abuela said firmly.

Rosie and Cheeto turned to her in surprise.

"At the hotel, we maids always go in the back door, by the Dumpsters. I'm never going to do that again." She lifted her chin. "*Ven, mis hijos.* We're going to claim our future. Through the front door."

Rosie and Cheeto looked at each other and shrugged. Claim their future?

"Too many *telenovelas*," Rosie mouthed.

Cheeto grinned.

They crossed the street to the Inforum, a big boxy downtown building with lots of glass. How many people had to buy losing tickets in order to pay for all this architecture?

Rosie smoothed her hand over her jacket pocket as she crossed the street. The ticket crackled through the polyester gabardine.

She should savor the moment. Thirty more minutes and her old "poor" life would be over. She would be reborn, wealthy.

"Are you the winners? Hey, ma'am, sir? Are you the winners?" The call was taken up by more of the news people.

Abuela glanced behind them, and her eyes grew wide.

People poured from every van and truck, calling out to them, some of them clutching coffee cups and doughnuts while others held microphones. The TV reporters fixed their hair and straightened their lapels as they hurried toward them, their cameramen following close.

"Do you have the winning ticket?" A woman thrust a microphone at Rosie like a weapon.

Rosie jumped in front of Cheeto, shoved the door open and slid inside, pulling Abuela after her. Cheeto closed the door behind them and held it shut as a uniformed guard hurried toward them. Reporters were pushing at the door.

"We're about to be invaded," Cheeto told the guard. "I'd lock the door if I were you."

The guard was ready, keys in hand.

"Where's your lawyer, Abuela?" Rosie saw only the receptionist and the security guard in the cavelike lobby.

Abuela shrugged. "He said he'd be here. Maybe he's trapped in the crowd."

The receptionist jumped up from behind a tall, barlike counter made out of polished stone.

"May I help you?" Her smile looked genuine, as if she was really glad to see them, but her gaze kept flashing nervously to the mob outside. Rosie's fingers traced across her pocket. Did she know? Was there some kind of chip in the ticket's paper that told everyone who she was, and what she had?

Abuela touched her shoulder. Rosie forced off the paranoid thoughts and leaned over the counter to whisper, "Is this where we bring a winning ticket?"

It was an effort not to glance around like a spy in a movie. Only the security guard was there, and he was speaking earnestly into his radio as he blocked access to the door. No one was going to snatch her ticket.

"Yes it is, for tickets over five hundred dollars." The woman matched her low tone. "We're kind of expecting the MegaBucks winners to come in."

"That's me." Rosie waved at Cheeto and Abuela, who were crowded close behind her. "Us."

The woman's eyes widened and she reached for the telephone. "Let me get someone to verify your good luck." She pushed a button, just one button, like the Batphone, said something too soft for Rosie to hear, then hung up. "So how many numbers did you get? We had two Georgia winners with four numbers and the Mega Ball. Those are worth two hundred and fifty thousand each, and then, of course, one ticket won the big one."

Rosie turned as a commotion sounded behind them. The security guard was shoved aside and the crowd surged in, jostling each other as they ran toward the reception desk.

"I thought he locked it," Abuela said, eyes wide. Rosie's mouth was dry. Would they get hurt? Would she lose the ticket?

"Come on." The receptionist flung open the "Employees Only" door behind the counter and pushed her in. Cheeto and Abuela quickly followed.

The crowd howled as their target disappeared.

"Are you the big winners?"

"What's your name?"

"Do the three of you work together?"

The door closed on the shouting journalists. Rosie and her family were now in a quiet hall lined with office doors. A striking woman in a red suit appeared. Her outfit was elegant, but still tight enough to look painted on, and she wore enough makeup to qualify for a chair on a televangelist's show. The woman extended a hand to Cheeto.

"I'm Linda Mayfield, prize coordinator. I'm so sorry about the riot. Security is sending more staff. What may I do for you?"

Cheeto looked at Rosie, his hand in Linda Mayfield's grasp.

"I'm Rosa Caballero, and I won the MegaBucks," she said. "I need to turn in my ticket."

Ms. Mayfield dropped Cheeto's hand and rubbed her palms together.

"You've signed it?" she asked. Her smile seemed fake, probably the aftermath of spending her working days verifying how lucky the rest of the world was.

"I signed it." Rosie pulled the ticket out of her pocket and turned it so that the signature was visible.

Ms. Mayfield held her hand out. Rosie pulled the ticket back, reluctant to relinquish the world's most important piece of paper.

"Ma'am, you'll have to give it to me for verification. Don't worry, it'll be safe." As she spoke, Ms. Mayfield gave Rosie a quick up and down glance as if she was toting up the dollar amounts of everything she was wearing. If so, the total would be a very low figure. Her whole outfit wouldn't buy even one of this woman's shoes.

"Thirty-five dollars on clearance at JCPenney."

Ms. Mayfield stared blankly.

"The suit. It seemed to me you wanted to know." Rosie gave her a big smile.

"Thank you. The ticket?"

Rosie glanced at Abuela, who nodded encouragingly, and she surrendered the ticket.

Ms. Mayfield turned it over and opened the fold. She glanced at the numbers, then looked at it again. Her eyes flickered up to Rosie's, startled. "Oh, my," she said. "Hold on a second, please, Ms. . . . ?"

"Caballero. Rosa Caballero," she said again.

"Ms. Caballero." She managed to look both respectful and suspicious.

"Ms. Mayfield, we need to put the Caballero family in the

conference room." The receptionist had reappeared, trailed by the excited roar of the crowd.

Something banged against the door.

"Reporters," Cheeto said. "Lots of them."

Ms. Mayfield's look turned from annoyance to alarm. "Follow me." She motioned them down the hallway, and they followed.

"We didn't tell anybody." That wasn't true. Rosie remembered the cheering landscaper escort. Cheeto's *lengua larga* had probably informed the press, too.

The receptionist patted her arm. "They've had the building surrounded since yesterday."

Ms. Mayfield leaned across the desk and picked up a nearby wall phone, dialed a number. "Where's the extra security? I don't care. They need to be here now." She hung up and sighed, then gestured toward a nearby door. "You'll be more comfortable waiting here." She pushed open the door and ushered them into a room that looked as if it belonged in the White House. The dark red carpet almost swallowed Rosie's flats. A long polished table filled the length of the room, and was surrounded by comfortable rolling armchairs. The walls on either side had giant whiteboards covered with posters of what looked like pictures from a lottery commercial.

"Please have a seat. Are you family, partners, or coworkers?"

"This is my grandmother, Josefa Caballero, and that's my cousin Enrique." Rosie sat, wondering if the cab they'd ridden in had left some kind of grime on her skirt that she'd now rub off on the expensive chair.

"I'll be right back." The ticket fluttered in Ms. Mayfield's hand. She caught Rosie staring at it. "Don't worry, this is totally safe with me."

If she didn't get it back, Rosie would hunt her down. The snooty woman wouldn't get far in her tight skirt and tall shoes.

The door closed behind her and Rosie sat back, trying to relax. The door opened again a moment later. It was the receptionist, with three bottles of cold water. "Thought y'all might be thirsty."

"Thank you," Abuela said. She twisted the top off a bottle and sipped. Cheeto rubbed his bottle over his cheeks, a landscaper's cooling-off trick. He looked nervous.

"I'm Vickie," the receptionist said, and grinned at them. "Y'all are going to make the national news. There are scads of reporters out there. Biggest lottery prize ever!"

"Maybe we should have brought disguises." Cheeto started to laugh, but it quickly faded away. He licked his lips.

"Would you like anything else?" Vickie put a hand on the door, ready to leave again.

"What's taking so long?" Rosie asked. Maybe Mr. Kim had sold her a bogus ticket. Boy, would he be in trouble. The lottery commission would have to wait in line behind her to beat him up.

"Linda's setting up the press conference, since the reporters are already here."

Rosie jumped to her feet. "Press conference? Oh, no. I don't want a lot of publicity."

The receptionist looked sympathetic. "Too late, honey. Just think how exciting for the folks watching on TV. Six hundred million dollars, and every one of them that bought a ticket thinks they could have won. They feel as if they know you."

Abuela frowned. "It sounds dangerous, Rosie." She spoke in Spanish. "If too many people know our faces, we could get robbed."

"Where's our lawyer?" Rosie whispered.

Abuela shrugged and patted Rosie's hand. "He'll be here. Maybe he got lost."

"This press conference thing is a trip, Rosie. I'm glad we weren't planning to go back home afterwards. We won't be safe." Cheeto looked worried.

"And everyone will ask us for money," Abuela added. *"Dios mío."*

Ms. Mayfield came through the door carrying a sheaf of papers bristling with colorful tabs. She'd stopped to put on a fresh attitude. She looked at Rosie as if she was someone who shopped at Wal-Mart because she wanted to, not because she had to. What a difference six hundred million dollars made.

The woman walked to the opposite side of the conference table and fanned the papers out on its surface.

"Just a few things for you to sign, and then you can get your picture taken with the big check."

Rosie reached for the first stapled packet that Ms. Mayfield pushed toward her. The little pink and purple tabs that stuck out of the papers read "sign here."

Cheeto clicked open a black pen and laid it on the papers. "You first, cuz."

Ms. Mayfield seemed taken aback. "There was only one signature on the ticket, so Ms. Caballero is the sole owner."

Rosie looked at her grandmother and cousin. "I'll sign, but we're family. It belongs to the three of us."

Abuela patted her shoulder and Cheeto grinned.

"May I congratulate you on your good fortune?" Ms. Mayfield chirped.

"Thanks." Rosie looked at the papers.

A sixtyish, potbellied man appeared at the door. "Excuse me? Is Mrs. Caballero here?"

"Armando." Abuela stood and walked quickly around the table. The two kissed each other's cheeks and Abuela turned to Rosie. "This is Armando Pujol. He's our attorney."

Mr. Pujol nodded at Ms. Mayfield, who sighed and extended a hand to him. "Mr. Pujol. I'm Linda Mayfield, the prize coordinator."

"How do you do?" His voice was deep, like a radio announcer's, with a strong Spanish accent. "Ms. Mayfield, are these the papers to be signed?"

"Yes."

"Ah." He put a finger to his brow. "May I?" He sat, pulled a pair of gold-rimmed reading glasses from his jacket pocket, put them on, then drew the stack toward him and began to leaf through the pages.

Ms. Mayfield blew air between pursed lips. "Great. Can you hurry? There's going to be a riot out there if your clients don't show up for their press conference."

Rosie agreed. She wanted to get this over with. Next to her, Cheeto crossed and uncrossed his legs. Only Abuela sat back, serene, as her friend skimmed each page, running his finger along the lines as he read.

After five pages, he said, "Ah," and pulled a sheet aside. Ten pages later, he said, "Ah," again and repeated the motion.

Rosie sighed. "This is going to take a year. What are you looking for?" She wanted her giant check. It was time to get the good life started.

Mr. Pujol looked at her over the top rim of his reading glasses. "Your best interests, Miss Caballero."

She watched the lawyer go through the stack, page by page, and pulled off her Payless pumps. Her toes hurt. No more ten-dollar shoes.

Cheeto had his head down on his hands, snoozing, when Mr. Pujol finally finished. Abuela had pulled her crocheting out of her bag, and Rosie was imagining the jewelry she would buy.

"Almost everything is in order," Mr. Pujol said. "After changes."

Everyone jumped at the sound of his voice.

"Please name the three parties equally on these forms. And my clients do not agree to making their personal information public."

"We were agreeing to that?" Rosie stared at the papers. "Like, our addresses?"

"What does it matter? We won't be living there for long." Cheeto sat up, then tilted his chair, balancing it on its back legs.

Ms. Mayfield gathered up the sheets and hurried out. "I'll be right back with these changes."

Abuela nodded approvingly. "Our lawyer, Rosie. See?"

She saw, but she wanted this part to be over with. "Yeah." She smiled at Mr. Pujol.

Ms. Mayfield returned with fresh pages and put a stack in front of Rosie, then another in front of Cheeto, and the last in front of Abuela. "You will each receive a check for your share of the winnings."

"Now you may sign." Mr. Pujol handed his fountain pen to Abuela. "There are tax forms, and permission forms, and the receipt of payment."

"I haven't received any payment," Cheeto said. "Are we done? It's been almost two hours."

"You're getting whiny, *primo*. Just sign." Rosie didn't even read the pages. She scrawled her signature across each line marked by a sticky note.

Rosie's mind was whirling around by the time she finished, and the room had gotten a lot more crowded. Lottery workers were coming out of their offices to stop by and congratulate them. Some of them looked really pleased at their good luck, but others looked at her as if they were dogs and she had the best bone. She could almost see their little gears spinning as they tried to figure out how they could get in on the cash.

When did she get so paranoid?

After all the signing was done, Ms. Mayfield led them back out to the lobby, where a little carpeted stage had been set up. Twelve TV cameras turned their way. Security guards were everywhere now, and two flanked them as they stepped onto the stage.

A silver-haired executive type was already on stage, talking to the reporters.

"That's the lottery commissioner," Ms. Mayfield said.

"Do we have to do this?" Rosie thought of the ten rules of lottery winners. At least three were variations on "keep your mouth shut."

"Everyone loves to hear about lottery winners. The press has been ready for this for weeks, but the total kept rolling over. Then a single winner was announced." Ms. Mayfield waved her hands toward the crowded room. "We were so excited that it was someone from Georgia."

"Okay then. Sure. Let's get it over with." And get me my money, Rosie thought.

Mr. Pujol gave Ms. Mayfield a stern look. "I am told that it will take only ten minutes, no longer."

"That's about right." She stepped onto the stage and motioned for Rosie, Abuela, and Cheeto to follow her.

Mr. Jackson, the silver-haired lottery commissioner, raised his hands and leaned forward to the microphone. "And here we have our lucky winners—the Caballero family. Rosa, Josefa, and Enrique Caballero." He grinned. "I sure hope I said that right."

Ms. Mayfield lifted a huge stiff poster that had been leaning against the back wall of the stage and passed it to Mr. Jackson, who turned it around. The crowd cheered.

Rosie felt tears in her eyes. It was the big check, the fake one that was always in the papers with the lottery winners holding it. Now it was her turn, and the check had "Six hundred million" scrawled across the front in large black cursive letters. Abuela's hand squeezed her arm tightly and Rosie put an arm around her plump waist. This was for real.

The three of them stood behind the giant foam-board check, holding it up as photographers' flashes blinded them. Rosie counted twelve cameramen from networks, some she'd never heard of before. Reporters yelled out questions that she couldn't hear above the echoing crowd.

A man in front called out, "Are you going to quit your jobs?"

Abuela leaned toward the mic. "I worked as a housekeeper in a hotel, but I officially quit." She beamed at the laughter that erupted from the room.

The excitement of the big lottery prize had infected everyone, Rosie thought. Abuela hadn't said anything funny. Or maybe they were laughing at her accent.

She looked from the cameras trained on them to her family's colorful outfits. By tomorrow they'd be a joke—the hicks who won the lottery. She felt sick.

"What are you going to do first?" a woman yelled.

Cheeto grinned. "I'm going to buy a big car, a big house, and take a big vacation. And I'm inviting all my friends to come along."

Whoops of appreciation echoed in the room. Rosie realized that not everyone in the crowd was a reporter.

"How about you, Miss? What do you want to do?" The woman raised her voice to be heard over the excited throng. A mic was pushed into Rosie's face.

She stared at it as if it were a weapon. "I want to get out of here," she said. Then impulsively, "Diamonds. I want diamonds."

Mr. Pujol waved to them. "*Vamos*, let's go." He signaled to the security guards, who opened the doors back into the hall, then closed ranks behind them.

Outside, the media that couldn't get in were pressed against the doors.

"*Dios mío.* How are we going to get out of here?" Abuela looked shocked. Cheeto looked over her shoulder, the giant Styrofoam check under his arm.

Rosie grabbed the closest uniformed officer. She glanced at the ID bar pinned to his pocket. "Bobby, get us out of here in one piece."

The man nodded to the other officers, who formed a barrier around them and herded the new millionaires back into the conference room.

Abuela was flushed, and Cheeto danced. Rosie wanted to act cool, but she was excited, and happy that they were on their way. "We have to get to the Ritz Carlton in Buckhead. Our cab is waiting for us. It's a Yellow Cab."

Bobby the security guard looked around. "Wait here. I'll call you when I have him."

He returned five minutes later. "I found the cab, but the driver can't get close to the building. You'll have to run for it."

"Are you out of your mind?" Cheeto looked at the crowd that was milling in front of the building.

Abuela tsked. "Be polite, Enrique."

"We'll never make it to the cab alone. Bobby, how would you like to make a little extra money?" Rosie rummaged in her purse for paper and pen.

He raised his eyebrows.

"I'll pay you two thousand dollars to escort us back to our hotel."

Bobby's eyes bugged out. "You got it." He slipped out of the conference room.

Rosie wrote an I.O.U. for two thousand dollars. It wasn't a check, but this way she'd remember. She had a feeling she wasn't going to remember much for the next few days. The first hour already had her reeling.

Mr. Pujol pulled out a cell phone and started to dial. "I'm calling the Ritz so that they know you are coming."

Bobby stuck his head in the door. "Okay, follow me."

The thrilling mix of fear and exhilaration made Rosie light-headed.

"Oh my God!" Abuela had her hands to her face, her eyes wide with excitement. "It's really true. Did you see that check, Rosie? I was so excited, and I don't think I really believed it before this afternoon. *Somos millonarios.*"

Her grandmother's excitement made her own come bubbling back. She wanted to dance and shout. And why not?

Rosie grabbed Abuela's hands and the two of them hurried after Bobby.

"Bring on the bling," Cheeto sang, holding the check over his head like a surfboard from an old movie. "Black gold, Texas tea."

Rosie punched him in the shoulder. "We didn't strike oil, we won the lottery. Living at the Ritz, wearing diamonds and designer clothes."

"Custom Hummers," Cheeto added. "Mansions in every city."

Abuela laughed, and looked ten years younger. "I'm going to take a cruise. I've always wanted to do that."

"Come on, Abue. Think big. Buy yourself a cruise ship. We have six hundred million dollars." Cheeto laughed and wiggled his hips in a quick merengue step. "What could go wrong?"

CHAPTER FIVE

Try to live your old life for a while.
There's plenty of time to ease into a
new standard of living.
—*The Instant Millionaire's Guide to Everything*

Bling Is Her Thing! The Trailer Park Diva Hits the Malls
—*Star magazine*

Ms. Caballero? Would you prefer the steak au poivre or the
pistachio-encrusted salmon?"

Rosie looked up at the waiter looming over her, dressed in
the sober black of the Buckhead Ritz restaurant waitstaff.
They'd checked in, starving, and had come straight to the restaurant for an early dinner. Bobby had been dispatched to their
apartments to pick up luggage, or in Rosie's case, grocery store
bags and one scruffy poodle. "Pistachios? You mean nuts?"

"Yes, the salmon is rubbed lightly with fragrant herbs, then
encrusted with a savory blend of mustard and Hawaiian pistachios." He seemed pleased to offer the bizarre dish.

"Steak, please." Mustard, nuts, and fish? Who thought up
these gross combinations? "Well done."

"I'll have the steak, medium rare." Cheeto took a sip of his expensive wine and made a face. "You have any beer? And can I get French fries to go with the steak?"

"Of course. What beer would you like?"

"Do you have Bud?"

"Of course. Ladies?"

"Same thing," Abuela said in English. She winked at Rosie. "But broccoli, not fries."

Cheeto laughed. "Rosie, you should see the look on your face."

"Wait a minute, you just spoke English in public." Rosie stared at her grandmother. "For years, I've done all the translating for you because you were afraid to make a mistake. Now you're speaking it into a microphone and ordering in restaurants."

Abuela shrugged and answered in Spanish. "Forty years in a country, you pick up a word or two."

Cheeto laughed and hugged Abuela. "You old sneak. I'm proud of you."

Rosie rolled her eyes at the waiter. *Family.* "I'll have fries, too, please." Rosie looked around the restaurant. The tables closest to the front windows were illuminated from outside, but here the only light came from the table lamps that illuminated the diners' faces. Everyone was absorbed in their meals or engaged in quiet conversation. This was nothing like the noisy restaurants she had gone to on dates.

Abuela frowned at them. "I can't believe you can order *papitas fritas* at a deluxe place like this."

"French fries are universal. And the waiter didn't complain, did he?" Cheeto looked around. "Is this place boring, or what? It's like a funeral. And what's with the harp music?"

"It's soothing." Rosie thought it was boring, too, but it was classy, and she wanted to fit in. She drew the line at fish in nuts and mustard, though.

"Oh, I almost forgot." Abuela pulled her purse from the empty chair next to her. "Armando said these were for us." She pulled an envelope out of its cluttered depths.

She held the envelope out to Rosie, who took it. A bill already? She ripped it open and pulled out two American Express credit cards.

"They're not credit cards. Gift cards, but you can use them just like a credit card." Abuela leaned forward to whisper. "There's thirty thousand dollars on each of them. One for each of you, and one for me."

Cheeto plucked his out of Rosie's hand. "Whoa. That's a good start." He waved it in front of Rosie. "Ka-ching!"

"Where did Mr. Pujol get the money?" Rosie turned the card over and examined the back.

"Through the hotel services desk. He said it was just until we could get to the bank. Wasn't that nice?" Abuela tucked her card carefully into her old wallet and dropped it back into her purse.

"Nice? They must be used to doing 'little favors' like this. We're paying a thousand dollars a night for our rooms. I can't wait to see them."

"Yeah. Look at all these rich people." Cheeto was staring at the other diners. Some of them were obviously wealthy, with jewelry and clothes to match. There was a famous TV announcer at the table next to them, and the family in the corner included a child actress Rosie had seen in several films. Mostly, though, they just seemed rich. Maybe it was the way they sat, or ate, or talked to each other, as if no one else mattered.

She tried to practice not caring about anyone but Cheeto and Abuela, but everything was too interesting. She couldn't help looking. She'd have to be content with being treated like a princess, even though she didn't act like one.

The waiter reappeared with a tray holding three tall glasses of beer. He set one in front of their grandmother, then did the same for Rosie and Cheeto.

Cheeto grinned. "Is this high-class or what?"

Abuela pushed her chair away from the table. "Excuse me, I'll be right back."

"Are you okay? You just went." Rosie was concerned. Abuela had vanished down a hallway as soon as they'd checked into the hotel.

"Oh no. I was making friends, then."

"Friends? In the bathroom?" She and Cheeto looked at each other then back at their grandmother.

Abuela looked at her hands. "The maids. I invited them to dinner, too, but none of them has come."

"Are you surprised?" Rosie laughed at her grandmother's crazy notion.

"I never mixed with the guests either." Abuela shrugged. "I thought I'd offer."

"You *are* a guest," Rosie reminded her. "Why don't you invite your friends from your old hotel job? At least they don't work here."

Abuela brightened. "I'll do that."

Cheeto rolled his eyes. "Yeah, and I'll invite my crew over. They'll wear their nicest T-shirts. Come on, we can rent a hall on Buford Highway and throw a major *fiesta* for our old friends." He motioned with his chin at the palm trees, ferns, and old wood. "This place would make them uncomfortable. It kind of gives me the creeps."

Rosie agreed, but she was getting used to it, and she'd only been an official millionaire for less than a day.

After dinner they went upstairs to their rooms. Cheeto raced past them when the elevator doors opened on their key-access-only floor, waving his key card.

Their rooms were at the end of a short corridor, one straight ahead, and one at either side, and they were supposed to open to create a giant suite.

Rosie slid her key into the slot, then pushed open the door. Tootie came running out from behind one of the sofas, barking. "Tootie, baby." Rosie scooped her up and petted her as she examined the room.

It was immense, but there was no bed. Sofas, a china hutch, a dining room, a grand piano. She opened another door and found an elegant bathroom. At the other end of the living room was yet another door. Here was her bed, huge, like the rest of the room, along with another bathroom. Her suite was bigger than her whole apartment.

She threw herself onto the king-sized four-poster bed and stared at the draperies above her. Tootie wriggled out of her arms, turned around twice, and lay down beside her. For the first time since she was little, she had nothing to worry about.

Not work, or bills. Nothing. Tears slid down her cheeks. It would be perfect if her parents were here to enjoy it, too.

The following morning they had their first bank appointment. Rosie wished she'd gone out to buy new clothes last night. She was in her old jeans and T-shirt.

She was going to burn the ill-fitting suit she'd had on yesterday, especially after she saw the front-page article in *The Atlanta Journal-Constitution*. She looked huge. And what was with her hair? A good cut was number three on her list, right after clothes. Number one was still Tiffany's. She wished she could excuse herself from the bank visit, but Mr. Pujol had insisted. He'd even sent a limo to pick them up, a grand gesture probably meant to impress Abuela.

"You've got to be careful, Abuelita. I think that old man is after your money." Cheeto was wearing jeans, too, but his shirt was starched and beautiful. "Courtesy of the Ritz staff," he said.

Abuela shook her head. "I'm too old for romance. If he's after my money, he'll have to think of another way to get it."

Rosie's stomach growled. "I'm starved. Can we stop for breakfast?" She'd slept deeply on her soft hotel room bed, surrounded by pillows. She'd put one of them on the floor for Tootie. "And can we stop afterwards to shop? I don't have any clothes, and I want all new."

"Me, too." Cheeto laced his fingers behind his head and leaned back on the soft leather seats. "Let's go to Lenox Square."

Rosie wanted to go to Phipps Plaza, across the street from

the hotel. Mall shopping had not been a part of Rosie's life, and this mall was totally deluxe.

Rosie scooted up the long sofa that ran the length of the limo and tapped on the glass. Their driver, Ted, agreed to stop for breakfast, and Cheeto gave him directions. "But you don't have to come all the way to the window, folks." He pointed out the telephone in the ceiling over the rear bench seat. "Call me on that phone."

Embarrassed that she hadn't known that, Rosie thanked him and returned to her spot next to Abuela. Cheeto slid back, too, exploring the beverage selections in the long bar as he moved.

"They think of everything," her grandmother said. "Next, we'll find out it has a bathroom."

"You have some kind of bathroom fixation, Abuela." Cheeto smiled and waved as they passed a group of girls on the sidewalk, pointing at their limo. His smile faded a bit as he realized that they couldn't see him through the darkly tinted windows.

They stopped on Buford Highway, since the miniscule parking lot at the old diner couldn't hold the oversized car, and Rosie wondered if theirs was the first limo to stop here. All the customers stopped what they were doing and pressed against the windows, staring. Fred appeared at the door, wet rag over his shoulder as usual.

"Cheeto, when you say you're buying a car, you don't mess around. You going into the limo business?" Fred eyed the car critically.

Cheeto threw an arm around the cook's shoulder. "Fred, we won the lottery. Remember we were just joking around? It really happened. Rosie bought the ticket."

Fred whipped around and kissed Rosie before she could step away, then he kissed Abuela, too. "This is the best day of my life," he cried. "My diner will be famous now. Come in, come in."

Ted joined them inside for eggs and grits and toast. He paid for breakfast, too. "Mr. Pujol said that I was to cover all incidentals."

"Are earrings incidentals? I really want some platinum hoops." Rosie laughed at Ted's shocked look. "Just kidding."

A woman approached their table shyly. "Are you the lottery winners? I saw you on TV."

"Really? On TV? I wish I'd taped it," Abuela said. "How did I look?" Abuela had fallen asleep early, exhausted by the day's excitement. Rosie had too, but she knew Cheeto would tease her if he knew she was keeping granny hours.

"You looked fabulous, Abuela. Like a rich woman." Cheeto grinned at the woman. "Want our autograph?"

The woman blushed, but her look was desperate. "I need your help. My son was in a car accident with no insurance, and we're going to lose our house. Could you please help us?"

"How much do you need?" Abuela asked. Rosie noticed that the other diners were staring now, and their expressions were a mix of envy and curiosity. One woman was staring appraisingly at their clothes, as if she thought they'd be dressed better than in worn jeans. Only Abuela was dressed well, in a navy dress that had a classic enough cut not to look too dated. Rosie wished she'd worn it yesterday, when the TV cameras had been aimed at them.

"Twenty thousand dollars," she said. "That would pay the biggest bills." She swallowed. "Anything would help."

Rosie remembered the magazine's advice to not give any money away, and the warning that people would come begging. She thought of the American Express card in her purse. The card was meant to cover incidentals, but there was enough there to resolve this woman's problems. But what if she was lying?

Before she could make up her mind, Abuela was offering the woman her own gift card. She whispered into the woman's ear. The woman's eyes widened in shock and she glanced down at the card in her hand as if it were a feather from an angel's wing. Then she burst into tears and hugged Abuela.

"Stop," Rosie said, looking at the assessing stares the other diners were giving them. "Please, just go."

The woman nodded and left hurriedly.

Cheeto took Abuela's toast. "As long as you're giving stuff away."

A movement behind Cheeto caught Rosie's eye. One of the other diners was taking their picture with her cell phone.

Crazy. Why would anyone want a picture of them eating breakfast? It wasn't as if they were real celebrities. She hoped that the excitement over the lottery win would fade so that they would be left alone.

They finished eating quickly, enduring more stares, and then left for the bank.

As they walked out Rosie overheard the waitress call them cheap for leaving a 20 percent tip.

"You'd think with all those millions they'd be nicer," the woman said.

"I thought twenty percent was a decent tip," Rosie said. "Fred doesn't expect more."

"Whole new world, cousin." Cheeto shook his head.

It sure was. She'd been prepared to be generous, but Abuela's gesture had been breathtaking, while all Rosie could think was that she didn't even have a new pair of shoes yet.

"*Cálmate,* Rosie." Abuela ducked into the limo. "People will be jealous of us now."

As they headed toward the bank, Rosie thought of the looks the restaurant's customers had given them, from curious to hostile. Was this what life was going to be like from now on? No wonder celebrities could be cranky.

Ted dropped them off in front of a big glass and granite building set in a sea of asphalt parking. He'd have no trouble parking here.

Inside, they stopped in the huge lobby, wondering which way to turn.

"We're supposed to go to the second floor," Abuela said. With Bobby close behind, they walked from one side of the bank to the other, looking for stairs.

Rosie spotted a tiny brass plaque that marked the way to the elevators in a thickly carpeted hall. Upstairs there was no lobby, no tellers, just wood paneling, old oil paintings, and a shushed atmosphere that made Rosie feel out of place.

"You must be the Caballero family." A model-elegant reception stood by a flower arrangement that towered over her, like a clerical goddess at her altar.

"Big money," Cheeto whispered, as they followed the long-legged woman past tapestries and more oversized flower arrangements.

"That's us." Rosie spoke in a normal tone, which echoed through the silent corridor.

"I don't like this place." Abuela looked at a vase filled with lilies. "It's like a funeral home."

"Except without the bodies, I hope." Rosie's cheerful voice seemed loud, but she wasn't yelling.

The Clerical Goddess didn't flinch at the volume, so it was probably okay. She ushered them into a smaller room more in human scale, but just as beautiful. In the center was a round table covered with a snowy cloth and holding a silver tray with a silver coffeepot and delicate, nearly transparent white cups and saucers. No coffeemaker in sight.

The woman motioned toward the table. "Would you care for coffee?"

"Sure." Cheeto sat down, and Rosie took the chair next to his.

"Yes, please," she said. It was un-Cuban to turn down coffee, even though they'd just had some with breakfast. Cheeto took his cup and held it as if it would break in his hands.

Mr. Pujol joined them, and they were introduced to the bank's brokerage staff and began going over the baffling paperwork, opening accounts, and discussing trusts and foundations. Finally they were able to call Ted to ask for the car, and headed downstairs.

They stopped to say good-bye to Mr. Pujol in the lobby. Rosie was impressed by their attorney. When she'd first met him, she'd thought he was one of the cut-rate ambulance chaser types whose storefronts filled Buford Highway and whose prices always escalated unexpectedly when there was money to be had. She couldn't exactly tell him that, though. Instead, she extended her hand. "Thanks, Mr. Pujol, for all of your help."

He shook her hand warmly. "You've taken a big step today. Have you thought about your plans for the future?" This last he addressed to all of them.

Cheeto shrugged, trying to look nonchalant. "Easy. I want to buy a car. After I get some new threads, I'm hooking up with some of my friends later to check out the dealerships." His hands clenched and unclenched in excitement.

"I'm going shopping, too. I need clothes, a makeover, and then I'll be ready to face the world as the new me." And a visit to a certain someone. Rosie looked at her grandmother. "You don't mind if we go without you, do you?"

"No, *niños.* Go ahead. My back is killing me. I'm just going to the hotel to take a little nap."

Mr. Pujol looked exasperated. "I meant with your futures, not this afternoon's plans."

"Oh." Rosie looked at her cousin and grandmother. Cheeto shrugged. He was an "in the moment" kind of guy. Not a big planner. But she'd given it a lot of thought in the past years, after avidly reading stories of people who'd won big lottery prizes.

"I'd like to help girls who can't get into college. You know, average students like I was, who don't stand a chance of getting a scholarship. They deserve to go to school, too."

Mr. Pujol considered her as if she'd surprised him. "An excellent idea, and you are very kind."

Abuela was staring at her as if she'd never seen her before. "Where did this come from, Rosie?"

"From me. I had to work full time and get student loans to go to college because my grades weren't good enough, and then after Papi died and Mami was in the hospital all the college money got used up. I'm in debt and never finished."

"Surely you can pay those debts now." Mr. Pujol's voice was soft.

"Yes, I can. Every one of them." She would owe nothing, owe no one. That was a pretty good feeling.

Abuela patted her shoulder, then kissed her cheek. "My good girl. You deserve this."

"Well, I'm going to the beach, and Disney World, and I'm going to buy a huge house," Cheeto said. "But first, that car is calling my name." He waggled his eyebrows. "I think you're going clothes shopping on your own, Rosita. I'm feeling greedy."

"I'd rather go alone anyway. And you're not greedy, you're honest," Rosie said. With as much money as they had, they could afford to be.

Back at the hotel a frantic Tootie made known that she hadn't been out since early morning, so Rosie snapped her leash to her collar and took her downstairs.

The ratty-looking dog drew stares in the lobby, but Rosie ignored them. She stopped at the front desk. "Can you recommend a dog groomer?"

The clerk looked through her computer. "I have three listed. Do you wish for me to make the appointment for you, Ms. Caballero?"

"Yes, please."

One of the doormen hurried in and raced through the door next to the front desk. The clerk looked up as he sped by, then schooled her face back to pleasant unconcern. "I will certainly do that for you. Is there anything else, Ms. Caballero?"

"No, thank you."

She turned and started to walk toward the front door when the doorman reappeared, followed by two more. Outside, a gray sedan had pulled up, followed by two other cars. A doorman raced to open the sedan's rear passenger door and a man walked out and hurried into the hotel.

Rosie froze. It was Brad Merritt, his face chiseled and perfect, just as it was on the cover of the *Star*. Her favorite movie star was staying in her hotel. She looked down at her jeans and T-shirt, an outfit that hadn't bothered her at the elegant bank, but now seemed impossibly unchic.

The other doormen were trying to intercept the occupants of the other cars, loaded with cameras and audio recorders, who were trying to rush the hotel.

A spidery little man hurried to meet Brad at the door and followed him through the lobby, talking rapidly. "Your room is ready, you may rest for thirty minutes and then a car will pick you up to take you to the dinner. At eight I'll pick you up—Zabo's for drinks with Mr. Chestnut."

They hurried past. Brad's eyes met hers and he rolled his

eyes and then unleashed that devastating, dimpled smile, aimed right at her. The world blurred and then came back into focus, her heart racing as if it could keep up with him. One of the photographers who'd made it inside and was snapping pictures the whole way stopped and stared at Rosie.

"You're the lottery winner." His voice carried through the lobby and everyone stopped and then turned to stare at her, including Brad.

Mortified, she tried to run outside, but Tootie's leash tangled around her legs. She started to fall and put a hand against the wall. One of the doormen rushed to help her, while another shooed the photographers back outside. When she looked up again Brad was gone.

Why did his agent think this trip was necessary? Brad Merritt had liked Atlanta the two times he'd been here, but it galled him to spend the one week the shoot was on hiatus traveling across the country when he could be catching up on sleep or relaxing on a beach remote enough that no one knew his face.

The scene in the lobby had been funny, although that poor girl could have been hurt. The animal she had on a leash had wrapped it around her. Brad had taken a step in her direction, but luckily the doormen had caught her before she fell.

"What were they saying downstairs about a lottery winner?" he asked his agent.

"Biggest prize ever, and this little Cuban kid and her grandmother win it. I think she has a brother or something, too." His agent grinned. "It would make some movie."

Brad laughed. "Not likely. There's not a part in it for me."

Rosie stared after her favorite movie star of all time. Was her luck holding, or what? If only he'd seen her after her makeover. Maybe he would. "Zabo's for drinks," the other man had said.

"I can show you another way out, Miss Caballero. You may not want to go out the front door for a bit." The doorman smiled kindly.

"Thanks. Was that really Brad Merritt?"

"It sure was. This is his favorite Atlanta hotel." The doorman led her through twisting back corridors, ending in a tiny, carpeted lobby with a glass door leading to a small garden and a gate to the side street. "Just use your key card to come back in this way."

She thanked him and walked up the street, then picked Tootie up and carried the little poodle across the street toward Phipps Plaza. A glance toward the front of the Ritz showed a knot of men with cameras lounging around their parked cars, waiting. She shuddered and turned her back to them.

Time to shop. It would be fun to buy everything she liked, but having tons of money had taken the edge off the desire to splurge. It was strange, as if not having money had made her want things more.

Her plan was to buy everything she needed for the next two weeks, and then she'd evaluate her wardrobe again. Living in a hotel meant she couldn't store a lot in her closet, but for sure she wouldn't look at a single price tag. And she'd eat chocolate-dipped strawberries and drink an expensive Starbucks drink. Something with a long Italian name and lots of whipped cream.

Tootie was dragging before they had reached the mall's front entrance, so Rosie stopped to let her hop into the canvas tote she used instead of a purse. The little dog nestled into the towel at the bottom and yawned.

"That's right, *viejita*. Take a nap, so Mami can go shopping." The lure of Phipps, and the Tiffany's store inside, was too much. She'd buy clothes later.

Rosie noticed a couple staring nervously at her. She glanced down at her outfit, jeans and her nylon coat over a T-shirt. Did she look poor?

Money was green no matter who spent it. That was either a saying by Confucius, or more likely from Feo, one of the gang lookouts at the apartments. He thought he was a philosopher.

She found the big directional sign all malls have and made her way to Tiffany's, deep in its retail heart, passing chic clothing shops, deserted at this hour on a weekday. The famous jewelry store was nothing like Rosie had imagined. She thought it would be dripping with diamonds and escorted by armed security guards.

Instead, it was the size of a clothing boutique; two open rooms filled with glass counters and inset glass-covered cabinets in the walls. The employees all wore suits and ties. If there was a guard, he was disguised as an employee.

She looked around at the quiet shop and respectful clerks. Jewelry was like a sacrament here. This was the Church of Bling.

A counter full of pearl necklaces drew her eye. They were beautiful, and she was staring at them when an older man behind the counter noticed her interest, identified himself as Jim, and asked her politely if she needed help. The two women who'd just had their question answered had started to move away, but one of them did a double take when she saw Rosie.

Rosie ignored them. "Yes, please. What's more expensive, pearls or diamonds?"

He didn't laugh, although out of the corner of her eye she saw the two women smirk and move closer. "It depends on the size and quality of the gems, ma'am. All of them are different." He opened the back of the counter and pulled out a black velvet tray, which he placed on the counter.

He looked down at the necklaces through the glass and chose one. Reaching in, he plucked it from the little velvet arms that offered it up to prospective buyers.

The creamy pearls glowed against the velvet tray. "This one is thirty inches long, the pearls are seven millimeters, and the clasp is eighteen-karat gold. Seven thousand, eight hundred dollars."

If he was disappointed at her lack of reaction, he hid it well.

"It's beautiful."

"Thank you." He put the necklace back into the case and went to another counter and returned with a slender strand of diamonds set in a silvery chain. He placed it gently on the black velvet, arranging it with his fingertips.

"This is the Tiffany Swing necklace. At sixteen inches, it's shorter than the pearls, but the diamonds total three and a half carats, and they are very good quality, and set in platinum. Thirteen thousand, five hundred dollars."

"I like it. Does it have matching earrings?"

"Yes. Several types. Would you like to see them?"

"I would."

He stepped away to get them, taking the Tiffany Swing necklace with him. Understandable. If she worked here she wouldn't trust anyone either. Especially the two women, SUV warriors for sure, standing a foot away now.

Rosie gave them a brilliant smile and her best Scarlett O'Hara drawl. "Don't you-all just *love* this store?"

The two women shared a look.

"I do," the blonde said. "My grandmother bought my first diamond studs here. And my husband bought my solitaire here when we got engaged." She held up a hand heavy with platinum and diamonds.

Her anorexic-looking friend leaned closer. They were both dressed in strange, skinny clothes that were too ugly to be anything but expensive designer stuff. "Do you do this often?" the woman asked her.

"What?" Rosie glanced around. Aside from an older lady talking to a female clerk in the other room, they were the only ones here.

"Demand to see all this jewelry, and then, oh, it's not what you had in mind, and off you go. This poor guy gets paid on commission, you know."

"What are you, the union rep?" Rosie looked them up and down, but then the Tiffany's sales clerk was back with several pairs of earrings.

"These are the Swing earrings." They sparkled on the velvet, enhanced by the soft golden light.

Church, Rosie thought. The light was just like in church. It made jewelry look really good.

She examined the earrings. "This pair is kind of big." They looked like chandeliers. "But these are cute. How much?"

The little platinum earrings had three diamonds set just like the ones in the necklace.

"Forty-five hundred for these, forty-three fifty for these."

She frowned.

"Here it comes," the blonde said, rolling her eyes. The salesman glanced at her, then back at Rosie.

"I'll take them all." Rosie reached into her purse. The women backed away and the salesman cringed a little. "What?" She fished out the gift card and handed it to the salesman. "The pearls, the Swing necklace, both of these long earrings, and a pair of pearl earrings to match the necklace. Do you have them with gold posts? They're for my grandmother and she's allergic."

The salesman stared at the card. "Thank you. It'll take me a moment to prepare your purchase."

Rosie tried not to smirk at the dropped jaws of the two women.

"The total is thirty-one thousand, nine hundred twenty-four dollars."

"That much? Wow. Hold on, the gift card won't do it." She handed him her black American Express card, expedited by the bank and delivered by courier that morning.

One of the women gasped.

She grinned at them. "What, you thought I'd pay for it with food stamps?"

They hurried to another counter. Rosie noticed they hadn't bought anything. Amateurs.

A moment later she was signing the receipt. Two other clerks had come to help fold tissue to cradle the robin's egg blue boxes that held her purchases. The blue tote bag they gave her was small, considering how many thousands of dollars' worth of jewels it held.

She hefted the bag a little and grinned. "Thanks, Jim. I'll see you soon."

He smiled in return. "I certainly hope so."

She gave the two astonished women a sunny smile and left, swinging her bag. Outside she paused and looked back inside.

It had been one of the most satisfying moments of her life, especially the reaction of the two women.

Two hours later, after hitting the clothing shops, fur salon, and shoe stores, she put her sleepy dog on the floor, stashed the jewelry bag in the tote, and covered it with Tootie's towel. The rest of her purchases would be delivered to the hotel.

Rosie snapped Tootie's leash to her collar and picked up her tote bag. "Time to walk, old girl."

They strolled to the end of the block, and then crossed the street to an outdoor shopping center that featured a sporting goods store and a bookstore.

She paid a delighted college kid twenty dollars to watch Tootie while she went inside.

He'd said, "Twenty to watch a Rasta poodle? Sweet," then put the loop of Tootie's leash around his ankle and returned to jotting notes in the margins of his book.

Rosie quickly found *The Instant Millionaire's Guide to Every-*

thing, paid for it and a big creamy caramel macchiato, and went back out to reclaim her Rasta poodle.

The reporters had abandoned the front of the hotel, so Rosie sailed in through the main door, said hello to the afternoon reception staff, then rode the elevator to her room.

Rosie noticed that the door to Abuela's adjoining suite was open. She unleashed Tootie, who made a beeline for the pillow Rosie had put on the floor for her the previous night. She fell over onto it, exhausted by the long day. Rosie could go for nap, too.

The phone was ringing, though, and she answered. "Hello?" More reporters. She stared at the receiver in disgust. Didn't they ever get tired? "No, we already did a press conference. No more interviews."

"*Niña,* is that you?" Abuela's voice came through the open door of the adjoining suite, sounding strange, low and rumbling, as if she was talking through a box fan.

"*Sí,* Abue. It's me. Are you okay?"

"I'm having a massage. Who was it?"

"Some TV show. They wanted to talk about being rich."

Her grandmother laughed. "And get asked by a million people for money the next day. How did they find out we were here?"

"Cheeto probably told everybody." She went into the other room and stopped, astounded by the sight.

Abuela was on a massage table in the middle of the living room and a man was working on her back. Not just any man. The guy was handsome, with curly dark hair and a square jaw, and he was dressed in a tight white short-sleeved T-shirt that showed off his muscles. He smiled at Rosie. He had dimples, too, though not as nice as Brad Merritt's.

The phone was ringing again. Rosie sighed. "I'm going to let it ring. Is Cheeto back yet?"

"No, he hasn't come back. He said he was going to buy a car with Herb Sanchez."

Abuela, who'd gone crazy when she'd first seen the heated towel racks, stacks of Egyptian-cotton towels, and extra-thick toilet paper, was having a massage from a man. She was acting as if she'd lived with this luxury all her life.

If Rosie hadn't gone shopping she'd be feeling left behind. "I hope the phone hasn't been driving you crazy. I'm going to order lunch, and I'll tell the front desk to hold calls."

"Thanks," Abuela answered, eyes closed. Rosie noticed her cheeks were red. Was she blushing? The guy had finished her back and was rubbing oil on her legs, stroking higher and higher.

Eek. Abuela needed privacy. She pulled the door closed, walked to her bedroom and stashed the blue tote bag in the wall safe inside her closet, then returned to the parlor, as the hotel called the living room, to sit on one of the elegant sofas with her coffee drink and her new book. She was eager to read it, but part of her mind wouldn't let her concentrate, the part that kept whispering, *Brad Merritt is going to sleep in this hotel,* and as if it was a connected thought, *your bed is king-sized.* It wasn't the hot coffee that made her break out in a sweat.

CHAPTER SIX

* * * * * *

Spend no more than 10 percent of
your total windfall on impulse items.
Have fun—but carefully.
—*The Instant Millionaire's Guide to Everything*

$37,000 in Diamonds, a Hummer, and Lavish Parties—
Details of How Lottery Winners Celebrate
—*Star* magazine

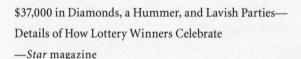hat evening, Rosie sorted carefully through the purchases that had
been delivered from Phipps and hung up in her closet by an
awed housekeeper.

She would not have noticed the discreet knock at her door if
Tootie hadn't barked. She walked to the door in her new silk
robe, enjoying the swirl of soft cloth around her legs.

A man with a bright yellow crew cut stood outside, with two
young women behind him, each carrying a large tool chest.

"You're Daniel?" Daniel Cross, that is, the city's foremost
hairdresser.

"In person," he said, bowing slightly, eyes on her head as if
assessing what he had to work with. He pushed past her and
looked around the suite, then pulled a chair from the dining
table.

One of the assistants laid a plastic sheet on the floor, then put the chair on top of it, covered with another sheet.

"If you will please sit here, Miss Rosie, we will begin."

Rosie sat on the chair and a swirl of plastic flew before her like a matador's cape, then was pulled up tight around her neck. "I'd like something a little more modern, maybe—"

Daniel appeared in front of her, hands on hips. "I am a master. Did you hear I was the best? Well, I am. And your role is to sit and submit to my artistry."

One of the girls smiled slightly and turned away, then looked back at Rosie and winked.

"Um, okay."

Apparently Daniel and crew were accustomed to coming to hotel rooms. They washed her hair right in the middle of the living room without spilling a drop on the plastic sheeting. One of the girls set up an easel in front of her with a huge mirror, then Daniel pulled scissors from a holster and got to work.

When he finished, he dried and then flatironed her hair. "I want you to consider color, Rosie," he said, tugging hairs this way and that. "Copper highlights, with gold threads."

"Sounds exotic."

"And fun. Very fun." He ran his fingers over her dark brown hair, now straight and silky as it had never been before. The cut emphasized her eyes and layers pointed to her cheekbones and jaw. She looked almost like a model.

"Your turn, Twylla."

The girl who had winked at her earlier opened her tool case, revealing rows of pots and pans of cosmetics. She set up jars of brushes, pushed back Rosie's newly cut hair, and set to work.

"Watch carefully so that you can do this when I'm not around," Twylla said. "Unlike Daniel, I'd like for you to know how to do your own."

Daniel, on the couch with a cell phone to his ear, ignored her. Rosie paid close attention to every brush stroke and color choice. When Twylla was done, Rosie looked as if she were about to pose for a magazine cover.

The trio packed everything up and left. Rosie went to her room, opened the safe, and took out the Tiffany's bag. The box the pearls were in was beautiful. She put the smaller box with the earrings on top and put her diamonds on top of the dresser.

She knocked on Abuela's door.

Abuela answered with her hair in foam curlers. Her eyes widened when she saw Rosie's hair and makeup. "My God, is that you?" She dragged her inside. "You're beautiful. Who did this for you? She's a genius."

Rosie laughed and hugged her grandmother. "Thanks. And she's a crew of three. I'll give you their card if you like what they did."

"I do, I do." Abuela held out tendrils of Rosie's hair. "*Bella.*"

"What time are your friends coming tomorrow?"

"Not until six, and I have some shopping to do first. I was just watching TV while my hair dries."

Abuela had invited the entire day shift of the Grand Hyatt, her former employer, and Rosie had volunteered her suite since it had a dining room. Afterward, Abuela's closest friends would join her in her suite for cards.

"Are you still going to stick to your plan for today?" Abuela didn't sound happy.

Rosie smiled. "Oh, yes."

Abuela shook her head. "You are a crazy girl."

"Crazy? Maybe I won't give you the present I have here." She waggled the blue gift bag.

The older woman looked surprised and pleased. "For me? Oh, you shouldn't spend your money on me. Come sit on the sofa." The TV was on and the remote control was on the sofa arm. The table before it was littered with brochures for Caribbean cruises.

"That's the old you talking. The new you is very rich." She put the bag down and pulled out the two jewelry boxes, holding them behind her in the old game they'd played since Rosie was a toddler. "Which hand?'" She smiled, anticipating her grandmother's reaction.

Abuela's eyebrows lifted in anticipation, then she closed her eyes. "The right one." She opened them again, and frowned at the flat, robin's egg blue box Rosie held out to her. "What's this?"

"Open it. I'm sorry I didn't gift wrap it."

"You didn't need to. The box is so pretty." Her grandmother opened the blue cardboard box and pulled out the leather case inside. "Ooh, what's this?" She looked up at Rosie, smiling delightedly.

"Just a little present."

Abuela unsnapped the tab that held the box closed, and then opened it to reveal the creamy pearls, perfectly displayed on a lush velvet tray within. She gasped. "*Dios mío.* These are real, aren't they?"

"Yes. And these go with it." Rosie produced the little square box that held the matching earrings.

Abuela's eyes welled up and she held her arms out to Rosie. They hugged tightly and cried. "Is it ungrateful to wish this had happened before, so that your parents and your grandfather could also have enjoyed this?"

"No, it's normal. I wish it, too." She barely remembered her grandfather, but the pain of her parents' absence was a scabbed-over wound, still raw just under the surface.

She helped her grandmother fasten the pearls, and after admiring them for a while Rosie slid to the floor at her feet, and the two sat quietly, lost in thought. She watched the TV Guide Channel scroll endlessly through the viewing choices. Her life had endless choices now, too.

The screen went to an ad for a coming show, one that highlighted celebrity gossip. A wedding flashed by, along with a few red carpet moments, and then there she was, with Cheeto and Abuela. "The winners of the biggest lottery prize in U.S. history came forward and *Bling!* has all the details," the announcer chirped.

"That's us!" Abuela leaned forward. "We're on TV." She telephoned Cheeto's room, but he didn't answer. They hadn't seen him all day.

Rosie stared at the TV, openmouthed. She looked like a blimp, like a sausage, and what she'd considered a professional suit made her look like a badly uniformed nanny from TV. She remembered the thin women at Tiffany's, and their casually rich clothes, and hid her face in her hands. What had they thought of her? Good thing she'd bought new clothes. She was ready to make a big impression.

"It's not so bad." Her grandmother was clearly pleased by

the press coverage, but Rosie thought it was just a matter of time before her family showed up on tabloid covers, too.

Rosie returned to her room and changed into one of her new outfits. The sales clerk had assured her that the pants suit was the latest style. Looking in the mirror, Rosie wasn't so sure, but it was expensive, as were the high designer heels. She carefully pulled out her pride and joy, a full-length blue-and-white-striped fox fur coat, an off-season bargain that even at half price cost as much as her necklace.

She was fighting the clasp on her diamonds when the front desk called to say that her car had arrived.

She grabbed her fur coat and put it on, posing in front of the mirror. Would it look better over her shoulders? On her arm? No, she put it back on, loving the soft coolness of the lining and the expensive-feeling weight on her shoulders.

She pressed the down button on the elevator, which stopped on two more floors, collecting more people. Each person that mounted the elevator stared at her and at least two seemed to recognize her, or thought they did. The doors opened at the lobby level and she walked out into the hall, then turned the corner to the lobby and out to where the stretch limo awaited her.

Ted hopped out and ran around to open the door for her. "Where to, Miss Rosie?"

"Do you know where Zabo's is?"

"Indeed I do."

By the time they got there, Rosie was almost breathless and had to force herself to breathe normally. The stretch limo was definitely the wrong choice to maneuver the crowded Buckhead party district, but it wasn't the only one, and everyone stared as she went by.

The colorful neon sign for Zabo's gleamed above a nondescript burgundy awning set in the side of a building that housed two bars. The crowd milling outside wore jeans and trendy tops. She might be seriously overdressed, but that only meant that he'd be sure to notice her.

The limo rolled to a stop and she waited impatiently for her door to be opened. A glance at her watch showed that she was only ten minutes late. He was sure to be here already. She sidestepped a grate in the sidewalk, shuddering at the thought of ruining her new heels, and strode past the gaping smokers hanging by the door. She smiled as she entered the bar. They couldn't take their eyes off her.

Brad played with the drink straw in his sparkling water and listened to Paul Chestnut and his agent discuss the upcoming film.

Another action movie. Why couldn't he do something different? He was a good actor, everyone said so. Well, not the so-called "serious" actors, but he was sure that if he was given a chance he could prove them all wrong. He should look into stage work, too. Now that was real acting.

A change in the noise level drew his attention. The people by the door had gone quiet and were staring, but not at him. A woman had walked in wearing a huge striped fur. Was that the Greek flag? She moved forward and the coat fell open, showing that she wore skintight satin pants and a top that dripped beads and ribbons down one side.

"So what do you want to do, Brad?"

He turned to Paul, who was looking at him expectantly. "I want to do theater. I want to act on Broadway."

His agent stared at him, eyes wide. "Brad—"

Paul Chestnut lifted a hand, silencing him. "If I get you on Broadway, will you do *Vector Five*?"

Brad glanced at his agent, who'd gone silent. He'd hear about this later, but so what? This was the chance he'd been waiting for. He was so excited that he barely noticed the woman in the bizarre fur as she walked past slowly.

"Yes," he said. "I'll do it." His dream was about to come true.

"Cartwright Office Supply in Chamblee." The voice on the phone was unfamiliar.

Rosie clicked her iPhone off and leaned her head against the limo door. She was excited, which helped her not to think about last night's fiasco.

She'd gotten a lot of attention, all right, but none at all from Brad. He'd stared right at her, and his expression hadn't changed, as if she were invisible. Whatever those two men were saying must have been very important.

It hadn't helped that she'd felt out of place in her diamonds and fur. But she'd sure gotten a lot of attention. Everyone had stared.

She wore the fur and diamonds today, too, although she had on jeans and a sexy top. She thought she looked sharp, and very rich. Lana was going to die when she saw her.

She'd turned her attention to her book, *The Millionaire's*

Guide, on the short ride north to Chamblee, trying to keep from getting nervous. None of the advice sank in.

When they were a block away, Rosie picked up the overhead phone. "Pull over on that side street, Ted. I need to make a call before we get there."

The limo slid to the curb, drawing curious stares from passersby. Now was the time to make the call. Rosie pulled out her phone and tapped in the number for Cartwright again. The same woman answered.

"Is Lana Cartwright there?" she asked.

"Yes she is. May I tell her who's calling?" The voice was young and perky.

"Rosie Caballero."

There was a startled gasp and then a quick, "One moment."

She listened to the office products hold message, then the line was picked up again.

"Rosie? I tried to call you at your hotel," Lana gushed. "I heard your great news."

"I figured you might have. I'm nearby. I thought I'd drop by to sign my termination papers and get my check."

The silence that followed her statement made Rosie smile. She could almost smell the little gears overheating inside her former boss's head. She was probably thinking, Do I say yes? Will that make her mad? Would she have given me any lottery money either way?

"Um, yes," Lana squeaked. "The papers are right here."

Rosie grinned. She pictured her old boss squirming. "I'll be right there." She hung up and then picked up the overhead phone and gave Ted directions to her old job.

The limo was almost as long as the low building was wide and there was no place to park it, so Ted stopped in the street. He got out and walked around to open the door for her. She stepped out, turning her face to hide her glee from the ghostly faces visible through the tinted windows. All twenty-five employees must have had their faces pressed against the glass, she thought. This was going to be so much fun.

The front door opened to reveal Lana, shivering as she held the door open.

Rosie straightened, winked at Ted, then nodded to him coolly for the benefit of the watching eyes. Ted touched his cap and bowed slightly. Rosie looked toward the front door and allowed herself a little look of surprise, as if she'd just noticed Lana, then sauntered up the walk, aware of the diamonds and furs against her skin, and not feeling the bitter March air at all.

Abuela's friends were arriving when Rosie got back to the hotel. Today hadn't been as thrilling as when she'd turned in the lottery ticket, but the memory of Lana and the employees of Cartwright treating her like a celebrity instead of the office drudge had been very satisfying. She'd signed her termination papers and received her check for two hundred and twenty dollars, watching out of the corner of her eye as everyone in the building made an excuse to walk past Lana's doorway to get a glimpse of her.

They'd all trailed after her as she walked out the door to her waiting limo. She'd waved good-bye to them, then Ted had closed the door, and the solid clunk it made cut off the outside sounds, as if severing her from her old life. Snuggled in the comfortable leather seat, surrounded by the hum of the engine and the limo's new car scent, she hoped that she'd never have reason to think of Lana or Cartwright Office Supply again.

That night she ate dinner alone. Abuela's housekeeper *amigas* were next door, playing cards and ordering room service, but she hadn't wanted to join them. With her job firmly behind her, she felt adrift. The guilty pleasure of ditching work was gone, and even though she knew that she didn't have to work anymore, she felt unemployed. Strange. Maybe work had been a habit; if so, it would be an easy one to break.

Rosie lay in bed listening to the noise that filtered through the connecting door, glad for the thick walls that kept the party from the other rooms on the floor. They were talking about cruises, and Abuela was having the time of her life. If Rosie's life had changed, so far it had been like changing the cover of a book, but leaving the inside the same. Was Rosie the only one who felt that? Her grandmother had taken to her new life as if, after years of hard work, she deserved it. Cheeto, of course, never worried about anything.

Maybe Rosie needed more worthwhile goals. She had beautiful jewels and clothes. She was living in a luxurious hotel, waited on by a staff. She had a limo and driver. What more could she want?

She needed a permanent place to live, a home base from which she could do whatever she wanted, just as soon as she figured out what that was. Friends, maybe. Her workaholic ways hadn't left room for friendships, and she hadn't dated much. She thought of the dates with Jorge, and the night Rick had left her during what she'd considered their big date.

Men were definitely not part of her plan, although she hadn't been able to resist trying to meet Brad Merritt. Who could? And so what if it hadn't worked—she'd been within touching distance of him twice. Her good luck was holding up.

An excited call from Cheeto woke her the next morning. "Come down and look at my new car, Rosie. Get Abuela and we'll go for a ride and grab breakfast at the Pancake House."

She groaned and looked at the bedside clock. Eight in the morning. "Where have you been?"

"Around. Are you coming?"

"Okay, I'll be down in a minute, but *you* call Abuela. She was up all night."

Cheeto laughed. "I definitely take after her."

Not even close, Rosie thought after she hung up. Her grandmother was mature. She was having fun, but she didn't just vanish, leaving no word of where she was going.

Rosie pulled a pair of her new jeans and a knit top from the closet. She'd tried on lots of jeans at the little boutique at Phipps. They seemed to think that size four was normal, and size twelve was fat. She'd finally found a pair that fit; tight, but they zipped. A personal trainer might take care of the extra curves that had made her look so awful on TV.

As she dressed, she noticed the diamonds on her dresser. She debated putting them away, then impulsively put them on, turning in the mirror to make them twinkle from her neck and ears. She'd never get tired of their glitter.

Downstairs she crossed the deserted lobby and went out into the drive, where a sleek silver Ferrari hummed in the circular brick driveway, although Cheeto was nowhere in sight. Did he expect the three of them to fit in the tiny two-seater? No way would she ride jammed in the back.

The door opened behind her and Abuela came out, wearing a sporty knit outfit. "*Buenos días, nena.* Where's your cousin?"

She kissed her grandmother. "Maybe he's inside."

Abuela clucked her tongue and shook her head. "And left his car running? He won't own it for long if he does that. This is Atlanta." Her words were engulfed by the boom of a boosted bass that thundered around them as a huge black Hummer climbed the drive and rolled to a stop behind the Ferrari.

Abuela covered her ears and the smokers lurking by the doorway looked annoyed. The sudden silence when the Hummer was turned off seemed almost like another sound.

The driver's side door opened and Cheeto jumped down. The hood towered over him. He polished the fender with his sleeve as he passed it. "Well, what do you think?"

"I think it's obnoxious." Rosie's peripheral vision caught the smokers nodding in agreement. "Did you actually buy it?"

"*Basta,*" he said. "This car is so hot you can't stand it. What do you think, Abuelita?"

Their grandmother was staring at it in horror. "This is a car for the street? It looks like a tank. I thought that was your car." She pointed at the Ferrari, which looked like a silvery sardine next to the massive Hummer.

"The guys at the dealership were psyched that I was the lottery winner. Did you catch the three of us on TV, night before last? We're all over the news. They practically gave me the Hummer."

"I hope you didn't sign anything," Abuela said. "Remember Mr. Pujol said not to sign anything." She motioned to a doorman to help her into the vehicle's tall backseat.

"Where have you really been?" Rosie whispered from the seat behind Cheeto as they toured the city, burning gas in *chorros*. She didn't want Abuela to ask the same question and maybe hear an honest answer that would upset her. As in, hanging out with women and drinking too much.

"No secret. Buying this car and a motorcycle, too. And accessories. Trailers, seat covers, the whole enchilada. I'm living it up, babe. I helped out some of my homies with some stuff, and I'm flying to Vegas tomorrow."

"Babe?" She laughed. "When did you start calling me babe? And what are you going to do in Las Vegas? You didn't invite us."

"What's so funny?" Abuela leaned toward them.

"Cheeto's going to Las Vegas. Easy money and easy women." There. Let him get blasted by grandmotherly advice against fast living.

Her cousin rolled his eyes and grinned. "Don't have to go to Vegas for that."

Rosie stuck her fingers in her ears. "La, la, la. I don't want to hear." She dropped her hands to catch whatever Abuela would say in response, but her muttered answer was unintelligible.

"I think you'd better do some good works, too, *primo* dear," Rosie said. "Or Abuela's going to sic the priests on you."

"I worry about you, *mi amor.*" Abuela patted Cheeto's shoulder. "You should find a nice girl and settle down. You can afford it now. Those bad girls will take advantage of you."

"I'm sowing my wild oats, Abuela. Aren't guys supposed to do that before they get married? And what about Rosie? She's older than me. Give *her* the settle-down lecture." He shot Rosie a "gotcha" grin.

She punched his shoulder. "No candidates. And who can I trust? Any guy that wants to go out with me will want my money."

"Not all, Rosie," Abuela said. "Cheeto's right. You need to make friends with boys who are like us."

"Cuban-American lottery winners?" Rosie slouched in the Hummer's seat. "Rare."

Abuela tsk-tsked. "Don't make fun, I'm serious."

"I want to travel," Rosie said.

"Not by yourself?" Abuela sounded doubtful. "Where will you go? I don't think you should go alone."

"People do it all the time, Abuela. Besides, I won't be in some barrio. I'll go to the islands, or to Miami. They probably have resorts with private armies of security guards." Okay, so now she had a goal, even if she'd just made it up.

"Let me give you the number of my travel agent," Abuela said. "If you work with them, I'll rest easy. They are very dependable."

"I didn't know you had a travel agent." She remembered the brochures on the coffee table. "You're one to talk about traveling alone if you're planning to go on a cruise by yourself."

"Not alone. I'm going to treat my canasta friends. You children are welcome to join us."

"That's a lot of people, if it's everyone who was at the party last night." Rosie couldn't imagine traveling with that many old people. They partied hard, too.

"Las Vegas for me," Cheeto said firmly.

"I think maybe I'll go to Mexico." It had been a flash decision, but the idea made her shiver in anticipation. Just like that, she had plans.

Back at the hotel, Abuela took Rosie aside. "I think we should put together a company, you, me, and Enrique, one that does good deeds and helps people, but with no strings. Like Mr. Pujol told us about at the bank."

"Don't we have one? Isn't that the foundation we started? Or at least, Mr. Pujol filed the papers." She kissed her grandmother's forehead. "Maybe our foundation can be dedicated to teaching the elderly to play canasta on the high seas."

Abuela snorted. "I'll take care of that particular group. They won't need any more help."

At the end of the week, when Abuela was packing for her cruise, Rosie decided to go to Miami with her. She'd never been outside of Georgia, which was ironic, since some Georgians would consider her a foreigner just because she was Latina. But she was a homegrown Southern girl. Her parents were, too, if "South" was anything below the Mason-Dixon line. Cuba was considerably below it.

Miami would be a baby step. Travel would be fun, although what she really wanted was to be one of the glitterati, those famous people whose party pictures from New York and L.A. were always in celebrity news. "Here's the *American Idol* winner," the caption would read, "with Rosie Caballero who won the MegaBucks." Or "Here's Rosie Caballero, the lottery winner, dancing with Brad Merritt." That would be one she'd frame.

It would not happen on a rented bus with a bunch of old folks.

She wanted to be a celebrity too, but in a good way, not in a tabloid way. Which reminded her that she needed to monitor the supermarket magazines, just in case.

She called the hotel's front desk and asked for a copy of each of the tabloids. They were delivered discreetly wrapped in tissue. The hotel was already accustomed to the Caballero family's weird requests.

Cheeto stopped by on the way to his room, laughing when he saw the magazines. "You never read that shit before." He leafed through one of them, stopping at the sexier pictures. He eyed them appreciatively. "Hey, here's one of you." He held up a magazine, and there she was on the cover, holding her dog and about to go into the Ritz Carlton.

She snatched it out of his hand, her heart sinking as she saw the awful photograph up close. She looked fat and dowdy, and Tootie looked as if she'd been plucked from Katrina's floodwaters.

"I hope I don't look like this anymore." Dismayed, she turned to the inside article, which displayed a photo of her entering the hotel. At least the article was brief, just two paragraphs describing her shopping habits.

Cheeto held out another one, making kissing noises. "Here's lover boy." Brad Merritt smiled at her from the cover. Cheeto poked her shoulder, still a big kid. "Be cool, Rosie. Relax."

She looked down at her face, grimacing at the difference in the tabloids' covers. Relax? How could she?

The next day the paparazzi clogged the streets in front of the Ritz. Everywhere Rosie went a guy followed her with a big-lensed camera. When she met Cheeto and Abuela for lunch at J Alexander's in Norcross, Cheeto reported that he'd been hounded, too. Before lunch was done a small knot of photographers had gathered outside.

"That guy who was following Brad Merritt must have told everyone he knew." Rosie was perplexed. "Boy, they work fast."

Abuela thought it was great. "They came into church this morning while we were planning the new kneelers and took lots of pictures. They were very nice."

"Did Ted drive you over there?" She imagined the stretch limo gliding into the parking lot at St. Patrick's. That would be an attention-grabber for certain.

"No, I took a cab. A very nice woman was driving, too. Can you believe she has two children and drives a taxi while they're in school?"

"How much did you give her?" She knew her grandmother.

"Just five thousand."

Cheeto laughed and high-fived her. "Ain't it great that you can say *just* five thousand?"

"Abuela, Mr. Pujol said that we weren't supposed to do that."

She shook her head. "What if there's a 'Church Lady Lotto Queen' headline? You'll be mobbed by people wanting money."

"So? You will be, too, and you don't give anything away," Cheeto said.

Rosie turned on him. "Laugh it up, Mr. Generous. Who have you helped, beside your friends?"

He pursed his lips. "Let's see. I bought my friends each a truck, and gave them ten thousand dollars to spend any way they want, then I paid off Gloria's bills and told her I wouldn't be dating her anymore." He turned to Abuela. "Mr. Pujol made sure she couldn't sue me for anything. See? I *am* being smart."

Abuela frowned. "You didn't have to give that girl anything."

"Just a little good-bye gift." Cheeto shrugged.

"That was really generous, Cheeto." Rosie had underestimated him. Maybe she should help someone, but who? Mirta, for certain. Fred at the diner, maybe. Mr. Kim, whose bodega had sold her the ticket already got a big cash prize, but maybe she could do something for the folks at the apartment complex. She'd ask Mr. Pujol what to do.

"I'm leaving for Miami on Friday and the ship leaves the next morning," Abuela was saying. "That's why I wanted us to get together today."

Cheeto hooted. "Seven days of seafarin' canasta. I'll think about you when I'm in Vegas playing twenty-one."

A short man in trendy clothes stopped at their table and offered his hand. "Cheeto Caballero? I'm Cal Wadsworth with the *Star*. Can I talk to you for a second?"

Cheeto released the hand he'd automatically taken and backed away.

A flash went off. The woman at the next table had taken their picture. Rosie stood, feeling naked. "Come on. We're out of here."

She grabbed Cheeto's hand and pulled him behind her. Abuela was already headed toward the exit. Fast learner.

"Rosie, how has your life changed?" Cal called.

"How did he know where we would be?" Abuela muttered something else after this, but her clenched teeth made it unintelligible.

"That's a good question." Rosie looked back at the restaurant. Who had tipped them off that they would be eating there?

Cheeto drove them back to the hotel, where the front desk clerk handed Rosie a large envelope. "Your messages."

"Thanks." Rosie clutched the fat envelope to her chest as she hurried to the elevators, followed by Abuela and Cheeto, and jumped into one already occupied by an older couple. Abuela quickly swiped her hotel room card.

Silence reigned when the elevator doors closed. Rosie wanted to lean against the mirrored wall. Being chased was tiring, and she hated being stared at as if she was an escapee from the zoo. Not even a dangerous and glamorous escapee, like a tiger. More like a penguin. The stares had been of the "what the hell?" variety.

The elevator stopped on the third floor and the couple prepared to exit. The woman turned to them.

"I'll bet you're having the time of your lives. Are you doing everything you've ever dreamed of?"

"You bet we are." Cheeto grinned.

Abuela nodded and Rosie smiled, the mirror reflecting her weak effort.

Upstairs the silence was broken by the sound of tinkling glasses and laughter coming from behind the doors of the combined suites at the end of the hall.

Abuela's friends were partying without her. Rosie said hi to the card players as she made her way to her bedroom. She wanted to kick them out, but didn't want to offend her grandmother. Maybe she should get another suite.

The envelope the clerk had handed her was full of little pink notes, most of them pleas for money and offers of investment help. She didn't recognize any of the names on the notes, so she dumped them in the trash, thinking of how much money her family had given away, while she'd sat on her portion.

When her folks had been alive she'd worked part time to save for school, then had taken out loans so that she wouldn't have to work while attending college. The loan money had paid for her parents' burials and some of their bills, and she'd been stuck with the loan debt and no degree.

Since then, her goals had been to keep the lights on and the rent paid. Maybe she should go to college now, although it seemed pointless since she wasn't going to need a job. Whatever she ended up doing, it wouldn't include handing out cash to everyone who said they needed it. She was no fool.

She stared at the remaining pink messages in her hand. One of the travel agents Rosie had contacted had called back with the information she'd requested for her Mexico trip. She set it aside, as well as another one from Mr. Pujol. The only other note she kept was a day old, from Lana at Cartwright, offering her congratulations. Three of the messages in her voice mailbox were from Lana, too.

Tough, Rosie thought. If you'd been nice, I'd have been nice right back. She went to check on her grandmother.

The suite was noisy with oldsters drinking margaritas and playing cards. She poured herself a margarita from the pitcher on the sideboard, then retreated back to her bedroom to return Mr. Pujol's call.

He sounded pleased to hear from her, although he seemed concerned when she told him about the photographer at the restaurant. "Do you have time for lunch soon?" She heard him move papers around. "It's not with me. I want you to make the acquaintance of a friend of mine, Dr. Eve Sloane."

"Sure. What's up?"

"I'm concerned that you're in the newspapers so much. Today was a disturbing example. I just want her to give you a little advice on how to manage yourself in your new situation. Consider her a life coach."

Her heart sank. It sounded like someone who would lecture her on what she'd been doing wrong. She'd never considered herself helpless before, but she was unprepared for this new life. Maybe she did need a life coach. Maybe she'd needed one for years.

That Friday the *Star*'s headline was, "Lottery Diva's Big Squeeze," with an accompanying photo of her in the dressing room of the mall boutique, trying to zip a pair of too-small jeans.

Mortified, Rosie let her breakfast coffee cup clatter back onto the saucer. "I am not leaving this room today. Someone might recognize me. And they got everything wrong in this article, too."

Abuela looked up from the *Financial Times*, which she'd taken to reading lately. "Don't make a fuss, *nena*. They're trying to sell more newspapers."

"Yeah, with my overweight backside. The woman kept bringing me the wrong size jeans. And I wasn't an unemployed waitress. They must have talked to Fred." She picked up her cup again for a long, fortifying gulp.

Fred had probably seen her only as Cheeto's cousin and his fill-in waitress. Everyone had an idea of who she was, how she fitted into their world. Rosie wished she had a clear view of her own life. Eve Sloane would help her take control.

"If you tell the paper that they were mistaken, they'll just tell you to talk to the reporters again in order to get the story right." Abuela sipped her own coffee. She frowned at the *Financial Times*'s pink pages.

"Even when I try to straighten them out they get everything wrong." Rosie felt grumpy. "I need to get away. I'm glad we're headed to Miami. I want to look at boats. I saw a TV show about luxury yachts and I think I want one."

"A yacht?" Abuela laughed. "Since when? Except for Lake Lanier, there's no place to put a big boat around here."

"You should see them. They have bedrooms and bathrooms just like houses." Thoughts of the boat cheered her. "Bigger than a lot of houses." In it, she could go out into the ocean for days, far from stares and whispers and photographers. It was one reason Mexico seemed so appealing. No one would know her there.

Abuela shrugged. "If you take a cruise, you can walk away from the ship afterwards. No upkeep. Much easier. Besides, you don't know anything about boats. Who would drive it?"

"I'd have to hire someone. A captain." That sounded romantic.

Abuela had gone back to reading her newspaper, mouthing the words as if she'd understand them better that way.

Rosie returned to her room, where she found Tootie nosing around the shopping bags she'd left there. She looked like a real poodle now, fluffy and white, with little red toenails and a diamond clip in her topknot.

"You're going on a little trip, old girl." She stroked the little dog's ears. At least it wasn't a plane ride. She didn't think she was up to that just yet.

Tootie licked her hand.

Rosie pulled a candy-striped patent leather tote from its swathes of tissue paper. "This is a present for you. A real dog carrier. No more canvas tote bags. Isn't it chic?"

Tootie's tongue lolled out, a sign that she was pleased. An elegant dog deserved an elegant carrier.

Rosie thought of the tabloid photos taken in the dressing room by a photographer she'd never noticed. She needed to go where they wouldn't recognize her. Miami Beach wasn't exactly the best choice. She had to look good and be on guard the whole time. Dr. Sloane might be her salvation.

CHAPTER SEVEN
* * * * * *

Avoid celebrity. There are thousands of
millionaires in the United States,
and most live quietly.
Above all, avoid notoriety.
—*The Instant Millionaire's Guide to Everything*

MegaBucks Lottery Winner Rescues Film Festival,
Five Hundred Thousand Keeps It Afloat
—*The Miami Herald*

Hurricane Rosie Hits Miami—
Bling Warnings Posted
—*Star* magazine

Dr. Eve Sloane was who Rosie wanted to look like when she was forty.
Slim, elegant, and perfectly groomed, she sat at a table for two
in the Buckhead Ritz lobby restaurant, reading the menu. She
didn't look up until Rosie stood by the table, then she rose
smoothly, diamond-ringed hand outstretched. Pure class.

They introduced themselves and shook hands. Rosie wondered if she imagined the little wince as Dr. Sloane looked her
up and down. Her outfit was new, jeans and a sweater she'd
only worn once.

Her favorite waiter came up, his rumpled face smiling.

"Hi, Lou. How's your mother?"

"Better, Miss Rosie. Thanks for asking. Would you ladies care for a drink?"

"I'll have a Coke and French fries. How about you, Eve?"

The woman frowned. "Give me a minute."

"Of course." Lou bowed a little and moved to the next table.

"Is something wrong?" Rosie watched her companion examine the menu. "I thought Mr. Pujol said you wanted to meet here."

"Indeed. He said that you wanted help so that you could assimilate financially and socially to your new life, with your new peers."

"Peers. Hadn't heard that word since high school." The woman's stern look reminded Rosie of her high school algebra teacher.

"Then consider this an advanced high school class. Are you willing to learn, and work hard?" The woman looked as if she had rebar running through her spine and Rosie remembered how much she'd hated algebra. She needed the advice, though. She hadn't done so well on her own.

"Sure," she said, and gave her a smile, although her insides felt sour. She was tired of being laughed at in the press because of the things she did and her taste in clothes, but what was she getting herself into?

She had to control her temper. "Okay, Eve. When do we start?"

"Right now. For starters, I am Dr. Sloane." She motioned

with one upraised finger, and Lou the waiter was instantly at her side.

"Change our order, please," she said.

Lou nodded expectantly.

"Water with lemon, poached salmon, and field greens dressed with lemon juice. For two."

"Would Madame care for wine?"

"Yes. Do you still have a bottle of Fleurie La Madonne Dudet? Don't remember the year, except that it was quite young."

"Madame's memory is excellent. We have that Beaujolais, and the year was 2004."

She beamed at Rosie, who'd felt her mouth fall open.

"You changed my order," she said after the waiter left. Lou hadn't even glanced at her to confirm. She was so astonished she wasn't even indignant.

"Coke and French fries are beach food. Picnic food. One orders better fare at this type of restaurant." She lifted her upper lip in a little ladylike sneer. "It's nutritionally important as well, and for, ahem, weight loss."

Rosie sat back in her armchair, stunned. Had Dr. Sloane just called her fat? Her thoughts must have shown on her face, because the woman's cool, thin hand hovered over Rosie's warm, tanned one.

"Don't worry, my dear. Once you can order wisely you may have whatever you desire." Dr. Sloane turned her smile to Lou, who'd returned with their water. Wafer-thin lemon slices floated in the glasses, not the thick yellow wedge Rosie was accustomed to getting in her tea.

Another server placed a tiny plate next to her, with two toast slices embellished with minced tomatoes, onions, and garlic. If this was salsa, it was so wrong. No one had ever served this kind of stuff to her before, and she'd been eating here for weeks.

"Bruschetta," Dr. Sloane whispered.

Rosie bit into one. Tasty, in a garlicky way. She reached for the other one, and caught Dr. Sloane's disapproving stare.

Her hand returned to her lap. She'd starve waiting for her signals, but she wanted to learn how to fit in. "I didn't know I'd hired Miss Manners to be my financial advisor," she said, unable to resist a jab.

"I'm not a financial advisor. My duty is to make sure you can handle your wealth. That includes blending in with others of your class. So, Rosie. Tell me about your job. Did you tell them the good news?"

"I was a receptionist," she said, wondering how this rude, imperious woman could teach her manners. "I quit the morning I found out I won."

"How free you must feel. Did you send them a little thank-you?" Her lipsticked smile seemed artificial.

"Like what, a card? Thanks for two years of misery and humiliation? Won't need your tiny bucks anymore?"

The older woman pursed her lips. "You may feel that way, but it's best to leave in a good light and not open to litigation."

"Litigation? A lawsuit? Over what? I've never done anything to my coworkers. They'll never find the voodoo dolls."

Eve Sloane's face froze.

"It was a joke, Eve. Actually I went back for my final check. You should have seen them. I wore all my diamonds, and my fur coat, and they just stared with their mouths hanging open. It was great." One of her finer moments, for sure.

"No doubt. And call me Dr. Sloane. I dislike familiarities." She dabbed her lip with her napkin. "Now that you've gotten that juvenile impulse to show off out of the way, you need to send them a basket of goodies and a card that reads, 'I'll always remember the good times we had together.' That's it. Nothing more." She must have noticed Rosie's look of shock because she leaned forward. "It'll drive them nuts, I promise."

"That's evil," Rosie said admiringly. "A blow-off basket."

"Good manners don't have to have mannerly results." She spread her napkin on her lap and Rosie mirrored her movements. Dr. Sloane smiled approvingly. "We'll do well together, I think."

Lunch was delicious, although there were awkward moments, while Dr. Sloane scrutinized her every move.

Rosie felt as if she'd just become apprenticed to a Jedi Miss Manners. The woman was a warrior.

As she paid for lunch she mentioned her plans for the afternoon. "I'm joining my cousin on his house search. He's desperate to build a nest. A really big nest."

"Have you considered buying a house as well? It's excellent for tax purposes, unless you'd rather buy a hotel. Your corporate advisory committee is working on that option."

"I didn't like making those decisions when I played Monopoly, either. And I didn't know I had a corporate advisory committee. I just want a vacation." She threw herself onto a tapestry-covered chair. "I've been superrich for weeks. When am I going to have fun?"

She felt guilty the minute the words left her mouth. The day she blasted Lana off her throne, her insanely fun trip to Tiffany's? Major fun. A few weeks ago, those seemed like impossible fantasies, and now they were dreams come true, but despite her guilt she wanted more. She had to make up for a lot of misery.

"Life is not all pleasure, Rosie. Not even with your wealth. You have decisions to make, or you may find yourself broke."

Rosie laughed. "Okay, I'll look into some real estate. But really, Dr. Sloane, broke? My share of the prize is one hundred million dollars *after taxes*. That'll last forever."

The next morning she accompanied Cheeto on his house hunt. Tootie enjoyed her view from a new Burberry tote, but Rosie sulked on her side of the Hummer. She'd been eager to show off her new driving skills to Cheeto, and he'd laughed at her. Dr. Sloane must have warned them about her "closed track" order. She'd never get any practice at this rate.

Rosie's bad temper evaporated as she toured homes with massive wine coolers, private tennis courts, and bedrooms larger than her whole suite at the Ritz. Cheeto's taste was off the charts, and not in a good direction. All of the homes he'd chosen to explore were enormous and full of exotic details.

"What would you do with this much room?" She craned her head back, looking up at a vaulted ceiling that had to be two stories tall. "Normal furniture would look puny in here."

No way she'd buy one of these monsters, especially the ones that had just enough grass around each house that it could be mown with a weed eater. Maybe the houses were so close together so that their owners could impress each other with their cars and stuff.

Everyone around here was crazy about golf, too, and she didn't get it. Hitting a ball with a stick was best done with something meatier, like a baseball bat. Rosie added Braves skybox seats and season tickets to her want list. Heck, she could have season tickets to every major-league team. That would make her popular with the guys.

"Why would anyone need a wine room on each floor?" Her voice echoed against the tall ceilings of the sixth house they'd seen.

"Some people really love their wine."

"Right." She'd ask Dr. Sloane later. Rosie stared at the anatomically correct cherubs painted on the ceiling. Dave the real estate agent had skipped on to the next room, talking as if they were right behind him. He treated Cheeto and Rosie as if they were his own kids, left over from when he used to be a doorman at the hotel where Abuela worked.

"If you have to have lots of wine bottles on each floor of your house, you have a problem," Rosie said.

"I can see the wine rooms. But a remote control for your sock drawer? A dry-cleaning rack? That I don't understand."

"Okay, now you're talking heaven," Rosie said. "I wanted to live in that closet."

The real estate agent was starting to look a little worn around the edges. "It's a good party house."

"That it is." Cheeto had discovered the cupids.

"Eight thousand square feet?" Rosie asked. "It's warehouse huge, and the outside looks like a public library."

"But in here it's all shiny."

He was right. Inside, the place gleamed. Every surface was either black and white polished marble, or gilded.

Cheeto's mouth hung open as he walked into the next room.

"A ballroom? For what, a big-screen TV and stadium seating?" Rosie wished she'd brought sunglasses. It was sunny outside and the pool and tennis court tour had given her a headache.

"I might want to throw a party." Cheeto floated through the room, entranced. "I'm picturing one now."

"The front gate has dual control," Dave said, sensing a deal. "Excellent for parties, when you have security at the front gate and the valet parking staff needs access."

It was the mermaid in the basement that cinched it. The basement held a home theater with a stage and raked floor, a hot tub room and spa, and a huge indoor swimming pool made to look like a stone grotto. They walked through the colonnade at one side of the pool.

Rosie could hear water gently splashing. Sort of pleasant, until she turned the corner and saw the source of the water.

A life-sized stone mermaid of voluptuous proportions writhed at one end of the pool, her hands holding out Pamela Anderson–sized breasts from which twin streams of water arced and tinkled into the pool.

Rosie finally found her voice. "The lactating fish chick has got to go."

"I understand," Dave said, although he looked disappointed. Having a beautiful long-haired girl holding her breasts up for a man's bathing pleasure was probably high in the pantheon of male wet dream fantasies.

"Maybe we can sell her," she said. She hoped that she sounded sympathetic and not grossed out.

"Over my dead body." Cheeto stared at her, fascinated. "Lactating fish chick stays. Draw up the papers, Dave. This house is so mine."

Dave grinned and looked around for a place to put down his folder.

Cheeto flipped open his cell phone and dialed. "Rock walls with orchids growing out of them," he said into it. "And little tiny mosaics like in Roman days, and a naked mermaid at the head of the pool. She is so awesome. Reminds me of you."

She didn't know who he was talking to, but she knew one thing. If a photo got out, the tabloids would love the mermaid, too.

CHAPTER EIGHT
* * * * * *

When traveling, hire an assistant
to facilitate your journey. Avoid
unnecessary hassles.
—*The Instant Millionaire's Guide to Everything*

MegaBucks Winner Worked for Me—
Diamond Rosie's Old Boss Tells All!
—*Star* magazine

{ six weeks later }

The shiny deck of Rosie's giant new yacht was like a huge reflector, and after two hours in the hot Miami sun, slathered in oil, Rosie was starting to broil.

She stood up and stretched, then slid open the door to her cabin and slipped inside, shivering a little as the air conditioning hit her overheated skin. It had been heavenly to float in Biscayne Bay, soaking up the sun, but it was time to get moving if she was going to arrive at the film premiere on time. She walked past her bed, covered in gold silk to match the draperies that turned the topside cabin into a dim, seductive cave.

She loved her yacht. It was super-luxurious, beautiful, and one hundred feet long, a floating luxury condo. It had cost her thirty-five million dollars, far more than Cheeto had spent on his house. Abuela thought she was insane, and even crazy Cheeto wondered out loud if it was worth it. It totally was. Besides, it had been a bargain. The seller had been so thrilled to unload it for his asking price that he'd thrown in a second boat, a forty-foot clunker that was docked in Apalachicola, wherever that was, and a small marina there.

She picked up the phone that connected her to the captain. No answer. Captain Manny was probably working on the engines again. They'd sputtered to a stop in the middle of the bay. Not a big emergency, since they had a smaller boat on board that could ferry her to shore, but still.

She opened the door to the little deck again. Somewhere below her bedroom balcony, Captain Manny Gomez swore in Spanish.

"I heard that," she called down. She looked out at the dizzying view of sparkling ocean that surrounded them, and seemed to be far below her little deck, one of three on four levels.

It was so beautiful out here. She didn't want to go back to shore, but she looked forward to tonight's outing, a film premiere and benefit for the Humane Society, one of her favorite charities. She was a big donor, but she'd come because she'd heard that Brad Merritt would attend. She was scared and excited to finally meet him.

"Everything okay, Manny?" She leaned over the deck rail, trying to see the captain she'd hired on impulse after she bought the ship. The bartender at the hotel's oceanfront bar had told her about his unemployed brother who'd lost his wife to cancer and his boat to a hurricane. She met Manny Gomez the next day and offered him the job of ship's captain, and he'd hired a crew of three to help him.

Luckily, Manny was as smart as his brother said he was. He knew engines, although he seemed to be baffled by some of the new ship's fancy electronics and the Miami-Dade police had given her the bad news about Manny, after Mr. Pujol had insisted on running a background check.

He'd lost his wife, all right—she was doing twenty federal years for being a drug mule, and not a bright one. Manny himself was labeled a habitual troublemaker by the cops.

She should have fired him, but he reminded her of Cheeto, who now spent most of his time in Las Vegas or throwing parties at his new place, dubbed the Lotto Palace by the tabloids.

Below, Manny leaned backward over the rail so that she could see him. "I'll get you there, don't worry." He hadn't bothered to button his stained short-sleeved shirt.

The PI that Mr. Pujol had hired to do Manny's background investigation thought that he might be trouble, but she was determined to keep the gregarious captain. Next week he was starting lessons on how to run and repair this kind of ship.

He wiped oil from his hands. "I think I flooded the engines."

She looked at the far-off coastline and shuddered. "I sure don't want to swim back."

"You don't want to swim here. *Picúas*. Barracudas. But I think I can get the boys started again. We'll be able to get back, it'll just take a while, and if not, there's the dinghy."

She shook her head and went back inside. Her bare feet sank into the cool, deep golden carpet. She crossed to the bathroom with its glass-walled shower that could hold her whole crew comfortably. Not that *that* would ever happen. She still had three hours to get to the theater for the premiere.

Tootie moaned in her sleep and turned over on her pink dog pillow, all four legs in the air. The pillow's sides had "Doggie Princess" embroidered in black.

Rosie felt like a princess, too. Her life had changed dramatically in just a few weeks. Her family was scattered now, each to their version of fun. Strange how much more together they'd been when they were poor. Was poverty the only thing they'd had in common?

Sunday lunch at Abuela's house every week, trips to the Latin supermarket, saving up to go to the baseball games so that they could afford hot dogs *and* a soft drink—those things had been fun. Even though they'd had to be careful with money, they were proud that they had jobs and a roof over their heads.

Maybe that was why she'd stuck to her parents' old apartment, she thought. She was as proud as her father had been, even if it meant scraping by, and she'd been determined to have her own space. Now she had too much space.

They each could do whatever they wanted, and it seemed what they didn't want was to be together. She sighed. Even if she tried to spend time with Cheeto and Abuela it wouldn't be the same, not to mention that the three of them were seldom in the same town at the same time. It would take careful planning to have a family dinner now.

Besides, Cheeto and Abuela had so many friends that even on phone calls they were always getting interrupted. Rosie looked around at the miles of water. Unlike her.

Beneath them the engines rumbled back to life. *Menos mal.*

She hadn't looked forward to the alternative, climbing down the long ladder on the side of the yacht into a little boat.

Rosie slipped into the shower and washed off the sunblock with her favorite shower gel. Maybe she'd give Manny a raise after he learned how to maneuver the ship.

Mr. Pujol called while she was towel-drying her hair.

"I need for you to be in Atlanta on the fifteenth of next month to sign the papers for the foundation. I've called Cheeto, but I can't get in touch with your grandmother."

"Abuela's not answering her cell phone. She's on her canasta cruise. You can get word to her by calling the *St. Anges Princess*."

"I thought that was two weeks ago." Mr. Pujol rustled papers.

"It was, but she liked it so much the whole group stayed onboard for another week."

"Did she keep all of her friends with her?"

"The whole herd of Silver-Haired Homies." Scary, all those old folks out on the open sea, playing cards with only the ship's doctor around in case they got sick. She had seen them off, Abuela in her colorful version of cruise wear, surrounded by her best friends.

They'd been like excited children on the plane from Atlanta to Miami, too, yelling for more drinks and throwing their hands in the air like kids on a roller coaster when the plane hit turbulence. It had been Rosie's first plane ride, and she hoped the next one would be quieter.

It was almost four in the afternoon before the *MegaBucks* docked at the deepwater marina in front of the Atlantic View Towers, where she'd rented a condo. Rosie climbed the short steps to the deck wearing a sundress and flip-flops. Manny was at the wheel, deftly docking the ship. At least he knew how to do that.

"See you, Manny. Good luck with your classes."

"I'll keep you posted, Miss Rosie." He saluted as she waited for the ship to stop.

She adjusted her hat and stepped onto the gangplank that led onto the cement pier.

She followed the flower-bordered path into the east tower, walked through a polished granite entryway, and crossed the Atlantic View's ballroom-sized lobby to the elevator banks.

She shifted Tootie in her striped tote to her other shoulder and put her key card into the elevator. She loved the silent whoosh as it climbed, and that it stopped automatically at her twelfth-floor apartment. The doors opened into her foyer, where fresh flowers had been arranged in a tall blown-glass urn.

The wall of windows facing the ocean was cool at this hour of the day. The folks on the other side of the tower got the rays of the setting sun. She got the sunrises.

Tootie climbed out of the tote, stiff-legged and yawning, and headed for the pillow in the bedroom. These days the old dog went from nap to blissful nap.

Rosie slid open the closet door and examined her clothing choices, although she was pretty sure of what she'd wear. She pulled out a long, layered gauze Stella McCartney dress that was two sizes smaller than pre-lottery. She'd lost weight since gaining a personal trainer and ditching the stress of unpaid bills and a job she hated.

Dr. Sloane had volunteered to get her a personal assistant, too. Abuela already had one. She'd hired a friend of hers who needed work, and loved having a helper.

She struggled with the gown's complicated straps, then checked herself in the mirror. The Stella dress fit perfectly. She slipped on high-heeled sandals and checked the makeup that she'd done on the yacht, using the techniques she'd been taught. She didn't look like the models that filled the South Beach dance clubs at night, but she looked like a tan and fit version of herself. She twirled in front of the mirror. She was ready for the tabloids.

Of course, no matter what she looked like, the photographers who hounded her would choose the least flattering images to run. At first it had been easy for them. She'd always looked fat, or like a hick. The last photo they'd run was of her driver's license exam. Her joy at finally having her license had been dimmed by the photo of her clutching the steering wheel, looking terrified. Or homicidal. Either way, she'd looked scary.

Cheeto, on the other hand, loved the tabloids and loved to have his picture taken, and the photographers who chased Abuela had quickly grown bored of shooting card games, water aerobics, and geriatric midnight salsa parties.

Rosie's paparazzi still sold the pictures that showed too much cleavage or captured her doing something embarrassing. It was not fair, but it no longer shocked her. Like dealing with requests for money, it was part of her new life.

The film festival gala opening was hot and overcrowded, and Rosie didn't know anyone. Her name was on the program because she'd donated a fat wad of cash to the festival when she read that they were about to go under, and they'd hired a publicist to attract some big-name celebrities. Abuela had hit the roof when she'd seen a report about it on *Entertainment Tonight,* and had called her from the cruise ship.

"Rosie, you can't just give money away like that. Yes, you have lots of it, but you'll be the target of every weasel out there when word gets out."

"You give away money," she said.

"I'm helping my old friends, and I'm old, too. I won't need the money for as many years. You don't know these people. They'll take advantage of you."

"They're not crooks, Abuela, and besides, we have millions, and I just used a little bit to help out a film festival. How is that worse than handing out cash to cab drivers or paying off your friends' medical bills? I'll meet interesting people at the party, folks who are fun to talk to." If some of them asked for money, why not give it to them? It wasn't as if she'd run out of the stuff.

She didn't want to admit out loud that she was bored and lonely. She never thought she'd say that. Her lack of friends hadn't been so obvious when she was poor and had spent all of her time working, trying to scrape together enough cash to make ends meet. Now she had the wealth she'd always dreamed of, and no one to share it with.

Maybe what she needed was a hobby, like Abuela's canasta. Something she could do with other people. Although, in her opinion, Abue carried that one a little too far.

Rosie stood near a group of film aficionados, listening to their excited chatter. She should walk up to them and join in, but once they recognized her as Diamond Rosie, talk would probably turn to the lottery and endless boring "how I almost won" lottery stories.

"Look at the cow wrapped in Stella." The woman's loud, Spanish-accented voice interrupted her thoughts.

She froze. She was the only woman around wearing Stella. She turned to see two very thin, beautiful women holding drinks. They were facing the front doors, but one glanced back, catching her gaze briefly. She recognized them. The Music Television Channel's famous VJ sisters, Lila and Ami Solas, and they had just passed judgment on her.

They had picked on the wrong cow. Rosie marched over to them. "You think that hurt my feelings?"

Ami, the taller of the two, looked her up and down. She was exquisitely dressed in red, with black ribbons interwoven in the fabric. She raised an eyebrow.

"Yeah, I'm talking to you," Rosie said. "You think calling me fat hurts my feelings? Well, think again." Rosie put her fists on her hips, parked but ready for action.

Ami rolled her eyes and walked away. Lila giggled. "You're crazy. I know who you are, lottery girl. If you want to be on our show, give a shout." She blew her a kiss, then followed her sister.

"Were you just picking a fight with Ami Solas?" a voice said in her ear. She turned to face a tall, familiar-looking redhead in a low-cut green gown. "That took guts."

"No. Just thinking that I should never come to these things alone." She tried not to stare at the woman's almost bare chest. There must be a lot of double-stick tape holding the cloth to her skin.

"I agree. Want to get a drink? You can tell me if you also like jumping out of planes without a parachute."

Rosie wondered just who Ami Solas was, and if standing up for herself had been a suicidal move.

They headed to the bar and waited in line. Rosie looked around, trying to see if she could spot Brad.

"I'm Kim Taylor." The redhead stuck out a very white hand. Of course. Rosie recognized her now. She was the star of a hit television cop show.

Rosie shook it. "Rosie Caballero. I should have recognized you, I'm sorry."

"I recognized *you*. From the newspapers. The Lotto Diva, right? Diamond Rosie."

"Right. Although Lotto Diva is much kinder than the headlines I've seen. Or what those two just said."

Kim laughed. "Don't mind them. Bitchy is their bread and butter. So why are you here alone?"

"I came to see my grandmother off on a cruise and stuck around after I fell in love with a yacht. You?"

Kim grabbed two flutes of champagne and handed one to Rosie. "Business. I saw you scouting out the guests. Who are you looking for?"

"Brad Merritt. I heard he'd be here and I'm a big fan." She didn't mention her prior humiliating almost-meeting with him.

"Well, girl, why didn't you say so?" Kim said. "I know where he is." She laughed at Rosie's expression. "Come on, let's meet some people, and we'll zoom in on his hidey hole."

She dragged Rosie from group to group, snagging drinks whenever theirs were empty. Rosie tried to make small talk, which, as she'd expected, turned to the lottery and what it was like to be instantly rich. To her surprise, most people seemed envious, even the celebrities. She couldn't concentrate on the conversations, though, thinking that Brad was here somewhere, and she would soon be introduced to him.

Half an hour later, dazed from mojitos and overdosed on celebrity, she was ready to kick Kim. "You're a sadist, aren't you? You promised to introduce me, then made me talk to everybody here."

"Not everyone," Kim said, sipping yet another glass of champagne. "Just the famous ones."

"I can't believe this many famous people live in Miami."

"It's a favorite," Kim said. "But most everyone will be gone tomorrow. Off to the west coast or on location."

"All the way to Miami for one night and then back to work? That sounds brutal." Rosie had snagged an icy bottle of water from an artfully arranged tub.

Kim shrugged. "It's the business. Beautiful palm trees, aren't they?"

Before Rosie could respond that the designers had done a great job, Kim grabbed Rosie's free hand and dragged her toward an island landscape re-created at one corner of the ballroom. A man's silhouette was barely visible through the palm fronds and voluptuous greenery.

Rosie felt cold prickles on the back of her neck. She knew that profile.

"Brad, I've brought someone interesting for you to meet."

Goose bumps rose on Rosie's arms. He'd been nearby the entire time. She really was going to kick Kim.

A groan came through the shrubbery. "Kim, just walk by and pretend you didn't see me. I've got a cold and I look like hell."

That voice, like corduroy and wood smoke. She shivered.

"Don't be vain." Kim pushed Rosie through the mass of potted plants. Rosie found herself in a secret alcove made by the surrounding greenery. It smelled earthy and alive, and was ten degrees hotter than the rest of the lobby. The man leaning against the palm turned to face her and her heart banged against her ribs.

It *was* Brad Merritt. His eyes were as lusciously blue as they were in his films. He shot her one of his heart-melting looks, the kind that made her blood fizz at the movies. She was fizzing now.

"Brad, I want you to meet Rosie Caballero." Kim waggled her eyebrows.

His eyes widened and he flashed his famous grin. "Hi, cutie."

"Hi." Brad Merritt had called her cutie. She tried to regain her composure. He probably called lots of girls cutie.

"I'm getting over a head cold and had to blow my nose." He sniffled. "I didn't want it to turn into a photo op. You hiding out from the press, too?"

"No, we saw you through the leaves." Kim adjusted her gown. "This reception is endless."

"We could ditch this place and go somewhere else." He blew his nose. Only he could make using a tissue look sexy.

Run off to hang out with Brad? Rosie rubbed her upper arms to smooth down her excited skin.

"Can't," Kim said. "I'm accepting an award for *Fly Away Home*. It's being released as a short film." She turned to Rosie. "Did you see that episode?"

"The one about the kidnapped boy buried alive? It was so scary. I didn't think you'd get to him in time."

Kim wrapped bony arms around her and kissed her hair. "You are my favorite person in the whole world, Rosie Caballero. Thank you for watching it. Oh, there's my agent. I'll talk to you two later." She slipped out of the green cave and walked across the theater lobby as if she'd been out there the entire time. Rosie could see every vertebra in the actress's spine.

She laughed to hide her shock at how thin she was. "I'm her favorite person? We just met."

"You don't know too many actors, do you?" Brad smiled. "We live for praise. You made her evening."

"Then it doesn't take much to make her happy." Rosie stared at the champagne in her glass, wishing it were a soft drink, or even water.

"How about you? What makes you happy?" He was making small talk, his eyes flitting to the crowd on the other side of the greenery.

She wasn't experienced with the world of movie stars and film festivals, but she knew men, and he was coming on to her. She shivered in anticipation as she answered his question.

"Lately? Not being on the cover of the *Star*. But you've been there, too. How do you survive the tabloids?"

"Want me to teach you?"

She tried to think of something normal to say, all the while imagining a tabloid photo of the two of them. "Brad Taught Me to Love, Says Diamond Rosie."

He waved a hand in front of her face. "Hello? Earth to Rosie?"

"Sorry. Zoned out." She lifted the champagne glass. "Not used to this."

He gave her an impish smile. "You are such a lightweight."

"I'm not from Miami." She was sinking deep into the Sea of Lame. Had she said that people from Miami were alcoholics? She wanted to die.

"Me neither. Louisiana." His smile widened. If it got any bigger, she'd fall in.

"Really? I'm from Georgia."

"I would have guessed somewhere more exotic."

"Yeah?" She tried to think of an exotic locale, but drew a total blank. Her mind was filled with him. "Wow. My family is not going to believe I'm talking to you like this."

He lifted a questioning eyebrow.

She waved around. "You know, normally."

"Ah. So you don't think I'm normal? Or is hiding in the shrubbery normal for you?"

"Of course not. I mean—" She had to think for a second. She was losing her bearings. "You're teasing me."

He looked amused. He must have this effect on a lot of women. "Are you in the business?"

"Acting? No, I won the lottery." Hadn't Kim said so? Maybe the cold had stopped up his ears.

His smile dimmed.

"No, wait. What I meant was—I'm sorry, I thought maybe you'd recognized me, too."

He looked interested again.

"I won the MegaBucks recently and I'm . . ." Her voice tapered off. His eyes glazed. Now he did look like someone recovering from a head cold.

"You're the *chica* who won the big prize. You made all the papers in L.A. Diamond Rosie, right?"

"It didn't have my picture, did it?" She thought of the tight jeans pic. Gross.

"Yes, although you looked different." He looked her up and down appreciatively, then leaned over and sniffed.

She laughed. "What was that about? I put on deodorant this morning."

"Wanted to see if lottery money smelled different from Hollywood money." He sniffed again, his breath warm on her skin as his nose hovered close to her breasts.

She wanted to swallow, and found she couldn't. "And does it?"

"Nope. You smell mighty fine, but money smells like horseshit no matter what the source." He laughed and swigged from his beer bottle.

"You must be playing a cowboy in your new movie."

His eyes widened. "Why do you say that?"

"Because you were so sophisticated in *Widow's Kiss* and when you did Jay Leno back then you wore a suit and talked just like your character, Jack Link. I love that character." She sighed, then noticed he'd moved closer.

"So you're basing your guess on my suit?"

"No, of course not. The next year you played a street fighter in *Billy Cork*, and wore torn jeans and slouched in your chair on the Letterman show, and then played Jack Link again in *Ninety Seconds* and it was back to the suit and the martinis. So now you're acting all cowboy, or at least that's what I'm guessing from the way you're holding that beer bottle and saying 'horseshit' like a cowpoke. It doesn't sound like something you'd normally say."

He stared at her for a bit longer then laughed. "Damn. Didn't think I was that obvious."

"It's your job to be someone else. It's not your fault if it keeps going after you're done working."

He nodded. "It's hard to get deep in character and then shake it just for a party."

"Just don't do a vampire movie. Or play a serial killer." She shivered and he laughed again. "So are you going to do more Jack Link movies? I love those."

He made a face. "I'm tired of them. I've always wanted to act on a stage, and that's why I'm here. We just wrapped up filming in Montana and I had to talk to a guy who wants me to star in a revival of a Broadway play, and he's here in Miami." His eyes had brightened as he spoke.

"I don't know anything about acting. Which one is harder, movies or stage?"

"Stage work is the hardest, no question. In film you get to do it over and over until you get it right. On stage you have one chance, and you do it live, in front of a paying audience." He shivered, but from his excited expression it wasn't from fear.

"You really get off on that," she marveled. "I think it sounds terrifying. Standing up in front of strangers, and memorizing words. My idea of torture."

He grinned, then reached over and pushed her hair behind her ear, totally shocking her. She rubbed her hands up and down over her arms to chase away the gooseflesh brought on by his touch. "And that's why I'm an actor, and you're not." He laughed.

She stared at him. *Brad Merritt touched me.*

He didn't seem to notice her reaction. "My flight doesn't leave until tomorrow afternoon. Want to get together for lunch?"

Now he'd asked her out. She really wished she had girl-friends. She imagined Dr. Sloane's reaction to a giddy phone call about meeting a movie star.

"Rosie?" He waved a hand in front of her eyes, smiling.

She thought of her schedule and groaned. "I can't. I'm leaving tomorrow morning. I have to go home for a meeting."

His disappointment seemed real. "Home to Georgia."

"Atlanta."

"Nice place. I've been there a couple of times." He stared into his empty beer bottle. "I'm heading back to Wyoming. Another shoot."

A camera flashed nearby and she glanced in the direction of the light, startled.

"Regret knowing me already?" He grinned, but the sparkle in his blue eyes seemed more anger than pleasure.

"I think press would be bad, especially for me," she said. "Can you see it? 'Diamond Rosie Snags a Movie Star.'"

He laughed. "I like you. You're real. Do you say everything you think?"

"My grandmother says I have no hairs on my tongue."

"Well, I hope not." He stared at her mouth.

"It's a Cuban saying. It means my mouth doesn't have an internal censor. I blurt it all out."

"It means you're honest. I need another beer." He laced his warm, strong fingers with hers and led her out of the greenery to the bar. Everyone looked, the cool ones pretending not to stare, as Brad walked her across the crowded room. In a corner, Kim lifted her drink and winked.

She smiled back. A camera flash captured them in its light, and just like that, she was one of them, the glitterati.

CHAPTER NINE
* * * * * *

Many lottery winners buy fancy houses in
expensive neighborhoods and then discover
that they have nothing in common
with their new neighbors.
—*The Instant Millionaire's Guide to Everything*

Brad Merritt Ropes Diamond Rosie!
—*Star* magazine

Cheeto called her a few days after he'd settled into his mega mansion. "Rosie, you've got to help me. They're killing me." He
sounded irritated.

"Who? What have you gotten yourself into this time?" Rosie
didn't panic.

His Vegas parties had been jammed with football and soccer
players, hip-hop artists, old friends and new. Cheeto loved to be
loved, and his house would always be full of music and fun. He
was careful about women, though. He didn't want to get caught
in any scandal that would make him share his wealth via a court
order.

A week later the tabloids were Rosie-free for once.

"Cheeto must be bribing these photographers." Rosie held
up the latest *Enquirer* cover so that Abuela could see it. "How

come he never makes the covers? They cover his latest party, but it's always his guests who get photographed."

"He's not beautiful, like you." Abuela looked up from her *Vanidades*. "It would be mean to pick on him."

"Hmph." Hard to whine when her grandmother had turned it into a compliment. "I'm thinking of going to New York City."

"New York?" Abuela closed the magazine. "Who do we know there?"

"It doesn't matter, Abue. I've never been there. I want to get away."

"Go stay with Cheeto."

"You're joking, right? I meant get away in another city."

"Go have fun in Miami."

"Been there. I want to see New York. Besides, I've got an appointment with our new tax attorney in Manhattan."

"Another one? What happened to the first ones?"

"I fired them. They said I shouldn't have bought the *Mega-Bucks*. They said it was a bad investment." *The Millionaire's Guide* had been absolutely right—she was getting advice from everyone, and why couldn't she spend money on things she wanted?

Abuela looked grumpy. "I thought we'd spend some time together. And don't ask me to go with you because I can't. I promised Analisa that I'd help her with the church bazaar."

"Hire someone to help her."

Her grandmother's eyes widened. "I promised them I'd help."

"Hmmm." Rosie tried to look sympathetic, but a glance at the mirror over the mantelpiece showed her face looking triumphant. She had no intention of asking her grandmother along. She wanted to party. There were so many celebs in New York that no one would bother her. That was her theory, anyway. "It won't be the same without you." That much was true.

"Well." Abuela sighed. "If you must, then you must. It's your life. Your decision." She sighed again.

Rosie folded her arms around her grandmother. All the salsa dancing had made her more muscular. She'd lost the cushiony feel that had meant safety to Rosie when she was small. Everything else had changed. Now the people were changing, too.

"Abuelita, I love you so much."

She patted Rosie's arm. "I love you too, *mi amor*. We'll shop in New York together another time, okay?"

"Okay." She only agreed because it was unlikely to happen.

Cheeto joined them for dinner in Rosie's suite, a rare occurrence these days. The hotel chef had outdone himself. When Abuela went to bed early, Cheeto excused himself, a familiar gleam in his eyes.

"Hot date?" She couldn't resist asking. He pretended to be such a player, but he was such a pussycat.

"Always. I'm staying at the LP tonight."

LP—the Lotto Palace. Cheeto loved the name the tabloids had christened his house with. She envied his relationship with the press, and with the opposite sex. "Not alone, I take it."

Cheeto grinned. "Just some friends. You can come, too, if you want. Hold on." He shoved a hand into his pocket and pulled out three message slips. "From the front desk."

Rosie glanced at them.

One was from Kim Taylor, wondering when they could get together. The second was from the tax attorney. She had papers for Rosie to sign—when could they meet? The third stopped her. It was from Rick Suarez. The message was "Call me, we need to talk" and a phone number.

She stared at the note. Here she was feeling sorry for her lonely self, and the one guy she didn't want to see resurfaced. Maybe he wanted to be friends again now that she was rich, as if he'd never left her to take a late-night bus home by herself.

Rosie crumpled the note and was about to toss it when she stopped, flattened it out, and then carefully tore it into confetti and threw it away. No sense letting the tabloid guys find out about her past indiscretion.

"Let me guess. You tore up the one from Rick."

Rosie took another sip of the cabernet that Chef Michael had sent up with the dinner. "It doesn't surprise me that you read it."

Cheeto grunted. "He's an ass. You aren't going to, right? He just wants your money."

"I don't want to see him ever again. It's funny, though. I never thought about money when I used to date."

"That's because you always went out with guys who didn't make any, like that gas station guy."

"Jorge." She hadn't thought about him in months. "You ever think about going back to visit?"

"To the hood? Hell no. My old friends know where to find me."

That's because he had a lot of old friends. At bedtime she thought of Rick again. Now that she had money, lots and lots of money, he needed to talk to her. Imagine that. She wouldn't call him, but she'd have fun imagining what would happen if she did.

She got ready for bed. For just a second, as she reached out to turn her lamp off, her fingers hovered over the phone.

"Pathetic." She switched off her light and lay in the darkness, thinking about the different girl she had been, the one who'd never tasted champagne, who didn't know what it felt like to wear diamonds, who thought guys like Rick were worth a date.

The Atlanta airport was crowded with business travelers: guys in polo shirts and khakis and women in suits with rolling briefcases. Most people looked calm, even bored, while they snaked through the long security lines.

At the gate Rosie stretched her legs out and tried to look nonchalant, a Starbucks cup at her side, as everyone stared at her.

"Ms. Caballero?" The uniformed woman looked like a cop.

"Yes?"

"Dr. Sloane asked us to look after you." The cop smiled hesitantly. "It took a while to find you. I'm with Jacobs Security."

A bodyguard? "May I see your ID?"

The woman produced a badge, laminated card, and a letter informing her of where to meet Rosie.

"Okay. Where should I go?" She picked up her pink tote. Tootie stuck her head out sleepily. "Back to sleep, baby." The poodle's head with its diamond-clipped topknot disappeared.

The uniformed woman beckoned and Rosie followed, slipping through the crowds in her wake. They stopped at an unmarked door. The guard opened it with a magnetic key and then ushered Rosie into a small private lounge. "You can wait here until your flight to New York boards."

"Great. I was feeling like a goldfish in the waiting room."

Rosie dropped into an overstuffed armchair, reached into the tote, and pulled Tootie out. "Need to stretch your legs, old girl?" The poodle shook herself, then explored the room, sniffing everything.

"I lived in New York for three years," the guard said. "Is this your first time?"

"Is it that obvious?"

"No. Just asking. Don't miss Brooklyn."

"Brooklyn?" Rosie almost laughed.

"You want to see how real New Yorkers live, get out of Manhattan. Everyone's too stuck-up there."

"Okay. I'll check it out." Brooklyn. Why not?

The guard glanced at her watch. "Your flight is boarding, Ms. Caballero."

"Great." She picked up Tootie. "Thanks. What's your name?"

"Jennifer." She patted Tootie's head. "Have a safe trip, Ms. Caballero. Don't forget Brooklyn."

"Right. Brooklyn."

The miserable-looking people waiting at the gate had gone. The gate area was empty as she walked down the jetway and slid into her wide, comfy first-class seat.

The flight attendants were smiling and nice, and they offered her a drink. She thought of Dr. Sloane's advice not to drink.

"Got any champagne?" she asked. The stuff wasn't bad, once you got used to the taste.

"New York City is incredible," Rosie told Abuelita on the phone that evening. "It's the most of everything. The dirtiest, smelliest, liveliest, most wonderful place in the world. It's the most beautiful, the tallest, the scariest—"

"Okay, okay, I get it," Abuela said, laughing. "You're having fun, right?"

"Yes. I'll tell you all about it tomorrow. But I've got someplace to be in a minute and I have to get dressed." Or undressed. Abuela hadn't seen the outfit she'd laid out to wear to this little party. Black, of course. Very cute, very short.

"Cheeto said to bring him a Knicks shirt."

"Okay, Abue. I'll bring back presents for everybody, don't worry."

"Be good, Rosie."

"I'll try." After settling in at her suite in the Grand Hyatt and leaving a message for Dr. Sloane, she'd gone shopping and had run into Kim at a store on Fifth Avenue.

"I thought you were in L.A." Rosie was at the cash register, waiting for employees to wrap up the lingerie she'd bought. "Congratulations on the award."

"Thank you." Kim looked luscious, although just as thin as she'd been in Miami.

"Oh my God, it's Diamond Rosie." The bony actress hugged her fiercely. "You should have stayed at the festival that night. But I wouldn't have been able to resist Brad, either."

Rosie shrugged, wondering what Kim was talking about. She and Brad had watched a couple of films, seen Kim receive her award, then she'd gone back to her condo alone when the media had descended on Brad.

"He's here in town, you know. He's got a shot at doing Broadway. Can you imagine Brad on the stage? I can't. But then, I kind of fell into acting from modeling, and he actually studied it in college or something." Kim was talking so fast that Rosie's ears could hardly keep up.

Her pupils were contracted to pinpoints, and Rosie suddenly knew the secret to the redhead's fabled thinness. She'd seen it before, at her apartment complex in Chamblee. Kim's brain was on chemical hyperdrive.

"Come to a party with me tonight," Kim said. "There's going to be a ton of people there."

"Okay," Rosie said. "Want me to pick you up?"

"I'll meet you there. It's in Soho. I'll text you the address. Brad said he'd be there, too." She winked.

Brad. She couldn't wait to see him again. Would he remember her? And maybe Kim would tell her why she thought that Rosie had spent the night with him in Miami. And why did she keep suggesting that she hook up with Brad?

CHAPTER TEN

* * * * * *

Get used to your new lifestyle before you
venture back into the world of your old one.
—*The Instant Millionaire's Guide to Everything*

Diamond Rosie Hits the Big Apple;
the Big Apple Hits Back
—*Star* magazine

The music thumped so loudly against the bare brick walls that Rosie thought she could feel it push against her skin. The loft was so crowded with partygoers that she had to edge around the ragged kitchen counter, a juice glass in her hand, wondering why the supposedly fabulous event was being held in such a dump. She didn't want to snag her new silky dress on the sharp metal edges that had peeled away from the Formica top, but she'd been bumped into and rubbed against by strangers since she'd arrived thirty minutes ago and more and more people squeezed in every minute.

She'd tried to join in some of the conversations, only to be stared at coldly. One woman had turned her back on her to exclude her. She was about ready to leave. The only good thing about tonight was the drink in her hand.

The loft was probably expensive real estate, but it was uglier than her Chamblee apartment. She sipped from her glass, then lurched forward as someone once again pushed her from behind. An arm snaked around her hips to steady her.

"Hey." She turned to protest and found herself nose to nose with Brad Merritt.

"Hey, cutie. Tired of Miami?" The edges of his eyes crinkled as he unleashed his famous smile. His arm held her loosely, as if he wanted her to know she could escape at any time.

A woman next to her turned, started when she recognized him, then stared at them jealously. Rosie tried to ignore her; easy, with Brad's blue eyes gleaming into hers.

"I heard you were here," Rosie said. Lame.

He made a gesture with the glass of wine. "Business."

"*This* is a party." She staggered a little on her high heels.

He pulled her against him and held her steady. Not an improvement. She was no longer in danger of falling, but she was close to having a heart attack. She felt his belt buckle against her navel. "I think I knew that," he said, his head pulled back so that he could look at her.

She smiled up at him. "Do you always cuddle women at parties?"

"Just the ones that might fall over any second. It's so much easier than hauling them up off the floor."

"You say the sexiest things."

"Are you drunk?" He said it as if it didn't matter if she was.

She laughed. "No. Are you?"

Brad put his glass of wine down. "If I said no, I'd be telling the truth."

"Are you calling me a liar?"

"What if I want to kiss you?" He leaned closer. "I don't take advantage of intoxicated ladies."

Her heart started to thump. "I'd say, bring it on."

He leaned closer, his eyes staring into hers. The corners of his mouth lifted. "Really? How do I know that's not your drink talking? How many of those have you had?"

"Two and it's just fruit juice and vodka." She put her cup down carefully. The room tilted a little.

He sniffed the cup. "A lot of vodka."

"You're acting like my cousin. Stop it."

"Why? How many of these have you really had?"

"What are you, a cop?" She saluted him mockingly. "Honest, officer, I've only had a couple."

He laughed. "I hope you aren't driving."

"Not in New York, I'm not." She looked around at the tightly knit groups and the growing number of eavesdroppers around them. "I heard you're here for some play. What's that about?"

He looked around quickly. "Who told you that?" he asked, voice soft.

"Kim."

He cursed. "Come on." He wrapped his warm hand around hers and started to push his way through the crowd, smiling and talking to fans and well-wishers, although these were a lot more discreet than the usual throng she encountered. If she were more sophisticated, she'd probably recognize some of them. She smiled triumphantly at the woman who'd shut her out, now staring open-mouthed at them. She was leaving with Brad Merritt. He was holding her hand. Okay, so something she'd said had angered him, but they still looked good together.

A second later she tripped on a loose floorboard and almost fell. The woman smirked, as if she'd learned a secret and couldn't wait to share it with her friends. Rosie turned away. With her luck, the woman was a gossip columnist.

The stairs were steep and smelled stale.

"Cabbage, I think." Brad wrinkled his nose. "And some pee, too."

"I've been in church halls that were nicer than this smelly, worn-out place." She sidestepped to avoid a dark shape on the stairs. "Is your cowboy movie over with? You said pee. Not a macho cowboy word."

"I was trying to be polite." He stopped as they reached a tiny vestibule at the bottom of the stairs. "Ready?"

"For what?" The door that led outside had a frosted glass panel that hid them from the street. Vague shapes moved on the other side. The music from upstairs still thumped around them.

"The media." He lowered his voice, putting on a horror movie tone. "The sharks."

She shivered. "More like rats."

"Smile, gorgeous!" He threw the door open and hauled her out into the night, which exploded with bursts of light and the dizzying switch from rhythmic techno to the chaotic yells of frenzied news reporters trying to get them to look their way.

She teetered after him on her tall heels, hauled along to a taxi door that miraculously appeared in front of them. He pushed her inside and dove in after her, almost landing on top of her.

The cab was moving before they could sit up. "What was that?"

"Just the usual. I think there's a network that telegraphs my movements ahead." It didn't sound like a joke, but Rosie laughed.

"I thought I had it bad." She watched the bright lights of the shops as they passed. "Everyone knows your face. How do you get any privacy?"

"Privacy? Never heard of it. But it's the reason I didn't answer you inside. Never announce where you're headed. There's always a media mole who'll call ahead." The famous face looked back at her, one corner of his mouth lifted in amusement. "You're cute. Even your name is cute. Rosie."

"Thanks." She'd rather be called sexy than cute, but she'd take it. "Where are we headed?"

"To my place. Is that okay?" He put his arm around her and pulled her close.

She pulled away. "If we were on a date back home I'd deck you for that, then go through your wallet for cab fare home." She was disappointed that her hero Brad was turning out to be all too human.

Just another guy, and he thought he was all that, too.

"I'm sorry, Rosie. I thought you wanted to talk about my play." He put a finger to his lips and pointed at the cab driver. "My townhouse is close by."

"Your townhouse? I thought you lived in California. Why don't you stay in a hotel?"

"It's an investment, and easier to secure than a hotel. Plus, I get to keep my own stuff around me."

She stifled a snort of laughter at the thought of her own stuff. Like what? The pressboard dresser and her grandmother's chenille bedspread? "Maybe I should've bought a house instead of a boat. I could fill it with my heirlooms." She fell against his shoulder, laughing.

He shook his head and put his arm around her shoulder, holding her close. "And I'd just about decided you weren't drunk after all."

They stopped in front of a lovely brownstone, its front illuminated by floodlights. It was narrow and tall, with flower boxes, now empty, hanging from broad bay windows. Black iron gates with spear points at the top blocked access to the front door.

"It looks like a dollhouse jail." The words popped out of her mouth before she could stop them.

Brad finished paying the cabbie and turned to look up at his house. "Yeah, it kind of does." He put his arm around her.

"Sorry. I'm not good at tact." Maybe she'd really had a little too much to drink.

"No hairs on your tongue. I remember." He laughed. "Don't change. It's what I like best about you. You're so different."

Different. Great. "Is that a good thing?"

"Of course. Like my dollhouse jailhouse." He squeezed her to his chest. "Let's see what you think of the inside."

Two women got out of a car and hurried across the street as he unlocked the gate. They stopped on the sidewalk, heads together, talking loudly enough that she and Brad could hear them plainly.

"It's really him."

"No, it's not. It just looks like him."

"Ignore them," Brad muttered. He pushed open the gate and motioned her through, following her, then locking the gate behind them.

The red door at the top of the stone steps opened and a man appeared.

"Yoo-hoo, Brad," one of the women called. "Look over here."

Rosie turned to glare at them. A flash went off. She groaned. "Not again. She took my picture."

"Just fans. Let's get inside. Herb, this is Rosie. Rosie, Herb's one of my guards."

Herb, a square-shouldered military type, motioned her inside. As she entered, the women called his name again.

He waved and smiled. "Later, ladies." He shut the door and sighed. "What do you think they got?"

"You unlocking the door and me looking at them."

"Not bad, then. It's not as if they got a shot of me grabbing your breast."

She glanced at Herb. "But you didn't—"

His face twisted until he looked like a cheesy movie monster. He reached clawed hands toward her chest. "Bring them here, little girl."

She laughed and backed away.

Herb shook his head and ambled down the hall toward the back of the house.

Why had she pushed him away before? This was what she wanted, what she'd dreamed of. Alone with Brad Merritt. The moment seemed unreal.

"Hey, are you okay?"

"Yes, of course." Despite her words, she couldn't smile, uncertain of how to tell him what she felt, or even if she should. He'd lump her in with the women on the sidewalk. Fans probably threw themselves at him all the time, wanting just one memorable night. Is that what she wanted, too?

He ran a fingertip down her nose. "What do you want, Diamond Rosie?"

She smiled as his words echoed her thoughts, and let her kiss answer him. He pulled her closer and deepened their kiss, then stepped back, smiling and a little breathless.

"Want a tour of the upstairs?"

She tilted her head. "Are you offering to show me your etchings? That's an ancient line."

"More like my eight-by-ten glossies." He leaned forward and whispered, "They're framed."

They walked down the hall, arms around each other's waists, hips bumping with each step. She held on to him a little more than she wanted, unsteady more because of his proximity than the two drinks she'd consumed at the party.

"This is my room." He pushed a wide, blue-painted door open.

She looked through the doorway and gasped. It was huge, paneled in wide, fragrant planks and with a football-field-sized bed in the middle. Huge antlers spread out on the wall over the headboard. Cheeto would love this place. Tacky didn't begin to describe it. She tried to think of something nice to say. "You brought Montana to New York City, cowboy."

"Yeah, and you can be my cowgirl." His blue eyes twinkled at her.

"Did you kill that deer?"

"The antlers are elk, and the animals shed them every year. I like fishing, but hunting's never been my thing."

"I'm glad." She didn't know what else to say. Her mind felt scrambled by the feel of his hard body next to hers, and by the sight of the bed that dominated the bedroom just a few feet away.

She knew how the night could end, that she could awaken in this room with Brad at her side. In a burst of clarity she realized that if she stayed here, he would react no differently than any other man. He'd said he liked fishing, which meant he probably liked a challenge, and she'd give him a fight before she let him reel her in.

"Show me the rest of your house. Did you decorate it all yourself?" She pulled free from his embrace and explored the other rooms. The one across the hall was done in a contemporary style. Contemporary to about 1975. She shut the door quickly.

"Some of it. I bought it furnished and I'm just starting to add my own touches, like my bedroom." He trailed after her.

She stopped. "Brad, you are charming and a talented actor and God knows you're good-looking, but if I were you I'd hire an interior designer. Like, right this minute. Do not attempt any more decorating."

"Ouch." He laughed and hugged her. "Rosie, you're not a breath of fresh air. More like a hurricane." He crowded her into the wall and kissed her.

It took what seemed like a full minute to recover.

"Thanks, I think. Can you call me a cab? I have a meeting in the morning." She tried to fix her hair to its original tousled state.

"Herb and I will drive you." He didn't argue, which was good, and even sounded a little disappointed, which pleased her. Her eyebrows went up at the mention of Herb, however.

She'd meant to put a little distance between Brad and the bed, but she'd looked forward to more hot kisses, and having a military chaperone wouldn't encourage any backseat fun.

She kissed him lightly on the cheek. "Thanks for showing me your house. Maybe someday I'll return the favor."

"Someday?"

"I don't really have a house right now, except for my yacht in Miami and a condo there. I've been living at the Ritz Carlton in Atlanta."

"I always stay at the one in Buckhead. It seems to me that a yacht, a condo, and a hotel room give you more homes than most."

"I saw you at the Ritz a few months ago. The day after I won the lottery."

"I don't think so. I would definitely have noticed you."

She remembered the longing she'd felt as he swept through the lobby, surrounded by his entourage. And how crushed she'd been when he didn't notice her at Zabo's that night. She'd come a long way from the person she'd been on that day.

"Well," she said, trying to push the painful memories behind her. "You know me now." She yawned. "Call me a cab, please? I'm exhausted."

Brad watched Rosie's profile on the cab ride to her hotel. She watched the city roll by as if it was done for her benefit.

She was different from the women that usually attracted him. For one thing, she didn't seem to want to sleep with him. And she'd admitted that she was a fan, too. Most actresses wanted to talk about themselves, or the parts he could get for them. Or they wanted his money.

Rosie had a lot more money than he did. He'd seen pictures of her yacht, the *MegaBucks*. And she thought she was homeless. He chuckled, drawing her attention.

"What's so funny?"

"Nothing. I was just thinking of your yacht."

"You were laughing at my yacht?" Her eyebrows rose, and her face darkened. What did that remind him of?

"No. I'd like to see it sometime."

"Oh."

She glanced up, face against the window again, then turned back to him. "You can come to Mexico with me if you'd like. I'm flying down to the beach there, and then I'll cruise home on the *MegaBucks* a week or so later."

"Are you serious?" A trip to a Mexican beach and a leisurely trip back by yacht. And with a lovely woman who admired his movies, and didn't want a piece of him.

"Sure." She smiled and turned away again. She had beautiful shoulders, and her skin was a creamy golden color that most women paid to be sprayed with in expensive tanning salons.

He wanted to touch her, but didn't know how she'd react. He felt like a shy teenager, and Brad Merritt had not been shy as a teenager. He sighed. "I can't wait," he said. And to his surprise, he meant it.

"Oh my God." Rosie held her coffee cup very still so that its contents wouldn't splash across the bedspread. On the bed in front of her was the *New York Post,* turned to a hideous photo of her and Brad dashing across a street in the Village, her skirt hiked up so that everyone could see her underwear (thank God she'd bought new panties that morning) and next to it the one of her fending off the photographer in front of Brad's brownstone. Those two *flojas* had sold the photos in front of his house. At least no one had captured a picture of their goodnight kiss in front of the hotel.

She needed some aspirin. The phone chirped on the nightstand, making her headache spike. She answered it. She could ignore the caller, but that ringing would make the pain worse.

"Rosie? It's Eve Sloane. Don't forget our meeting this morning. Dress appropriately."

Rosie made a face into the receiver. "I'll be there."

The phone rang again almost immediately after she'd hung up.

"Rosario, what are you doing up there in New York?" Her grandmother's voice was shrill and that "Rosario" was a warning of what was to come. "I hear on the news that you are, what did they say?"

A muffled voice behind her supplied the word. "Ah, yes." She continued. "*Cavorting* with a movie star. *Niña,* I don't know what that means, but from the picture, which shows your *pantaloncitos,* I don't have to guess."

She listened to twenty more minutes of angry grandmotherly advice with her eyes closed. It was almost restful, and hey, she was connecting with her grandmother again.

The next call was from the producer of a reality TV show, wanting her to consider starring in a lotto winner show. She hung up on him.

"You wanted to be a celebrity." Cheeto was the last call of the morning. "And you hit the jackpot. Straight to the top with that one. Brad Merritt. Wow."

He said "celebrity" the way Tia Hortensia used to say "dulce de leche." Tia weighed about two hundred pounds when she died. Dug her grave with her teeth, Abuela said.

"I had a good time last night. You don't have to be snide. Brad's really nice." Her head felt a teeny bit better. "Not conceited. He's not fake, like Hollywood people you read about." And he probably thought that she was immature. Last night it had seemed like a good idea to go to his house, knowing what he would expect. He'd been a gentleman, even when she'd asked to be taken home.

She'd thought about him when she awoke this morning, visualizing what it would be like to wake up with his body next to hers. She shivered at the image.

"Did you think that the photographers wouldn't be waiting for you, or were you planning on it?" Cheeto sounded amused.

Rosie remembered the wild mob scene outside the party, with photographers arranged in feeding order around the door. Big fish, little fish, obnoxious fish.

Brad hadn't cared. He'd acted as if they were just annoying, like white cats that deliberately brushed against you when you're wearing clean black pants.

"Brad's used to it, and I figured I'd better get used to it, too." Of course, hanging with Brad Merritt had probably made it worse.

"Good thing you feel that way. The 'lottery winner' headlines were getting old, and you've given them a whole new angle." Her cousin laughed.

Rosie wasn't thrilled at the thought of being forever followed around by a pack of hyenas, but maybe they'd get bored when they discovered that she and Brad were not an item. Yet.

She poured herself another cup of coffee from the English china pot waiting at her bedside, then doctored it up with cream and sugar cubes, loving the tiny silver sugar tongs. "At least they didn't call me Trailer Park Diva this time."

"Diamond Rosie is no improvement. Maybe we should hire you a bodyguard. Do you really like this guy?"

"Yeah. I really do, Cheeto."

"Then go for it, *prima*. I've got to go, my friends are here. We're heading to Idaho. Fly-fishing."

"Brad said he likes fishing, too. Be careful." She ended the call and picked up her coffee cup. She was jealous of Cheeto, who'd always had lots of friends, even when he'd worked as a landscaper. She headed to her very luxurious bathroom. Time to start her day, headache and all.

Rosie's bag was Prada, picked up on a whim, and her dress by an unknown designer whose window display in Soho had caught her eye. She'd gone beyond brand names. She'd come full circle and could shop at Wal-Mart and make it seem chic.

What a world.

Dr. Sloane was on her way in a hired car, and while she waited for her she called her grandmother. Abuela's assistant, Melba, answered the phone.

"Rosita, *mi amor*. It's been so long. I'm keeping your Abuelita's house for her while she's away." The woman's Spanish had the lilting accent of Mexico's northern provinces.

"I thought I'd called her cell phone."

"You did. She left it here by mistake. She's on a cruise. They're playing canasta."

"Oh, I just talked to her. She must have called from the ship." How many canasta cruises could a person go on?

Melba laughed. "*Ay*, Rosa, Josefa said you were funny. You can call her if you'd like. She's on the *Caribbean Princess*. I'll give you the number."

Rosie wrote it down, and left her grandmother a message to call. She was on her way to the meeting when the call came through. Dr. Sloane had been on the phone almost nonstop since she and her driver had picked up Rosie, so she answered without an apology to her backseat companion. Their ten-block trip was taking forever in the morning traffic, but the day was crisp and cold, and the store windows were full of Christmas displays.

"*Nena*, what's wrong?"

"Abue? Nothing's wrong. Are you okay? You left your cell phone behind. Melba answered it."

"*Claro que sí*. I let her know I'd left it behind. I'm having a ball. I'm on a winning streak, the bartender knows how to make good mojitos, and one of the gentlemen playing here is from my cousin Fefa's town in Oriente back in Cuba. We've been talking old times."

"How old is he?" Rosie thought of the masseuse at the hotel.

"What does it matter?" Her grandmother laughed, as if reading Rosie's mind. "He's almost seventy."

Rosie sighed, relieved. She hadn't realized she was holding her breath. The massage guy at the Ritz had been in his twenties, tops. The thought of some guy latching on to her Abuela for her money made her want to rent a helicopter and fly out to kick his butt. But if he was seventy he probably wasn't a gigolo. Maybe.

"So when will you be home, Abuela?"

"Before the end of the month, but then I'll stay in Miami for a while. I think I'm going to buy a condo in that South Beach tower where you rent yours."

"Stay in mine. I don't know when I'll be back in Miami."

"No thanks. I'd like a place of my own."

That stung. She'd said the same words to her grandmother after her mother's death. "Are you going to let me visit?"

"*Mi niña,* there will always be a room just for you."

The warmth that enveloped her at those words reminded Rosie of how much Abuela meant to her. She knew that Abuela loved her, but she needed to hear her say it.

"I love you, too, Abuelita."

She hung up and listened to the sounds of New York City traffic outside her window. Very different from South Beach, where the cruising cars had better-maintained, quieter motors, and ambulance sirens didn't sound every few minutes.

She couldn't believe that she was still almost at the beginning of her new life. One of the tight necktie guys at the meeting today had said so. Her trusts and foundation and land purchases were not complete. It would never really end, but they weren't even through the planning stages. Managing the Caballero family's wealth was going to employ a lot of people for a long time.

It seemed years since she'd trudged down the red clay paths along Buford Highway to answer phones all day, and then return to her apartment to play eenie-meenie-minie-mo when it came time to pay her bills.

Cheeto was fly-fishing out west, Abuela was playing cards in the Caribbean, and she was partying with movie stars in New York. What next?

She remembered what she'd told Brad in the cab. She'd seen a billboard for Mexican beaches and had made up a story about spending time on the beach and cruising home on the yacht. Well, why not? She'd find a little villa on a beach in Mexico, and Manny could come pick her up when she was done. She might even take Kim up on her offer to visit California while she was at it.

She didn't know anything about Kim's private life. Did her loved ones know about her drug problem? Maybe she didn't have any family.

What had been interesting tabloid news was now her real life.

Rosie had never been to the West Coast. They could shop on Rodeo Drive and drive up the Pacific Coast Highway. She needed fun. No, she thought, she'd had lots of fun already. She needed a friend.

"What you need is an assistant," Abuela said before heading out to a spa retreat on an exotic island with her girlfriends. "Someone who knows how to do all of those things that make you crazy, like keeping track of your appointments and making plane reservations."

"Actually, Dr. Sloane wants me to interview a bunch of candidates today."

"You need one. Remember that you're hiring an employee, not a friend." Abuela blew her kisses over the phone.

Dr. Sloane was helpful, but Rosie definitely didn't consider her a friend, and she was equally determined to have Rosie off her "to do" list. Rosie's questions aggravated her, especially her quest to find a villa in Mexico.

Mr. Pujol had flown up to meet with the tax attorneys, and he and Dr. Sloane had been meeting for hours. Neither of them had mentioned the pictures in the paper. Mr. Pujol had looked distracted.

It wasn't Rosie's fault. She didn't know how to use the Internet and the travel agent she'd gone to see didn't understand what she wanted and had kept trying to sell her a package deal. Meanwhile, Brad had gone back to California and the people she met at parties all seemed more interested in her money than in her.

She was beyond bored, and it was obvious that she needed a plan for the next years that included a job she could do. Maybe one of the candidates she would interview today would be able to guide her. It would be cool to have someone in charge of all the tedious chores, like air travel, as long as it was someone she could get along with, and trust.

Two days later she wasn't so sure. She returned from working out in the hotel gym and found her suite crowded with women holding résumés. A couple of them glared at her as she came in, as if she was competition. All of them looked like versions of Dr. Sloane, elegant women of a certain age.

By midmorning of the third day the suite's striped silk sofas and armchairs seemed to hold every out-of-work accountant and retired lady professor in the city. Dr. Sloane seemed to like many of them.

Once the last of the day's would-be fascist babysitters was back on the lobby-bound elevator, Rosie confronted Dr. Sloane. "Are you trying to tell me something?"

"These women are all highly qualified." Dr. Sloane's finger paused, holding her place on the line of the thick spreadsheet she was reviewing. If it was the list of applicants, it was disheartening.

"Maybe I can find my own assistant."

"Of course. That's why you're interviewing them." She turned a page. "I asked you to write down what you wanted to see in an ideal candidate, but you never responded."

"Any of them male, six five, with long black hair and a face like Orlando Bloom?"

"No." Dr. Sloane smiled a little.

Rosie sighed. "Well, then it's pointless. I'll do okay on my own, honest."

Dr. Sloane gave her a look. "Rosie, please. You've come a long way, but you're still very naïve about some things and I want you to keep out of trouble, and an assistant should be able to help you with day-to-day errands."

"Can't you find any normal people?"

"These *are* all normal people. They have superior organizational skills, as well as the know-how to handle all kinds of situations and requests."

"You're saying I'm disorganized and needy?"

Dr. Sloane shrugged.

Okay, so she was, but it kind of hurt to have to acknowledge it.

Rosie poured herself another cup of coffee and waved the coffeepot in the air toward Dr. Sloane, who shook her head no. Rosie put it back down and got busy with the cream and sugar. Dr. Sloane shuddered and looked away. She hadn't been able to break Rosie of all her bad habits.

"You know, Dr. Sloane, I'm aware that you don't like me." She flopped down in the armchair opposite the consultant's. "Pick your favorite candidate and I'll hire her. You'll be rid of me, and I'll head to Cancún with my new assistant and we'll see if it works out. Make sure her passport is valid."

Dr. Sloane's eyebrows had climbed toward her hairline. "Cancún? Since when?"

"Since I told Brad that I'd be heading to Mexico and asked him to come along." She tried to look innocent, but if she'd been a cat, little yellow feathers would have been sticking out of the corners of her mouth.

Dr. Sloane shook her head, looking as if she was trying to clear it, rather than disapproving. "That's not the way to avoid the attention of the press."

After two more sips of coffee, Rosie uncovered the tray on the breakfast cart and helped herself to toast and juice, leaving the eggs and bacon.

She'd watched Dr. Sloane eat, and she didn't actually consume so much as she destroyed her food. The woman was the size of a pencil, so Rosie decided that she'd try it out. It beat Kim's deadly diet.

She sipped juice, watched the morning news, and shredded toast between her fingers. An hour later when she headed to the shower she'd had about four ounces of juice and a nibble of toast.

Funny thing was, she wasn't particularly hungry anymore. Maybe leisure gave you more time to coexist with your food, rather than have to choke everything down and head back to work.

She showered and dressed in black slacks and a cute black and white top she didn't remember seeing before. It was her size, and had tags on it, so she must have bought it, probably in one of those grab-everything-off-the-rack-and-try-it-on-later shopping trips she'd done after the tight jeans photo had been published and she'd vowed never to try on clothes at a store again.

The outfit was cute, but her hair looked out of place, all drippy and limp. It had grown out since she had it done in Atlanta. "I'm getting my hair cut today," she called out.

Dr. Sloane's voice came from the other room. "Fine. I'll have the hotel send someone up."

"Oh, I got one." Rosie stepped out of her bedroom. "Someone from the hotel recommended her. Lizzie Suarez told me about a real artist and I've got an appointment at three."

A pleased smile crossed Dr. Sloane's face. "You called the concierge and asked for a recommendation? I'm proud of you, Rosie. You're becoming independent."

Had Rosie said she'd called the concierge? She didn't want that smile to go away, and knew it would the minute she told Dr. Sloane that Lizzie was the maid who'd done up her room yesterday. Instead of answering, she shrugged and went back to getting ready. No sense getting Dr. Sloane all upset. Besides, she was proud of herself, too.

Lizzie's friend, Celeste, had her salon in Brooklyn, and since Rosie couldn't figure out the train and bus system, she had the doorman call a cab, then paid the cabbie to stop a couple of blocks away from the salon. She felt like walking.

The New York she stepped out into was totally different from the one where the towering hotel stood. There, everyone moved quickly, their beautiful clothes a testament to their success, and they all seemed to be on their way to somewhere else.

This neighborhood seemed more like a destination. The streets were a swirl of color, scent, and sound. Loud Latin music, loud Spanish conversations, and the smell of ripe produce and fabulous cooking filled the air, along with an occasional whiff of garbage.

Rosie's head whipped back and forth like a tourist's as she walked the two blocks to Celeste's salon. This neighborhood probably wasn't in the usual guidebooks.

It was an old-fashioned salon. The name, Sami and Celeste, was stenciled in black script on a big glass window lined with pink curtains. Inside, black and white tile that had probably been laid way before Rosie was born made a patterned backdrop for the two women busy clipping hair.

Several women waited in a row of old armchairs, idly leafing through magazines, mouths going a mile a minute in contrast to their slow movements.

The stylist closest to the door looked her over and smiled. "Be right with you, *corazón*. You're Rosa, right?"

"Right."

"Cool. Lizzie told me you'd be here at three. You're a little early." She fluffed hair around her customer's face.

"I didn't know how long it would take to get here." The women in the armchairs were looking at her, but their conversation continued. A sign over their heads announced that a wash and haircut was thirty dollars, a lot less expensive than the team that had done her hair in Atlanta, not that it mattered. She would have paid a lot more for this adventure.

Grabbing an old issue of *People,* she sat opposite one of the women and started looking at photos of relationships that had soured long before the warm weather had arrived. Brad was featured in several of them, smiling into the camera with a beautiful girl at his side.

Rosie ignored the curious looks of the others until the older of the two stylists called her over. "I'm Celeste. Go with Sarita to get a shampoo, then we'll get to work."

Sarita, a young girl in low-cut jeans, showed her to the back of the salon, draped her neck in warm towels, and shampooed her hair. Bliss.

Peppermint-scented and drowsy, she sat in Celeste's chair.

"Well, *mi amor,* what do you want?"

"I'm in your hands, Celeste. I heard you were great. I need a trim."

Celeste examined her hair. "How about something shorter? Your little face is just swallowed up by all this hair."

"Why not? Just don't do anything that makes my nose look any bigger."

Celeste matter-of-factly picked up strands of Rosie's hair, pulled them out to the sides of her face, and even examined her scalp. If she killed a chicken and sprinkled her with its blood, Rosie was out of here.

Finally, Celeste nodded, agreeing with some internal voice, and started to clip. Rosie didn't look. She kept her eyes firmly set on her smock-covered lap.

She listened to the snipping of the scissors and felt the slight tug as each strand of hair was combed out and cut. No turning back now. Her mind wandered as Celeste worked.

She thought of her family, of Brad and Kim, and of the stern applicants for her personal assistant job. She needed to find a flight to Cancún. Or should she just charter a whole plane? It seemed wasteful.

She could buy one, but Dr. Sloane had told her that it cost money to store it and to have a pilot on call. She felt safer on a big commercial jet. Lots of people, government regulations. Definitely safer.

She'd never left the country before, but luckily Mr. Pujol had convinced them to apply for passports shortly after they'd won the lottery. Her ignorance regarding just about everything was sort of embarrassing. How did other people learn these things? The right fork to use, how much to tip, whom to trust? What would she have done without Dr. Sloane? She needed to buy her a thank-you gift.

"Okay, tell me what you think." Celeste sounded triumphant.

Rosie opened her eyes. Her reflection looked back at her, amazed. She looked like Audrey Hepburn. Well, Audrey Hepburn if she had been Latina with a strong nose.

Celeste had cut her hair jaw-length, with lots of long layers, and shorter ones around her eyes. The result was that her eyes looked huge and her nose looked smaller. And her neck seemed to have grown about three inches longer. She stared, silent. She'd paid hundreds of dollars for her previous haircut, and here this Brooklyn hair artist had worked magic for thirty bucks.

"What do you think?" Celeste must have been getting worried.

"I love it." Rosie jumped up and hugged her, skidding on the discarded hair around the barber's chair. Celeste hugged her back. Their commotion drew the attention of the old crows sitting by the door, and they took the public display of delight as an invitation to chime in with their opinions.

When she walked out of the salon fifteen minutes later, she felt like a queen. She'd been petted and admired, and she loved her new look.

She walked three blocks to a large intersection, stepped into the street with her arm raised, and scored a cab in under two seconds. She was on a roll. In her previous life, luck this good would have prompted the purchase of a lottery ticket. No need for that anymore. She was set for several lifetimes.

The hotel room was empty when she burst in yelling, "Ta da!" Disappointed, she walked around, looking for anyone to share her new look with. No one. Not even a mirthless applicant.

She called housekeeping and asked for Lizzie. The housekeeping manager said that Lizzie had worked the early shift.

For a long time she sat in an armchair, alone in the giant suite. A timid knock on the door had to be repeated before she heard it.

"Come in," she said, then jumped up. She wasn't supposed to let anyone in. What if it was a reporter for the *Star*? Ready to run into her bedroom and barricade herself in there, she watched a tiny person creep into the room.

She looked as hesitant as Rosie felt.

"Are you in the wrong room?" she finally asked.

The woman opened a leather portfolio and consulted it. "No."

"Okay. May I help you?"

"I'm here to see Dr. Sloane." Her English was perfect, but she didn't look Anglo, or Latina, either. Maybe Cambodian mixed with something else. Definitely Asian.

"Dr. Sloane's not here now. Are you applying for the assistant position?" Rosie didn't clue her in as to who she was.

The agency must have made a mistake—she didn't fit the profile Dr. Sloane had posted.

"I waited for all the others to leave. I can't stand them, and I know you can't either." The woman opened the black leather portfolio she carried. Inside was one sheet of paper, which she handed to her as if she knew who Rosie was.

Rosie didn't know why she bothered to look at it. Dr. Sloane would hate her. She was right, though. Rosie hadn't liked the brigadier-general types who'd been in earlier, and this woman seemed different.

Her résumé showed that she had some spunk hidden somewhere. She'd graduated from NYU and had worked steadily for the past five years, as a travel agent, an administrative assistant, and for the past two years as the personal assistant to a retired movie star who had recently died.

Rosie looked up at Leony Chandra. Her lucky streak was unbroken. "So you worked as a travel agent?"

She nodded.

"Listen, Ms. . . ." Rosie consulted the résumé. "How do you pronounce this?"

"The way it's written," she said.

"Okay, Ms. Leony Chandra. Can you relax? I promise I won't hit you."

Ms. Chandra looked affronted for a second, then smiled and seemed to force herself to relax. "Okay. Sorry. Call me Leony."

"Good. Let's sit down." They sat in facing armchairs. She tucked one ankle behind the other. Her Abuela would love this *chica*. "Demure" is not a word that was ever used to describe Rosie.

They chatted for half an hour about this and that, then got around to Leony's background, and as time passed Leony loosened up, even laughed once.

"I'll tell you the truth, Leony. I don't know anything about anything, and I need someone who knows the ropes and can help me out."

"So I would be working for you?"

Darn. She hadn't meant to let that out. Before she could answer, Leony leaned forward and looked her up and down as if she was the one being interviewed.

"I know who you are," she said, more animated. "The Trailer Park Diva."

The Trailer Park Diva. No matter what she did, she'd always be the Trailer Park Diva.

Tootie staggered out of the bedroom and collapsed at their feet. Her doggie grin told Rosie she was okay, just a little stiff.

"What a cute puppy," Leony said. "What's her name?"

"Tootie. She was my mom's."

"Aw, come here, Tootie." Leony left the chair and knelt next to Tootie. The fickle poodle lifted her legs for a belly rub, which Leony promptly supplied. As far as Tootie was concerned, she was hired.

"So why are you looking for another job as a personal assistant? Did you like working for Betty Schuler?"

"It was hard work," Leony said, still rubbing Tootie's tummy. "But I'm good at it. Ms. Schuler did a lot of stage work after she retired, and she had an active social schedule. I managed her calendar and her personal life."

"How do you know this one would be the same? Your employer might be a demanding bitch." She threw that last word in to gauge her reaction. Leony didn't even blink.

"But if you're the employer, that won't be the case." She smiled. "I'd heard horror stories from some of the other candidates. They said I was supposed to interview with Dr. Sloane."

"She's my consultant. You looked kind of scared when you came in."

Leony winced. "I didn't think it showed."

"That's okay. We know each other now." Rosie leaned close to the candidate. "How about we try a little test? I'll ask you a question, and if I like your answer, you're hired."

Leony nodded, but her expression was wary.

"I've been trying to get a quiet little place on the beach in Mexico, but the travel agent I talked to didn't impress me. Can you recommend someone? Cancún or Cozumel, I haven't decided which." Rosie was testing her. She knew both resort areas were crowded and busy.

"Neither," Leony said quickly. "They are so commercial. If you want a lot of other tourists around, then sure. But you said quiet, so I'd recommend a little beach town."

"Can you get me a good hotel? Or a house?"

"You don't want a hotel," she said. "No privacy. You need a private villa with staff."

Staff. Rosie grinned. She was loving her already. "When can you start?"

CHAPTER ELEVEN
* * * * * *

You can never go wrong investing in real estate.
—*The Instant Millionaire's Guide to Everything*

Brad on Broadway? Rumors Are Flying . . .
—*New York Post*

The sea sped by just forty feet below the helicopter's skids. Rosie's mouth was stuck in a permanent scream. Not that anyone could hear. The wind and engine noise were loud, worse than a nightclub or an Atlanta overpass at rush hour.

She clutched the armrest, closed her eyes, and pushed herself back into the seat. She hadn't counted on a terrifying helicopter ride.

"How soon before we get there?" She had to yell to make herself heard.

The chartered helicopter's pilot laughed. "Relax," he yelled. "Ten more minutes, max."

She opened her eyes and glared at Leony, who leaned close to the glass on her side of the chopper, looking at the water speed past below them.

It made Rosie sick just to think about the blur of glittery waves. She moaned. "We should have taken the train."

"There's no telling when the transit strike would be over, Rosie. This will get us there faster." Leony was already indispensable. She was unflappable, too. Rosie had been baffled by the transit strike that sidelined the train that would take them from Puerto Vallàrta to the tiny town of Playa Tierna. Leony had hired the helicopter with just two phone calls.

The idea of arriving at the beach house so quickly sounded terrific, but the reality of the flight had Rosie on the verge of hurling. She'd endure a six-hour car ride before she did this again. Or else they could knock her out and wake her up at her destination. Not a bad idea.

A line of spindly trees seemed to speed toward them. The helicopter slowed, then banked left, sending billows of white sand into the air. The house beyond the beach was low and gray, like a big cinder block. Beyond it was another one, taller and glittering with glass walls that faced the water.

When at last they landed on the beach, Rosie waited until the pilot signaled that it was safe to exit, and then she jumped out of the helicopter, duckwalking until she was out of the rotors' reach. Only then did she cautiously straighten to examine her surroundings.

The sand was white, with rock outcroppings, and the water was very blue. From here the long, concrete building seemed to perch on a small rise above the beach. Her heart fell. Except for the flower-filled trees, it looked like a concrete bunker. She'd expected a little charm, and with all this land, why were the two houses so close together?

Leony was pointing out which suitcases went where when a tall, thin man came out of the house and ambled toward them.

She hoped he was going to tell her they'd made a mistake and that her house was down the road.

"*Buenas tardes,* Señorita Caballero. Welcome to Casa Maravilla," His Spanish was crisp, and he smiled broadly.

She forced a smile. "And you are?"

"I'm Efraim Alarcon, the houseman," he said in English. His accent was flat and Midwestern.

"You sound like you're from the U.S."

"Yep." He grinned. "Nebraska."

"I'll bet you enjoy doing that to your guests. Your Spanish is flawless."

His grin pushed all of his sun wrinkles into extra origami folds. He grabbed a couple of suitcases, waved good-bye to the pilot, then started up a rustic stone path set in the sand.

The ocean breeze was tangy and carried the scent of flowers. The delicious perfume made her think that she could live in a shack as long as the sand was like sugar, the air smelled sweet, and the water was close.

"Señoritas, you'll want to be inside when the helicopter takes off."

The two women hurried through the front door, huge and made of dark, splintery timbers with bright red hardware. This was no shack. She glanced at the house next door. She hoped it was vacant. She didn't want to share the beach, and if anyone called her Diamond Rosie or asked her how it felt to win the lotto, she'd start back home, even if she had to grab a ride with a farmer.

Efraim pushed open the door and brought in the suitcases.

The cool darkness was pierced by bright shafts of sunlight

reflected from the sand outside. She'd expected huge mission furniture, like in an old movie, but the house was furnished in a spare modern style. So far nothing about Mexico fit her preconceived notions.

She stepped out of her shoes and enjoyed the coolness of the tiles as she followed Efraim to a large bedroom done all in white, an echo of the beach she could hear through the louvered shutters over the door and the windows that faced the sea. Through the connecting door she saw Efraim dropping Leony's suitcases on the floor of the adjoining room.

"I hope you'll be comfortable here," he said. "Have you eaten lunch? My wife Jana is the cook."

She glanced at her watch. Almost four in the afternoon back home, but just after one here, and she'd only eaten the cinnamon roll and coffee the flight attendant had served at the beginning of her flight.

"Starving," she said. "But tell your wife not to go to any trouble. Coffee and some fruit would be great, and see what my assistant wants."

"Very well. I'll serve it on the lanai." Efraim left to get the other suitcases, leaving her alone in the bedroom.

She pulled out her cell phone and dialed Cheeto's number.

"Rosie, what's up?"

"Hi, *primo*. I didn't think I'd actually talk to you. I was going to leave a message."

"I always take your calls."

"Guess what? I'm at my house in Mexico. The chef is bringing our lunch out to the lanai."

"Lanai!" Cheeto laughed. "Sounds like a cuss word."

"Come over if you want, Cheeto. Plenty of room."

"I got stuff going on here, *prima*. But thanks."

They chatted some more, then Rosie changed into a bikini and a wispy cover-up and headed out to explore the house. It was a palace. Everything from the hand-painted tiles in the kitchen, which was dominated by an oversized dragon of an Aga, to the ocean-facing rooms arranged for entertaining was luxurious yet felt like home, even the four bedroom suites and little apartment for a nanny.

A blond woman carrying a pile of folded towels came out of the apartment. She smiled.

"How are you, Miss Caballero?" Her accent was European, but she couldn't place it.

"Fine, thanks. You're Jana?"

"I am. I'll bring a snack out in a bit." She pointed the way to the lanai.

"Thanks." She went to the end of a second wide hall and found herself on a porch. Leony was already there, looking cozy in a rattan armchair, a book in her hand and her cell phone on the table next to her.

Leony smiled up at her. "Like the house?"

"It's beautiful, Leony."

"It came highly recommended. Robert DeNiro loves the place."

"Robert DeNiro stays here?" Rosie wondered if her bed had a Robert DeNiro–shaped dent in it. Had her life changed, or what?

"His nanny knows a friend of mine. She comes down with the family."

"You're so connected." Rosie spotted a wide, striped-canvas hammock edged in netting and slung from a stand. "Hey, I've always wanted to sit in one of these." Rosie grabbed the hammock's stiffened edge and backed slowly until her rear was all the way on it. She lifted her legs carefully, and the hammock started to swing wildly. She squealed and held on, trying to balance herself.

Leony laughed. "You need help there, boss?"

"I think I got it." Rosie's second attempt was successful, and she arranged pillows around herself. "This is like the trip down here, it makes me want to stay forever, because the journey was such a pain."

Actually, it felt heavenly. She was supported above the ground, and cool breezes flowed around her, as if she was floating, surrounded by puffy pillows, the only sounds the surf and the distant call of sea birds. She soon drifted to sleep.

When she awoke, a tray had been placed on a nearby table. A tall pitcher of icy water flanked a bowl of chilled sliced mango. A plate of cheese and crusty bread and a porcelain coffee cup with a little covered coffeepot were on a separate tray.

It looked like a photograph from *Coastal Living* magazine. She admired it until her stomach growled, reminding her that she needed to eat.

She slipped her fingers through the netting and sat up, then carefully let her legs drop over the side. Piece of cake. She'd be hopping on and off of this thing in no time. Leony was gone. Maybe she was in her room catching her own nap.

She thought of Brad and wondered what kind of hammock skills were needed in order to make love on it. That thought conjured lots of colorful mental pictures.

The mango was delicious, sweeter than any she'd eaten in Atlanta. Abuelita would love it. Rosie missed her, but not enough to take a canasta cruise. Maybe Abuela could join her out here, and bring Cheeto.

With no agenda and no reporters around, Rosie felt free. The sound of the surf was hypnotic, and the beach looked inviting. She returned to her room, got her sneakers, put her hair up, and hit the hard-packed shore.

The wind tugged at her topknot and made the curly tendrils at her neck dance and tickle.

The smells and colors brought back a memory of Papi holding her hands as she floated in the warm Atlantic water, and how he'd towed her around in lazy circles, telling her stories about life in Cuba. She'd drowsed as she floated, safe in his large hands, his voice, heavy with nostalgia, swirling around her like the eddies he made with his turns.

On the shore, her mother had anchored a bedsheet with rocks and was unpacking a picnic, looking glamorous in her two-piece bathing suit, her long hair up in a ponytail.

The wind carried a shout to her and the memory vanished. She looked around, but she was alone. Another call, thin and quickly blown away. She turned around.

A tiny Efraim stood by the model-railroad-sized house. He waved his arms and called again.

Lost in thought, she'd wandered farther than she meant to. Maybe Abuela had called. She walked back, enjoying the sound of the waves, the smell of the salt air.

Efraim waited on the sand until she was close enough to talk to without yelling.

"You didn't have to wait for me. It's not dangerous here, is it?" She waved toward the other houses, scattered far apart, all the way to the point that glittered close to the horizon.

He shrugged. "Nowhere is safe anymore, Señorita Caballero, and here, the big houses attract people with unfortunate goals. You are a woman of means, and would be a valuable prize. You need to keep near the house, or have someone go with you."

A woman of means. His old-fashioned term made her sound like a crusty society matron. She made a face. "I don't want a keeper. I'll be careful."

At least in Atlanta she could walk wherever she wanted to go. How much worse could the local bad guys be than Dog the dealer? Of course, when she'd nodded a daily good morning to Dog back in the day, she hadn't been worth millions.

"I will bring you a cocktail." He looked up and down the beautiful deserted beach once more, then went back into the house.

Little white-foamed blue waves slapped the shore gently, then receded. The hazy bright sky was almost white. Up the beach, a vulture was circling high overhead, wide wings waggling as it soared. Not a good sign.

She changed her mind about a swim. If the sugary sands were dangerous, what would the waters hold? She could deal with two-legged predators, but she wasn't sure about the ones in the deep.

Spooked by thoughts of sharks, kidnappers, and vultures, she started up the stone steps. A movement drew her eye. Someone walked past the wide glass doorway of the house next door, but she couldn't see who it was. A caretaker, maybe?

Leony waved from the lanai. "Kiki the manicurist is here."

"Be right there." Rosie hurried, glad she'd skipped the swim. Thirty minutes later she sat in her lounge chair, eyes closed and toes separated by fat cotton wads. She listened to the gentle waves break on the sand below as the teenaged nail artist worked on her feet. This was heaven. A facial and a mani-pedi on her front porch.

She heard a muffled shout, then a louder one. She opened her eyes, blinking to clear her lashes of the cucumber and avocado puree mask glopped over her face.

"What's going on over there?" The noise was coming from the glass house.

Kiki giggled. "Señor is practicing."

"Oh my God. A neighbor?" Darn. She'd wanted the house to be empty. "I thought I saw someone, but I thought it was a caretaker."

Kiki shrugged. "He arrived a few days ago."

Rosie tried to see him, but a huge frangipani blocked her view. She could still hear him, though.

"I've got a stake in this game," he shouted. "And I don't give a fuck what you think."

Her eyebrows jumped, cracking her forehead mask before its time. Kiki frowned, recapped the Tangerine Splendor nail polish, and came at her with the spatula and the pot of mashed herbed avocado puree.

"Señorita, you need to be still," the girl said, spackling her forehead once more. She added a thick layer to her cheeks while she was at it. The stuff felt cool and heavy, and Rosie settled back, ready to doze once more.

"Asshole!" The roar made the frangipani blooms tremble. "You get off my land, and if I ever see you near mine again, I'll be the last person you see."

Silence.

"So he's an actor?" Rosie asked through clenched teeth. Either that or a psychopath. She adjusted the towel that covered her hot-oil-treated hair.

Kiki grinned. "*Sí.* He is so awesome." She'd been speaking in Spanish, but the "awesome" came out in English.

"You fuckers don't belong here," he moaned. "You don't belong here. I had it all, and you took it." His words blurred, then ended abruptly with a gunshot.

Kiki squealed and sat down hard on the lanai's polished aggregate floor.

"That's it." Rosie got up and, walking carefully on the outside edges of her feet to spare her pedicure, picked her way over the sun-warmed tiles that led to the glass house.

Her potty-mouthed neighbor was pacing away from her toward the other end of his pool, a script in his hand and a huge sombrero on his head.

"You need to take your rehearsing indoors," she said. He turned and stared, mouth open.

The sombrero was ridiculous, a threadbare velvet specimen of the spangled hats that mariachis wore, but it didn't disguise the astonished face below its sequined, upturned brim.

Brad Merritt.

And here she was with a pound of guacamole on her face. She meant to say "excuse me" but made a noise that sounded more like "eep" and scurried back to where Kiki stood, eyes round.

"You are very brave, señorita. That is Brad Merritt, the movie star."

"I know who it is." Please don't come over here, she prayed. Maybe he didn't recognize her with a towel on her head and two inches of avocado mush smeared over her features. "Let's finish my nails inside, okay? I'm roasting out here." She pulled her robe tighter and stepped into the cool, air-conditioned house. "Jana, I'm not at home if anyone calls."

Jana stared at her as she went by, fragrant as a summer salad with acetone vinaigrette. "Of course. Not at home." She shrugged, as if she was used to insanity from the guests.

The invitation came right before siesta. Drinks and an evening walk on the beach with Brad. He'd recognized her.

"I thought walks on the beach were dangerous." Rosie looked at the black scrawl that covered the note he'd sent over.

> *I knew it was you. Chicken. Drinks and a*
> *walk tonight?*
>
> *Brad*

"Señor Brad often walks on the beach. He always has guards with him," Efraim said.

"Guards. Of course. I have my personal assistant, my chef and manicurist, my butler, but I totally forgot my bodyguards." She rolled her eyes.

"Don't worry, we'll bring some next time." Leony sounded totally serious. She'd been making calls inside this morning and had missed her humiliating moment, but Kiki had filled her in, showing an amazing capacity for observation.

"So what are you going to wear?" Leony frowned at her own perfect nails.

"A sundress and sandals, hold the avocado."

"You look beautiful by moonlight." Brad walked next to her, stepping carefully on the soft drifts, barely illuminated by the moon. It was so dark that she saw nothing ahead but the curve of the beach, marked by the glimmering wavelets.

"Thanks." She didn't add that he looked good enough to drag into the bushes. He had probably heard it so many times that he didn't believe it anymore. The breeze had picked up and Rosie was glad her hair was shorter so that it didn't whip across her face.

"Did I bother you when I was running my lines this morning? You looked pretty angry."

She felt her face grow hot, remembering exactly how she'd looked. "I'd just sat down for a spa treatment."

"Ah. That explains the face thing." It was too dark to see if he was laughing at her.

"Yeah. That was a pretty intense scene. What are you working on?"

He was silent for a long moment, and she wondered if she'd made a mistake. Maybe he was the kind of artist who didn't want to discuss his work until he deemed it ready for public viewing. "It's okay if you don't want to talk about it."

He walked closer to her and his hand touched her waist. "I'm not angry."

When she didn't move away the touch moved up until his arm was around her shoulder. He wore a long cotton shirt unbuttoned over a T-shirt, and the loose shirt flapped in the breeze. It was just like the boat scene of *Manon's Riches*. Totally scrumptious, and walking on her beach with his arm around her.

"I was just thinking how different you are. You don't ask about my film projects. Most women I meet would want to know everything about my new role, or else they'd be campaigning for a part in the movie."

"Not me," she said. "It's bad enough to have my picture in the paper."

"I don't think so. I love making movies. I get to be another person, just slide into their skin."

"I noticed. Remember I told you that you talk and dress like your character even when you're not in front of the camera. Do you ever get confused?"

"Not so far."

She remembered the anguished cries that she heard from the other side of the frangipani tree. This role was different from the spies and cowboys he'd played before. She didn't want to sound like the other women, the ones he'd complained about, so she changed the subject.

"I know I invited you to stay at the beach with me, but how'd you find this place?"

"My assistant called your foundation, and got the number of a Dr. Sloane." He looked at her and laughed. "You should see your expression." He grinned, eyes glinting with reflected moonlight. "I hope that was okay. I've been getting a lot of work done."

She wondered what Dr. Sloane had thought when a world-famous movie star had called her. "I'm glad you came."

That was an understatement. She wanted to jump into his arms and show him how much she appreciated that he'd come here because of her, to be near her.

Or was it because of her? Maybe he just needed a place to work on his acting. Had he really told her anything else?

He'd told her that she looked beautiful in the moonlight, but that could be just a line.

"I can't stay out late. I've got to get back to work. See you tomorrow?" He picked up her hand, lacing his fingers through hers.

Better. She admired his perfect profile. "Sure. Maybe you can show me what you're working on."

"Don't wait until tomorrow. Come see." He pulled her back the way they came, walking quickly. The lights from her house glimmered in the surrounding dark, looking vulnerable. They walked past it and up the stairs to the walkway, then over to his swimming pool, which glowed turquoise against the velvet night.

A table next to the pool held a bound script, which he picked up and offered to her.

"It's a play," he said, watching as she opened it and scanned the pages.

It looked really serious and emotional. "Not a movie?"

"No, Broadway. I'm being considered as a replacement for Murphy Murrow, who defined the role. It's my chance to leave action movies behind, Rosie."

"Anything I can do to help?" She thought of all the great

movies he'd made, where his comedic timing had made heroic tough-guy roles unforgettable.

He looked at her, as if seeing something he'd never considered before. "Maybe there is."

"What?"

"Help me run my lines."

She made a face. "I can't stand fish."

"Running lines is what actors call reading the other parts so that I can practice mine."

"Oh. I can do that." It had sounded like some kind of fishing. He probably thought she was an idiot. Every toddler in Los Angeles probably knew the term.

He smiled. "Can you be poolside at seven tomorrow morning?"

"Seven?" So much for her beauty sleep.

"Don't sound so dismayed. Rise early, and you'll enjoy more of the day, as my dad always used to say." He grinned at her, the rat.

"Okay, I'll be here, but there'd better be coffee involved, or I'll be incoherent."

"I promise." He leaned forward and kissed her, his mouth warm and slightly salty. "Tomorrow?"

"You bet." She ran back up to her own house and skipped into the lanai and dropped into a chair at the table opposite the one where Leony was spooning up a rich-looking sorbet.

"Ooh, I want one of those." She grinned at Leony.

"Okay, I know you're my boss and all, but girl, spill. I just saw you kissing Brad Merritt. Was all that *Star* stuff the truth?"

Efraim appeared behind them, holding another crystal bowl

of delicately colored sorbet. "Cherimoya," he said, placing it in front of Rosie. "Pardon, Señorita Rosie, but I couldn't help overhearing. Mr. Merritt arrived two days ago. His staff asked us to keep his presence quiet. He said he is a friend of yours?"

Rosie ate a big spoonful of sorbet. "Yum." She closed her eyes and savored the melting sweetness. She opened them again and smiled at Leony. "Those tabloid guys have to be right some of the time. Actually, Dr. Sloane told him where to find us."

Leony gave her a raised-eyebrow look. "At least we know this wasn't a weird coincidence." Her cell phone rang and she excused herself.

Rosie wondered what all the calls were about. Leony seemed to spend more time on the phone here than she had back home.

Rosie ran lines with Brad for the next three days, and with each hour of work she grew more frustrated. He was making a terrible mistake, and she didn't know how to tell him. Friends told each other the truth, didn't they?

"Gregory, you are a fool," she read aloud. "You have ruined your sister's life."

"No, Mother. I have done what is right, what is fair. Sophia must be content." He growled the words, his face twisted.

Rosie put down her copy of the script. "Why are you making that face?"

He frowned. He hated interruptions. "I'm showing regret. I'm regretting my actions. My voice says one thing, my actions another."

She stared at him. "Brad, I'm kind of regretting your actions, too. Your face was saying that Gregory is so constipated he's ready to shoot himself."

A small snort drew their attention, but Leony, sunning herself in a nearby lounge chair, seemed to be asleep.

"I think I know more about acting than you do. May we continue?" Brad took a deep breath, glanced at his script, and prepared for the next line.

"Maybe you should do another action movie. I love your Jack Link movies. Do another one of those. Maybe Jack Link can chase terrorists through a theme park. Kids, bombs, chase scenes." She stopped waving her arms, aware that his expression had darkened.

"Rosie, I'm tired of Jack Link. I want to be known for something more than blowing up the White House. Stage work is a surefire way to do that."

"*Fatal Mistake.* My favorite Jack Link movie of all time."

He shook his head. "Let's get back to Gregory."

Rosie sighed and turned to the page they'd been on. "Go ahead."

He acted a few more lines, then stopped. "Rosie, I can't do this if you keep shaking your head every time I say another line."

"I'm sorry, Brad. I think you should try another kind of play. This isn't you."

"It *will* be me. You don't have to work with me if it pains you." He looked hurt.

Rosie started to tell him that it would be okay, that he was really good, but she didn't. It wasn't true. He sucked, and someone had to tell him the truth.

She put the script down and stood up. "Brad, you're really talented. You're good in all kinds of roles, but this one isn't one of them. Either that, or you're trying too hard." She poked Leony, who sat up too bright-eyed to have been asleep. "Come on. We need to let Brad work."

"Sure." Leony's feet groped for her flip-flops, and then the two women walked across to Rosie's house, leaving Brad alone by the pool, his script clenched in his fist.

She hardly slept that night, worried about Brad's future. He was making a big mistake. Leony had work to do the next day so Rosie held a mini Jack Link film festival on the breezy lanai. She'd found that all the Jack Link movies were in the house's DVD collection. Maybe Brad would come and watch himself do what he did best.

She was halfway through *Reckless* when Abuela called. She paused the DVD. "What's up, Abuela? How's the cruise?"

"Beautiful, fabulous, and I think I could live out here forever."

"An eternal cruise. Sounds too much like the *Flying Dutchman*."

Abuela chuckled. "I would be content to stay on a cursed ship, if it offered all-day canasta, and mojitos at cocktail hour."

"Hey, sign me up, too. Why the call? Everything okay?"

"Yes, of course. Everything is fine here. Cheeto just called, though. I didn't understand what he was saying but he sounded upset, and telephones are iffy out here. *Nena,* would you call him and find out what's wrong?"

"Sure." She was instantly in worry mode. Abuela sounded too calm. Cheeto hardly ever called, and if he'd called Abuela on the cruise ship something must be very wrong. "Don't worry about Cheeto, Abuelita. I'll call him." She hung up and raced to find Leony.

CHAPTER TWELVE
* * * * * *

It sounds unromantic, but investigating
a potential partner, whether in business or
marriage, is good sense.
—*The Instant Millionaire's Guide to Everything*

Diamond Rosie's Mexican Beach Hideaway—
Who's Her Secret Guest?
—*Star* magazine

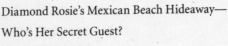

I took care of it," Cheeto said. He sounded beyond tired.

"You were in jail?" Rosie couldn't believe that her straight-arrow cousin had been arrested by the Atlanta police. He was crazy, yes, but not criminal. He'd answered the phone on the first ring when he recognized her number. "How did you get out? Did you call Mr. Pujol?"

"I couldn't find him. I bonded myself out. It was just five thousand dollars."

"How did you get home?"

"Cab. I'm sorry I called Abuela. I was so scared. What are you going to tell her?"

"That you're okay." Rosie could imagine the crowded and smelly holding cell, the uncertainty of not knowing what would happen next. "I'm so glad you're home now. Was there any press?"

"No, I got out of there without a single flash going off." He laughed.

"Lucky you. So, what happened?"

"I was set up. I was at El Toro with my friends, just chillin', and this chick starts bugging me for a dance, so then this huge dude tells me I'm hitting on his woman and that's it."

"You hit on a girl in front of her date? Dumb."

"I think they were both in on it. I've been trying to find Pujol to tell him that a lawsuit might be on the way." He sighed wearily.

"Dr. Sloane said we'd get sued a bunch of times this year. It's like everyone knows we have money and they want a piece of it. Weird about Mr. Pujol, though. Maybe he's on vacation. Leony's been looking for him, too."

"What's Leony look like? Is she hot?"

Rosie rolled her eyes. "She's my assistant, so hands off."

"I'm just messing with you. How's Mexico?"

"Beautiful and peaceful." Except for a certain movie star who confused her and made her heart sing.

"I'm totally jealous, *prima*, but don't worry about me."

"I'm glad to hear you're not in jail. I'll call Abuela, but you call her, too, okay? I think she's really worried. And stay out of the papers. You've been lucky so far, but a millionaire bar fight would make all the tabloid front pages. Maybe the regular papers, too."

"I try to stay under their radar." His voice took on a

mischievous tone. "It's you they love to harass." He hung up before she could strike back.

She didn't speak to Abuela again until the next afternoon, when she and Brad had taken a break from rehearsing. He was trying to enrich his character, as he called it, trying on different accents and attitudes. It made her nuts, and not in a good way.

"I talked to Cheeto, *m'ija*. Thanks for making him call me."

"I didn't make him call you. He probably felt guilty." Her protest sounded weak.

Abuela chuckled. "I know that boy. So tell me, do you believe him?"

"You mean that he was set up? Sure, why not. Cheeto never lacks for women hitting on him. I don't see him chasing a girl down like that."

"I think so, too." Abuela sounded more relaxed.

"Our attorney is missing in action, too. No one can find him. Did he tell you where he'd be?" Rosie stirred the pitcher of mojitos that Jana had brought outside. Thick mint leaves whirled in their cloudy, lime-flavored rum bath. She poured herself a tumblerful and sipped. Heaven.

"Don't worry. He's probably on vacation. He worked so hard right after we won the lottery. How is your beach house? Do you like it there?"

"It's cool. Everyone speaks English, thank goodness, since my Spanish is kind of shaky sometimes, but the house is gorgeous inside, and the beach is beautiful. Sunsets are incredible here."

"It sounds lovely, but I thought you'd be polishing your Spanish."

"Like a total-immersion vacation? Too much like work." Rosie laughed. "I spoke more Spanish in Miami a couple of weeks ago. Besides, Leony's here." She didn't mention Brad, knowing that her nosy grandmother would press for details.

"Oh, well. An old woman can dream."

"Why don't you join me here? I'm flying back to Miami, so you'd be there again in a few days." She crossed her fingers, hoping for a no.

"I'm in the middle of the ocean, *m'ija*. How am I supposed to get there, swim? And when I get back to shore I have to fly to Savannah for a Red Hat Society fling. That reminds me. I need a purple feather boa."

Jana came out to the patio. "Señorita Caballero! Miss Leony told me that you were finished with Señor Merritt for the day. We are having grouper Veracruz style for dinner. Do you want me to serve beer or white wine?"

"Wine, please." She hated wine, but she wanted to look sophisticated for Brad.

"Of course."

Efraim was silhouetted against the sunlit sand that surrounded the helipad. He waved at her in welcome and she waved back, a little tentative because with his rifle slung over his shoulder he looked like a sniper.

Brad called her name from next door, then appeared from the other side of the frangipani tree, freshly showered and wearing a robe and apparently not much else. He smelled delicious.

He lifted her hand and kissed it. "Have I told you how much I appreciate your help?" Those deep blue eyes came closer, and then her arms were around his waist and she was rubbing her cheek against his, urging him to kiss her mouth.

"I want you so much," he murmured. She groaned in agreement. Through his thin robe she could tell he was really happy to see her, physically, at least. Good thing Leony was inside. They sat side by side on the end of one of the oversized lounge chairs.

He kissed her again, and she leaned into him.

"At least we can be sure that there aren't any photographers out there. We have total privacy."

"Except for Ephraim and his gun."

"We need the security. I can have my men take over. They're so good at what they do, I forget they're there."

They'd have fun for the rest of their stay here, and afterward, who knew? He was a movie star. She shouldn't get her hopes up.

"I'm going to have drinks with some neighbors tonight. Want to go?"

"A *real* date?"

"Yeah—a short one. And why the face? You look like you've found something awful in your mouth."

She shrugged. "Sorry. Just remembering the last date I went on. It ended badly."

"Like, call the cops badly, or just hurt feelings badly?" His hand stroked her bare shoulder. He probably meant to comfort her, but the caress left a trail of heat that made her shiver.

"It was humiliating, that's all. He ditched me." Now his touch was comforting, and she moved closer to him, seeking more as she remembered the cold, miserable bus ride in her pretty dress and fancy shoes.

"Poor kid." He drew her into his embrace and pressed a kiss on her forehead. "Tonight you'll be able to erase that memory. We'll drive down the road to the Pinnellis' compound, have a couple of drinks, then drive back for dinner and another moon-lit walk on the beach."

"That sounds wonderful. Are the Pinnellis old friends?"

"Nope. Just neighbors. They found out I was renting here and issued an invite. Joe Pinnelli owns Fever Records, and his wife Crystal apparently dragged him here for some R and R."

"Fever Records. I'll bet they know lots of famous people," she mused.

Brad laughed. "Listen to yourself. Rosie. *You're* famous people."

"Infamous, you mean." She leaned against him, enjoying his solid warmth and the scent of his skin. "I'm chased around by annoying photographers, but I haven't done anything to deserve fame. I'm not talented like you."

"You mean you don't think you deserve fame because it was luck that landed you here?"

She nodded.

"Then maybe you'll have to figure out what you want to do if you want to make your mark on the world."

Brad's words were still moving through her mind as she dressed for her date.

Leony sat on the bed, her laptop open in front of her. "You haven't heard a word I've said, have you?" She sounded exasperated.

"I'm sorry. All that money talk bores me. I don't get it."

"If you don't learn how your finances work, people will take advantage of you—"

Rosie cut her off. "I know, and I won't make wise decisions and I'll miss opportunities and end up poor."

Leony smiled. "I hardly think you'll end up poor, but yes. Make an effort."

"Later. I've got to go. Just do whatever you want."

Leony threw up her hands. "Fine. But you have to decide what to do about the yacht."

"The *MegaBucks*? I thought Captain Manny was done with his classes."

"He is. It's the other one, the *Belle*. We've got an offer for it."

"Sure, why not. Manny said its engines were about to blow."

"I'll get the sale started. And you own that buffalo ranch in Wyoming now."

"No kidding? Since when?"

"Now I'm worried." Leony looked serious. "I asked you about it last week. You said you'd agreed to go into this ranching investment deal with your cousin."

She vaguely remembered talking to Cheeto about it. "Oh yeah. Wait till I tell Brad. He loves to play cowboy." She grinned at the thought of riding next to Brad in a cool Wyoming evening. Then she thought of horses and how big they really were.

They'd terrified her the few times she'd seen them in parades. She shuddered. No horses. She'd stick to the water. At least there, if you fell off the boat, you could swim.

The Pinellis' compound was a group of buildings inside of a high stucco wall topped by a thin, cruel strand of razor wire.

A guard waved their Mercedes convertible through, using his machine gun to point the way.

"Isn't that overkill?" Rosie looked nervously at the man's weapon. "That guy looks like something out of a drug lord movie."

"There are bandits around," Brad said casually. He wore oversized sunglasses that probably cost two months' rent at her old apartment. She still didn't know all the brands, and she didn't care anymore.

They drove around a curving, sandy drive bordered by beautiful landscaping, and passed cottages and a swimming pool bordered with rock, fed by a stacked stone waterfall. Cheeto would love it. Of course, if he lived here it would have to have a mermaid statue.

The main house was a large traditional colonial. It looked old. The car crunched to a stop and a boy ran out and opened the door for Rosie, then jumped into the seat that Brad had just vacated and drove the car off, raising a rooster tail of sand as he turned the corner toward the back of the outbuildings.

Brad's hand held her elbow as they walked to the front door, which opened before they reached it. Rosie wondered if his proprietary touch was a show for the Pinnelli family, or if it was meant to tell her something. The tough part about dating an actor, she thought.

A huge man in a Cuban guayabera came out, arms spread wide in greeting. "Brad Merritt and the beautiful Rosie Caballero. You honor my home."

He enfolded Brad in a meaty embrace, then before Rosie could step back, it was her turn.

"Thank you for including me, Mr. Pinnelli," she said after she got her breath back.

"It's Joe. Don't offend me with that mister crap." He held the door for them and ushered them inside.

The front room was cavernous, with tall ceilings painted bright blue and peach-colored woodwork. The floor was cool tile, just like in her house.

Crystal Pinnelli appeared, a tall drink in her hand. She had very straight long blond hair, and wore a white knit halter that showed off perfect, globelike breasts.

Rosie tried not to stare. Were they real? She felt a little inadequate in comparison. When Crystal turned, Rosie saw that she had an intricate tattoo down the center of her back.

Not the country club crowd, that was for sure. And Rosie wondered why that thought relaxed her.

She could say that she was used to having a movie star around, but it wouldn't be true. She was sure that every time she looked at him she would see not the guy she met at a party in Miami or kissed in New York, but the guy whose face was on *People* magazine covers as one of the hunkiest men alive.

It just wasn't normal. But what about her life had been normal lately? Maybe he felt the same way. Maybe he needed her money. She didn't care. She couldn't imagine having kids or sharing a dog with Brad Merritt. It would be like marrying Batman or James Bond. He was bigger than life.

Her bank account might be world-class, but she was still Rosie Caballero from Chamblee, Georgia. That didn't mean she couldn't appreciate her situation. *Dios mío,* could she appreciate it.

And this heaven would last a week, unless he got tired of her, but she was pretty sure she could keep him interested.

At dinner, Jana's herb-baked grouper was fabulous. Brad's company was even better. He was so normal. Brad chewed, talked, and made faces just like a regular guy. Well, an abnormally good-looking and very self-conscious guy.

"A lot of girls think I'm this hot star and they expect me to be just like the people I play in the movies. Then they're disappointed when I act like a real person."

"But you are a real person. I guess the same thing happens to me, when people read what trailer trash I am and then find out I'm just a person."

He laughed. "Trailer trash. That's funny."

"I don't think so. It hurts my feelings."

He half stood, reached across the table, and kissed her mouth. "Mmm. Grouper kiss."

"A yummy grouper kiss." She lifted her wineglass to his. "To misunderstood friends."

"Amen." He clinked his to hers.

She sipped, then looked at her glass in surprise.

"What?"

"It's good. It's the first time I've ever liked wine."

"Rosie Caballero, you're one weird chick. Not all wines are the same. You were bound to find one you liked eventually. Some, anyway. I'll have to teach you to appreciate it." He waggled his eyebrows suggestively.

"Oh boy." She fanned herself as if she were overheated, then leaned forward. "What's the worst picture of you that anyone's ever published?"

"I was at an Oscar afterparty, eating fried chicken, and the *Enquirer* ran a shot of me chewing with my mouth open."

Her fingers shot up to shield her lips. "I saw that one. You looked like a frat boy playing chew 'n' show."

"That's right." He lifted his wineglass to her. "Did it do wonders for my career? You bet."

"No. It helped you?" She was astonished.

"Yep. When you're in film, unless it's a bad review, any random photograph like that helps your career."

"Random being . . . ?"

"Anything not associated with criminal activity or creepiness."

"Whoa. So my cousin Cheeto's hillbilly chateau is actually a good thing?"

Brad's eyes widened. "Hadn't heard about that. You'll have to tell me the whole story."

"Great." She rolled her eyes and he laughed.

After dinner they walked barefoot on the beach, then came back to sit sleepily side by side on the big wicker chaise. The cushions were soft and the night air was cool.

Brad pulled a cotton throw over them and pulled her close.

They lay there, snuggled together, and she forced herself to relax, although she remained hyper-aware of him. Of the smoothness of his skin, the smell of his skin and his shampoo, and the sound of his breathing.

And every second, as she busily catalogued these sensations for the future, she was also afraid of what that future would bring, and was steeling herself for the coming good-bye. She'd never cared this much before. Here was an instance where lottery money didn't do a bit of good.

"Rosie," he murmured. "Let's go to bed." His tone suggested two people, one bed. *Oh, yes.*

She wanted to climb on top of him, even with the chance of someone walking in on them. He must have thought she'd tried to move away, because he pulled her closer.

"Stay a moment."

"I thought you wanted to go to bed?"

His heart thumped against her ear for a couple of minutes, sounding faster than it had moments before, then he got up abruptly, pulling her to her feet in a smooth motion. "Let's go somewhere more private." He held her hand as he led the way to her bedroom.

They passed under a rustic chandelier filled with unlit candles and she wondered if he could hear her heart thumping. New York had been a sexy, fun-filled night, but she'd cut it off before they could make love. It hadn't felt right. When she had a moment, she'd think about why this felt so different.

She shivered, feeling like a virgin bride. *Ridiculous.* She let Brad lead her across the sparsely furnished bedroom. The bed had a mountain of colorful pillows instead of a headboard.

Brad stopped and pulled her in front of him, smiling his famous smile, then slipped the little straps off her sundress and pressed his warm, soft lips on the top of her shoulder. She let her breath out in a hiss and pushed herself against him. He pulled on the cloth of her dress, slowly, steadily, and her bodice lowered, catching briefly over her strapless bra. A swift move unfastened it, and then her breasts were free. It was so fast she didn't have time to wonder if she should feel embarrassed.

His fingers, which had been rubbing the rounded tops of her shoulders, slid lower, caressing until nipples hardened and her breath caught. The look in his eyes told her he approved of what he saw. He could have been faking the whole thing, since he was an actor, but she didn't care. He made her feel beautiful.

His shirt was open, and though she'd run her hands over every one of the muscles on his chest and stomach as they lay outside, now she got to explore for real.

She tossed his shirt to one side and hooked her fingers in the waistband of his shorts.

He grinned, and she tugged down. They didn't budge. She pulled the drawstring loose and then they slid down, but stopped, held up by his gloriously curvy ass.

This opened an opportunity for further exploration. She reached behind him to push them down. She leaned forward, and her breasts brushed against his bare chest.

The feel of his bare skin against hers jolted her. His gasp echoed hers, and then they both forgot the sexy striptease and quickly ditched their clothes.

She found herself under him on the bed. "How'd you do that?"

He shrugged. "Magic." He kissed her right breast. "Maybe something I picked up on a movie set." He kissed her left breast. "I learn new stuff all the time." He licked her right nipple. It was getting harder to understand him through the roaring in her ears.

When his lips moved to her left breast and his fingers moved lower, Rosie totally left the real world.

She opened her eyes later, in his arms. They were both wet with sweat, although the ceiling fan was making it feel more clammy than sexy.

Brad was out, eyes closed and mouth open slightly. He'd performed like a superhero. Feeling like a sex goddess, Rosie scrounged on the floor for one of the discarded sheets and covered them both.

What he'd done to her with his tongue was so far beyond fireworks that they'd probably heard her cries in Atlanta.

Brad's profile was silhouetted against the wall by the exterior security lights that burned all night. For protection against bandits, Efraim had said.

A shadow moved in the darkness. She held her breath. Bandits. Ransom. Her mouth felt dry as she thought of how isolated they were, and what an attractive target they made.

But Robert DeNiro rented this house, too. It must be safe. She wondered where Efraim's rifle was. The shadow moved again, and she realized it was in the room with them. If she screamed, Efraim would come running, but since his room was on the opposite side of the house, he might be too late.

Suddenly she hated Brad for being asleep while she was scared.

She closed her eyes. Maybe if they were both asleep, the guy would just take her jewelry and go.

A hand covered her mouth. She bit hard, then shrieked as her mouth was freed and the burglar cursed. Brad leaped out of bed, from snoring to alert in a second, and jumped on the burglar, who fell heavily.

"Oh my God, I'm dying," the burglar cried out. "*Madre de Dios,* Rosie, stop him."

Rosie? The thief knew her name? She tasted salt on her tongue. No, not salt. Cheese powder. She snapped the table lamp on. Brad was naked on the burglar's chest, fingers digging into the man's throat, strangling him. The guy's face was purple, his bulging eyes turned on her beseechingly, then, as they saw her naked breasts, assessing.

"Cheeto!" She pulled a sheet up to cover herself. "Brad, let him go. It's my cousin."

Brad looked up, a lock of blond hair falling over his eyes. He reluctantly let go of Cheeto, who started to gasp, then when Brad got up, turned over and threw up on the rug.

"Your cousin?" Brad kicked Cheeto lightly in the rump. "Dude, I could have killed you. I thought you were paparazzi."

"You almost did," Rosie said admiringly. "I never saw anyone move so fast in my life."

Brad did an "aw shucks" move, which reminded her that he was naked. He looked at where she was looking and grinned. "Whoops."

Cheeto dropped back down on the floor. "My ass was kicked by a bare-assed Brad," he said hoarsely. "They'll never believe this."

"You barfed on my rug. Invaded our privacy. And if the cops find out you're here, jumping bond, you're going to be in so much trouble." Rosie wondered if airport security would notice that he'd left the country. Would they report his flight to the police? Probably not.

He shook his head, eyes closed. "I know, I know."

"Why are you here, Cheeto?"

"Cheeto? Is that really your name?" Brad looked interested.

"Enrique," Cheeto said. "Henry. I'm sorry, Rosie. I couldn't stay in Atlanta. The press was following me everywhere."

"You didn't have to stay in your house. But you left the state. The country, even. That's so against the law."

"Nice house," Cheeto said, assessing the room from the floor and totally ignoring her.

A polite tap at the door preceded Efraim, gun in hand. "Everything okay?"

"We caught a burglar," Brad said. "But turns out it's Rosie's cousin Cheeto."

Cheeto gave a finger wave from the floor. "Hi, Efraim."

Efraim nodded. "We met when he arrived. You look like you could use a beer, *amigo*."

"Hell, yes."

Brad helped him up.

"Fabulous," Rosie muttered as the three men left the room. They could say they were doing so out of respect for her privacy, since she was still clutching a sheet to her chest, but she knew testosterone solidarity when she saw it.

Rosie turned the light out and prepared to go to sleep, alone.

She banged the pillow with her fist and then threw herself down on it.

She thought of Cheeto, Efraim, and Brad, drinking beer somewhere in the house, or on the beach. Brad had never put on his pants.

For some reason, that took all the sleep out of her for another thirty minutes.

Rosie woke up late the next morning. Jana served her homemade yogurt, sliced fruit, and some of her amazing coffee.

"Did you meet my cousin?"

"Mr. Cheese Puff? Of course."

"Cheeto."

"Of course. And Mr. Brad. They went deep-sea fishing."

Deep-sea fishing? Didn't that involve a lot of equipment, like a boat? "Did they say when they'd be back?"

"Yes, of course. They leave a note for you." She pulled a folded sheet from her apron. It was lined memo paper, with dancing teddy bears along the bottom.

> We've gone fishing. Back tonight with dinner.
>
> Best,
> Brad and Cheeto

"Best," she said. "How nice." She gave the note to Jana. "Here, keep this for your grandchildren. Brad Merritt wrote it himself."

Jana tucked the note away again, apparently unimpressed.

Best. If she'd been a fan asking for an autograph he'd probably have written, "All my love always."

She stomped around a while, getting in Jana's way, then retreated to the desk she'd scouted out to be her office to check her e-mail.

Lots had happened to their little empire while she was away. It took a full hour to catch her up on events, mostly boring board of trustees and stock stuff.

She told Brad about it as they walked down the beach late one afternoon, as they headed back to the house. Efraim had promised daiquiris on the lanai at seven.

"I had news, too. I have to leave today," he said.

"So soon?" She felt sad, but not as badly as she thought she would. "I have to get back to Atlanta, too."

He laughed. "I figured." He put his arm around her shoulder and pulled her close.

His sun-warmed skin slipped against hers on a cushion of tanning oil. She could just eat him up. Even though Jana didn't recognize him, millions of women did, and their relationship meant that she would never be free of press coverage. The peace and quiet of her previous life was the only part she missed, and she thought it would come back, once the media tired of her, but not as long as she and Brad were an item.

Brad's lips brushed hers, then pressed harder. Rosie smiled into the kiss. She'd never had so much fun.

"We have time for a quickie before my helicopter comes." He wiggled his hips against hers.

"Is that all you ever think about?"

"Sure. That's why we're so much alike."

She laughed, but the beating sound of rotors made her look up. "Time's up, *amigo*."

"Cheer up. I'll see you at Christmas. Cheeto invited me."

He what? She was going to kill Cheeto. Much as she loved being with Brad, she didn't want her Christmas to turn into a circus. She forced her frozen smile into a grin. "Great."

The helicopter appeared over the other side of the bay, skimming low over the water.

Brad squeezed her close. "I feel like I've dipped a toe in the Caballero family water. I can't wait to dive in, though, gotta tell you I was relieved when Cheeto said that he was the only crazy one."

She laughed. "There are all different kinds of crazy, Brad."

"Hey, I know. I live in Crazy Central, remember?"

The chopper swung overhead then started to drop, blowing sand. They turned away, protecting their eyes from the blast of sandy air.

"I'll call you tomorrow," Brad yelled into her ear. He kissed her hard, shouldered his bag, and took off in a crouching run to the open doorway.

Rosie watched with eyes half-closed against the sand-filled air, her heart beating hard. Riding the helicopter was terrifying; the spinning rotors looked like they could quickly chop a head off. Then he was safe inside, and the skids lifted.

She waved good-bye as the helicopter swung over the trees and across the water.

Cheeto ran up from the beach. "Darn, I'm too late to say good-bye." He stood next to her, watching the chopper, tiny now, lift to clear the hills on the other side of the bay.

"You invited Brad to Christmas with us. What were you thinking?" She punched his shoulder.

He danced away so that her fist only brushed his bare arm. "He's cool. A regular guy. I think Abuela will love him."

Abuela. Rosie felt queasy, thinking that this might revive her grandmother's dormant matchmaking schemes.

"Hey, Efraim and I are going into town for supplies. Need anything?"

Rosie shook her head. If she got into a car with Cheeto she might commit murder. "Have fun."

She was going to put on her tiniest swimsuit, grab a fruity drink, and sit on the beach to get a dangerous tan. Atlanta and endless meetings were only a few days away, and she planned to make the most of her time here.

A week later, Rosie was back in her suite at the Atlanta Ritz. The formal draperies and chintz-covered furniture seemed familiar, like coming back home. When had stiff formality become homey to her? She'd always thought she was a bohemian kind of girl.

Of course, why had cracked linoleum and bugs in her cupboards seemed like home? She'd been used to it, that's all. Things were different now. She had a choice, and even if she went back to life the way it had been, she had changed.

She wouldn't be content to live in a vermin-ridden apartment complex. She could get a better job, live in a better place. She thought of the beach in Mexico. She could even live there. Being a housekeeper for rich folks in a place as beautiful as Playa Tierna would be wonderful. Her options had widened with her travels and new acquaintances.

She pulled on a firecracker-red jersey dress that looked great with her tan. She added a long platinum chain with a Peretti heart dangling from it and put on fat little platinum hoop earrings encrusted with diamonds, then slipped into heels and headed for the elevator.

Abuela was back in town and Cheeto was joining them for dinner. Just the family, just like old times.

She longed for the closeness they'd shared before. She hadn't had a kiss or a hug from her grandmother in weeks. They didn't talk as much, either. And Cheeto hadn't even been grateful that she sneaked him back to the States without the courts finding out he'd been in Mexico.

Her cousin would be the last person to say that the yacht was an extravagant purchase. He'd gotten in a lot of fishing from the back deck as they'd headed back to the States.

Cheeto had set up the dinner tonight, maybe the first of many. Maybe the family was getting back on track.

The quiet new restaurant he chose was in Roswell, far from the Buckhead crowds. A wreck on 400 held her up. She called Cheeto's cell phone.

"Don't tell me you forgot." She could hear talking behind him.

"I didn't. I'm stuck in traffic. Are you there? What's all the noise?"

"The Braves are playing on the monitor over the bar, and there's a birthday party going on."

"I thought you said it was a quiet place." She didn't feel like having an evening of yelled conversation.

Cheeto laughed. "It is, back in the dining room. We're waiting for our table." His voice lowered. "Wait till you see the old lady. You won't recognize her."

"I'll bet she's all relaxed and happy. I'd be seasick if I went on back-to-back cruises. You didn't tell her about Brad, did you?"

"Maybe." The line went dead.

She glanced at the cell phone's display as traffic started moving. Her phone hadn't dropped the call, he'd hung up. She wondered how much of his Mexican adventure he'd shared with Abuela. Actually, how much of *her* Mexican adventure he'd shared.

The restaurant, like many others in historic Roswell, was in a renovated shop dating from the beginning of the previous century. She walked into the warm, candlelit interior, not sure what to expect.

She could hear the baseball game from an alcove doorway. The tables in the main room were all full.

She walked into the alcove, which opened into a long paneled room lined with booths on one side and an enormous antique-style bar on the other. Cheeto was talking to a slim blond woman, a beer on the bar in front of him.

He saw her and waved, and the blonde turned to look at her. Rosie reeled back, slipping a little on her high heel. She caught herself on the doorframe, her eyes on the woman. It was her grandmother.

The woman beamed at her and put a hand to her hair. "What do you think?"

She crept closer, as if the blonde speaking in her grandmother's voice was about to pull out a knife. "Is that really you?"

The woman frowned, and suddenly it was her Abuela. The same peeved expression, with wrinkles making little swooshes between her eyes.

"What have you done?" She walked closer and stretched a hand out to touch the golden hair. Not a wig.

"I colored my hair, and got a good cut and a makeover, just like you did."

"No shit." Cheeto snorted. "Don't feel bad, *prima*. I didn't recognize her, either. She looks like a society lady, doesn't she?"

Abuela turned to him. "You say that like it's not a good thing. I'll take it to mean that you think I look successful and vibrant."

A server approached. "Caballero, party of three? Your table's ready."

They followed him to a table in the middle of the room. Cheeto looked around at all the people.

"This won't do, Miss. Can we have one by the wall? We're surrounded here."

The girl looked flustered. "Oh, sure, but it may be a minute." She looked around, their menus in her hand.

"We'll take those," Cheeto said, and pulled the menus from her hand. "It'll save time."

"What's wrong with this table, Cheeto?" Abuela looked around. "It's far enough from the bar that the noise won't bother us."

"Too many people."

The people sitting around them were starting to look. Their server was turning slowly, checking out each table. She looked like she'd lost her car in the Macy's parking lot at Christmas.

Finally she brightened. "Okay. I think I have the answer. Five more minutes in the bar, and you'll have your table."

The five minutes gave Rosie more time to examine her grandmother. She'd never seen the old lady wear so much jewelry, and it was rich, diamonds and colored stones on bright yellow gold.

Abuela looked at her. "What, *nena*?"

"You've changed so much." What else could she say? You've dropped so much weight you look scrawny? Your makeup looks like it was airbrushed on? Your hair's the color of I Can't Believe It's Not Butter—how did you achieve that faux-margarine look?

Her appearance wasn't the only thing that had changed. They'd been together almost ten minutes and she hadn't gotten a hug. Even the posers in New York would have air-kissed her by now. Well, she had lips, too.

She put her arm around her newly scrawny grandmother and pressed her close, then kissed her cheek. For a second, Abuela leaned against her, then she pushed.

"*Cuidado*, Rosie. You'll smear my face." She looked at Rosie. "Do you moisturize? You should see Señor Armando in Miami. The man's a genius."

"Is he the one who did your face?"

Abuela smiled beatifically. "Yes."

"I'll make an appointment. When I'm forty."

Cheeto snorted beer out of his nostrils. Rosie handed him

her napkin and turned to look for the waitress. "Didn't she say it would be fast?"

"I hope so," Abuela said behind her. "I have a date later tonight."

"A date?" Great. Her grandmother was someone else entirely now. "Who with?"

"A friend," Abuela answered and put up her menu, hiding her face.

Dinner was saved by Cheeto's teasing laughter and jokes. His retelling of the helicopter ride to Casa Maravilla, and how he thought he'd fall out of the sky, had them both laughing as he cringed in his chair, pretending to be terrified.

After dessert and coffee, Abuela said she had to go.

"Your date?" Rosie teased.

"I have an early appointment tomorrow, too." Her grandmother hesitated. "I'm looking for a condominium. I'm going to let Melba keep the apartment in Chamblee so I need to clear it for her."

"I didn't think you'd ever move back there," Cheeto said. He didn't seem bothered by the news, but Rosie felt devastated.

Her parents' apartment was gone, all her memories, good and bad, bulldozed with them. Her grandmother's apartment was the only connection left to her past.

"Why are you moving?"

Her voice must have sounded anguished, because some of Abuela's old gentleness returned. "*Niña,* I've changed. I knew I couldn't stay there forever, and it's served its purpose. It's just an apartment. I need more space, and room to entertain, and it can't be in those old apartments."

"Oh, I get it. You need to move because of your friends. Josefa the social butterfly needs room to spread her diamond-encrusted wings." She'd done it again. Her grandmother's face reddened and Cheeto's eyebrows rose. She tried again.

"I'm sorry. I should have said, good luck finding the perfect place. Let me know when, and I'll get you a housewarming gift."

"Hey, you never got me a housewarming gift." Cheeto pouted.

"How about I donate my fox fur to your mermaid so she won't get cold?"

"Her fishy nature likes it on the cool side." Cheeto's hand was on Abuela's shoulder.

Good thing Rosie didn't want to try acting. She sucked at pretending, at faking her feelings, and her family always called her on it. She couldn't fool them at all.

"Abuela, why don't you come to the beach at Casa Maravilla? We could spend some time together. We could play canasta every day." The good thing about having millions was that they could buy out any standing reservations.

"I don't have time now, Rosie. Maybe in a couple of months. Have you heard from Mr. Pujol?"

"He's MIA, according to Leony. Why? Do you think I should invite him to Casa Maravilla?" She made a face.

"Hey, we haven't discussed Christmas." Cheeto looked expectantly at Rosie.

Surely he didn't want her to lead the conversation in this direction. Not now.

He dipped his head, like a bull lowering his horns.

Crap. She was the one who'd complained about the family drifting apart. "I'm cooking dinner for *noche buena,* so neither of you make plans for that night, okay?" Rosie tried to smile, but she only managed to twitch the corner of her mouth.

"You're cooking?" Cheeto grabbed his throat. "Holy cow. I'm too young to die."

Abuela elbowed his ribs. *"Cállate."* She turned to Rosie. "So you've learned to cook?"

"It's something I've taken up." She would, too, just as soon as she left this building.

"Tell her who's coming." Cheeto leaned forward, eager to see his grandmother's face when Rosie told her.

"Brad Merritt. He's a friend of mine."

Abuela's eyebrows rose. "The movie star who was in the panty photo with you?"

Rosie cringed. She should have realized Abuela would remember it. "He's really nice. Just a regular guy."

"A regular guy who's followed around by reporters everywhere he goes. What are you thinking, *nena?* Find a nice regular boy."

"Regular? Like us, you mean?" Rosie felt her face burn. "I'm sorry, Abue. I meant to tell you about him, but—"

The old woman, who no longer looked old at all, held up her hand. "No need to explain or apologize, Rosie. But think about this. You complain about the press all the time, and this relationship isn't going to make the *periodistas* go away."

"It won't go away no matter what we do."

Abuela shrugged. "Christmas at your house sounds wonderful, by the way."

Rosie smiled, relieved. "Really?"

Abuela patted her hand. "Of course, *mi niña*."

Cheeto smirked and nodded. Rosie wanted to slap him.

"Just one thing, Rosie. Where are you going to have this?" Abuela held her little notepad ready, pencil in hand.

Damn. A house. One more thing to do.

CHAPTER THIRTEEN

* * * * * *

Don't fall into the boredom trap. If you didn't
have a hobby before, find one now. Become an
expert at something you love. You have the time
and the money to make it happen.

—*The Instant Millionaire's Guide to Everything*

Lani Prester and Brad Merritt? Diamond
Rosie's Spitting Mad

—*Star* magazine

The next week Rosie was on a plane to New York, where she'd en-
rolled in private cooking classes.

With a late-season storm system threatening the Gulf,
Cheeto had been anxious to hit the road for his fishing trip before air traffic was turned upside down for the whole country,
and Rosie had given Manny the week off while the *MegaBucks*
was in dry dock getting its annual checkup. She kept an anxious eye on the weather.

Brad had a film obligation to complete before he began re-
hearsals on the play, and he'd gone into isolation on a shoot.
Rosie had a week to learn cooking basics in a small group, and
had signed up for more cooking classes back in Atlanta at the
Cook's Warehouse. With that, and some devoted watching of

the Food Network on TV, she thought she might be able to pull off Christmas Eve dinner.

Leony suggested that she hire a top chef and just enjoy her guests, but since Brad would be there, as well as her grandmother, some of her grandmother's friends, Cheeto and his friends, and some of the foundation's employees, she'd opted to do the cooking herself with a couple of assistants.

All she needed now was an actual kitchen to cook it in. Her return to Atlanta was a mix of cooking classes and finding a permanent place to live. "Permanent" was such a heavy word. She liked flying around whenever she wanted to. Permanent sounded like houseplants to water and a cat to feed. Tootie was easy to bring along. She was about all that Rosie could handle.

Tootie was asleep in her tote and Rosie was curled up in an armchair at her favorite coffee shop, deep into a magazine about upscale Atlanta properties, when she felt the little hairs on the back of her neck stand straight up.

Not that she was psychic or anything, but she had the weird feeling that she was being watched. Maybe it was a sixth sense she'd developed from dealing with the paparazzi. She kept her face down, but let her eyes flick back and forth, trying to spot who the person was.

A man was waiting for his drink by the counter, toying with a sugar packet. Did she know him? The back of his head looked familiar. Medium height, dark, lean. Of course he looked familiar. He looked a little like Brad. She smiled. She had it bad.

"Do you know that guy?" The speaker was so close to her ear that his breath puffed across her cheek.

She shivered, then turned. Rick leaned over the back of her

chair. Handsome as ever and still a dickhead. She pasted on a fake smile.

"Rick. What a surprise. Still living in Chamblee?"

"I am." His smile wasn't as warm. Maybe he expected a different reaction. A maidenly blush perhaps. Or a faint "oh my," with a hand on her heart. Or maybe he'd read about her romance with Brad. Everyone else had.

Except he didn't know that Brad hadn't called her in two weeks, deep into his film. Her smile grew bigger as she put more effort to keep it in place. Rick took it as encouragement.

"I'm glad I saw you here. I've been seeing your picture in all the newspapers."

Her smile dimmed. "You mean the tabloids."

"I know just how you feel. I'm alone now, too." He swung around her armchair and sat in its twin across from her. His face sagged and he shrugged, as if shaking off a painful memory. "I'm sorry about that night, Rosie."

Could it be that he'd grown up a little? She didn't trust him. Their one date had burned her enough. "I'm a big girl. I got over being ditched."

He laughed. "You were always stronger than you looked." He smiled affectionately. "Cute, too." He sighed. "Did you hear that Nieves left me? I guess I got paid back for being a heel."

She felt a twinge in her chest. Alarmed, she jumped up. No way was she going to allow herself to feel tenderness toward this creep. "I need another coffee. Stay here." She needed time to pull herself together. Rick was a user. Users didn't change.

What was she doing, smiling at him and getting all emotional? She wasn't a tall skinny blonde, and never would be.

There wasn't a team of plastic surgeons big enough to trans-
form her into Rick's favorite kind of woman. And why would
she want to change, just to please him? He was an old crush,
that's all.

And no sense believing he'd changed, either, she thought
again. She couldn't remind herself enough. She ordered a small
skim latte and turned to look at Rick while she waited for it. He
was staring at her, and the look in his eyes was hungry. Her
breath caught. He was definitely sexy.

Was it wicked to want revenge? You bet. And it would be so
sweet to bring him down, even if Nieves had done it first. If Dr.
Sloane were here she'd tell her to leave, fast.

She returned to their table and picked up her purse. "Want
to have dinner next week?"

His eyes widened. "Sure. Just say when."

She lifted her latte in a salute. "Okay, then. I'll call." She
walked out, laughing at the look on his face. Hope and avarice.
Not a pretty sight.

The next day she went to Abuela's apartment in Chamblee,
where she found her grandmother shoveling out her closet, pre-
paring for her move. Even though she didn't have the condo yet,
she wanted to be ready.

Her bed was covered with shoeboxes, each one containing a
pristine pair of Payless shoes. She had been the Imelda Marcos
of the Kmart set.

"What's up, Abue?" She kissed her soft cheek, glad to see it
free of careful makeup. She still looked terrific.

"I'm giving all this to *el* Goodwill. Why do I need so many
cheap shoes?"

"Especially since at least twenty pairs are brown or blue pumps," Rosie said. "You could start a museum."

She laughed. "*Ay, loquita,* who'd come to see them? No, someone else will enjoy these shoes. And the suits."

Rosie gasped. "You're giving away your Sag Harbor suits?" She knew that she had a whole new classy wardrobe, but jeez. Her suits. The ones she'd worn to *misa* on Sundays, and to school pageants and holidays. It was the end of an era.

"I'm not shopping at *el* Value anymore, so why keep the clothes I bought there? We've moved up in the world, *mi niña.* Time to give away the old stuff."

Rosie thought of her parents' thrift-shop furniture, now in thrift shops once more. Her memories would last longer than cheap veneer. "It's a big move. I thought I'd never get rid of my old furniture."

"What would you have done with it, leave it to your children? They'd think you're *tostada.* Nuts."

Talking about the old days made Rosie nostalgic for her old neighborhood. She drove by the apartment where she used to live. Blue curtains hung in the windows that faced the street. Someone had moved in.

Rosie stood next to the cab, taking in the sad decay of the buildings around her. Weeds sprouted from the foundations of the buildings, and the parking lot was cracked, its ancient patches looking like infected scabs.

"Ma'am, you going to be here long? It's not smart to stand around." The cabdriver sounded nervous. "A lady like you doesn't belong here."

She snorted. He must not ever read the tabloids.

"Rosie? Oh my God, it *is* you." Mirta Gonzales was pushing a stolen grocery cart full of folded laundry.

"Mirta, hi. How have you been?"

Her old neighbor shrugged, trying to be nonchalant. "Not as well as you." She gave up and gave her a grin full of crowded teeth. "You're famous, Rosie. I've seen your picture in the *revistas. El Estar.*"

"The *Star*? Oh, yeah. You saw some great pictures of me." She shook her head. "They only print the ugly ones."

Mirta clasped her hands and tilted her head. "But you're always so beautiful. Look at you, dressed like a *princesa,* and with diamonds in your ears." She leaned forward.

Rosie touched her right ear. She'd forgotten about the big diamond studs. Bad idea to wear them to the hood. Mirta sighed. "It must be wonderful to be rich. Do you ever think about how your life used to be?"

"I think about it all the time," Rosie said. "And I miss your cooking. You always used to bring me dinner when Mami worked late."

"Thanks, baby, but I'll bet you thank your stars that you aren't stuck here anymore." She laughed, a hearty bellow that Rosie remembered from the Laundromat, when Mirta and her mother had shared gossip as they sorted socks.

After her parents' death, it had hurt to be around Mirta, who reminded her so much of her mother, and then she'd gone to work and her socializing had been limited to time with Abuela, and with Cheeto when he could pull himself away from his friends.

Rosie felt bad that she hadn't thought about her mother's old friend for so long. "So, Mirta, how are things? Is there anything that you need?"

Mirta's laughter faded. "What are you talking about? You think I stopped for a handout?"

"No. Of course not. I just thought you might need something."

"Like a stick of gum? A bucket of chicken?"

"Or a stove. Or a car."

"You think we can't be friends because I'm poor, is that it? Give me big presents, and you'll feel better about leaving the hood." Mirta parked her fists on her hips.

"Get out. You're kidding, right? I don't care about stuff like that."

Mirta laughed. "Yeah, I am. You should see your face." She leaned against the cart, tight pants accentuating every overflowing curve. "You've moved on, baby. You're not coming back here, not even if you were poor again."

Mirta was right. She couldn't see going back to her old life, but it was because she'd changed. Even if she lost all of this money, she'd now know there were many possibilities to pursue. She didn't have to be a receptionist and put up with a bad boss, thinking that her only other option was to be a waitress in a diner. If she lost it all she'd find help, borrow money and go to college as she'd planned back in high school when her parents were alive.

Rosie looked around the dismal apartments. "This place could use some work."

"You don't have to sound so surprised." Mirta waved her arms around. "Nothing's changed here."

"Just me, I guess." Rosie took in Mirta's cheap outfit and her clawlike acrylic nails. She'd always considered Mirta to be fashionable and put-together. Mirta hadn't changed, but Rosie sure had. She thought of the little boutique in Miami where she'd bought her outfit, and had been pleased to spend "only" three thousand dollars for two outfits.

Mirta glanced at her watch. "I've got to get to work. I got a second job at the mall. Remember the cookie place at Perimeter?"

"The one that makes the whole mall smell great when the cookies are baking? I was only at Perimeter a couple of times, but I remember the cookie place."

"Come by and I'll give you a free one." She vanished from the doorway, and Rosie heard the hollow thumping of her sneakers on the cement stairs.

Her mother's friend was working two jobs, and she had to be in her fifties. Rosie could imagine what her life was like, because she and her family had lived the same way. Well, all that was going to change. Mirta would have everything she needed from now on. Rosie would tell her when she went to the mall to take her up on that free cookie offer.

She smiled and picked up Tootie, who was tiptoeing over the cracked asphalt of the parking lot, nose twitching at familiar scents.

One of the buildings across from where Rosie stood had boarded windows, and electrical wires dangled from the corner of another. Her smile vanished. It wasn't fit to live in.

When she'd lived here it had seemed shabby, but not so bad. Tears pricked her eyes. She'd get the Caballero Foundation to buy the buildings and refurbish them, keeping the rents low.

Dr. Sloane had told her that throwing money at her friends wouldn't solve anything. Maybe it was true, but Rosie remembered going through the sofa cushions for the one quarter that would make the difference between eating her breakfast cereal with milk or with water.

And what had she done with all her lottery money? Except for the foundation, she'd spent it on trips, a yacht, staff salaries, and big attorneys' fees. She needed to do something to help those she'd left behind. This would be her legacy, a great place for the Caballero Foundation to put her money to good use.

She picked up Tootie and got into her cab, watched by the wary gangbangers who guarded their turf. She didn't belong here anymore, and she'd moved on, but she vowed that she would never forget where she came from. She stared at the broken-down buildings as they glided out of the parking lot, imagining them shiny and bright, with a playground in the weedy lot between the farthest buildings. She'd do it for the memory of her parents, who'd tried to make a better life for her. And she wouldn't expect to be thanked.

Two days later she slipped into her favorite corner booth at Nino's Restaurant on Cheshire Bridge Road. She had turned down Rick's offer to pick her up, so that she could get away if she had to. Not that she'd need an escape route—she was ready to put a ghost to rest. She felt confident in her favorite bronze-colored Mizrahi dress and black Bruno Maglis.

Five minutes later Rick showed up, looking sexy in black. He stopped just short of their table to stare at her in appreciation. Very gratifying.

She knew the dark color of her dress set off her skin, and

that her shoulder-sweeping silver earrings twinkled in the low light. Her hair was pinned up in sexy disarray, courtesy of her stylist.

"You look terrific." He looked impressed, but there was that same oddness to his expression. He looked—greedy. She expected no less from the weasel.

"Thanks." She motioned gracefully toward the bench seat and he sat down at the other side of the semi-circular bench, across from her. At least he hadn't scooted up next to her. She unfolded her napkin and spread it across her lap as he looked around for the server. A uniformed man slid silently up to him and Rick ordered a beer.

"Your phone was disconnected," he said, focused on her again. "I called your attorneys looking for you."

"I hope no one gave you my private numbers." She lifted her glass of wine.

Rick's smile spread like massage oil on warm skin. "I can always find someone who'll tell me what I need to know." He lifted his beer in a toast.

She touched her wineglass to his lager glass, thinking that some cute thing at the lawyer's office had just lost her job. "I was at the beach."

"Time to yourself? You probably had a lot to think about." He nodded as if he understood, then his gaze softened. "I could use some time to myself. Nieves and I split up."

"So you said. And now you're on your own?" Not likely, she thought. Nieves was a *fiera*, a wild beast, but she knew there was a long line of skinny blondes, all waiting to take Nieves's place. After Rick's betrayal had quit hurting so much she'd thought that maybe the two of them had deserved each other. "Any plans?"

He shrugged. "I'll see how it plays out. Right now, I'm having dinner with you."

She felt anger start to rise. Typical Rick. He sure knew how to make a girl feel special.

He changed the subject and they talked about old school friends as the waiters covered the table with plates of old-fashioned Italian delicacies and fresh drinks.

He moved closer to her on the curved bench, his lean hip pressed against hers. She didn't move away, but it occurred to her that even one night with him would leave a toxic aftermath.

"Rick, why didn't we ever go out together when we were in high school?"

"I don't know." He was digging into a serving of fried calamari.

"I had a crush on you starting when I was twelve."

"Well, there you go. That would have been so wrong."

"What a dorky thing to say." She put her fork down, appetite gone. "I'll tell you why we didn't date. You had a hard-on for every skinny *güera* around. If she had yellow hair and long legs, you had to have her."

His fork was frozen next to his mouth, which was hanging open. "What?"

"You think that women owe you total devotion. Well, some women can think for themselves." It was like everything she'd ever wanted to say to him was bubbling up. Her normal blunt manner of speaking had never surfaced around Rick, held at bay by the shyness generated by her crush on him.

"Hey. Why am I being attacked here? What did I do to you?" Rick took a long swallow of beer and grinned at her. "I can't help it if girls like me."

"Yes, you can. You sure can help it. And you were definitely more serious about Nieves than you were about me. I heard you two had even gotten married. Hard to believe that's over." She looked down at the bread she'd shredded on her plate.

"Well, it is, and I don't love her anymore. You said it wouldn't last." He smiled. "You were right."

"You knew I was right back then, too. How do you think that made me feel? Or Nieves? God knows I don't care about her, but you must have hurt her, too."

He watched her, mouth open.

She signaled the waiter, handed him a one-hundred-dollar bill, and got up to leave.

Rick didn't protest. "I can give you a ride back to the hotel."

"That's okay. My cab is waiting. I think you should take a cab, too."

"A cab? No limo?"

"It's my driver's night off."

He swayed a little and tried to protest that he was okay to drive, then got a shifty look in his eyes. "Okay. I'll come with you now."

Oh, brother. She wondered if she should make him ride up front with the cabbie, but decided that was tacky.

Mistake. The minute the cab started up he was all over her, blowing beer breath on her face and feeling up her breasts.

"Stop, Rick."

"Rosie, you are so hot," he said, after slobbering on her ear.

This was the guy she'd thought was so smooth? "I've missed you, baby."

"Get your hands off of me."

"Rick will make you feel so good, baby." His hand swept up from her knee to her crotch. She grabbed his wrist to block it.

"Rick will not make me feel anything but pissed off. Pull over, driver."

The cabbie's eyes were glued to the rearview mirror, so he didn't see the car that came up alongside. Lights flashed from its interior; the startled cabbie swerved to the right to avoid it.

Metal ground on metal as the cab hit a minivan on its other side and went into a spin. Rosie screamed as they were thrown against the curb. Rick's body jammed hers against the door.

"Damn. You folks okay?"

"Yeah." Rosie pushed Rick off of her. Those flashes had been from a camera.

Rick sat up, woozy. "What happened?"

The driver tried to open his door, couldn't, then jumped out of the passenger side. Rosie got out, too, eager to get away from Rick.

The other driver, a ponytailed soccer mom, was out of her SUV. "You idiot, you were swerving all over the road!"

The cabbie was shaking his head, staring at the damage to his door. "I just got the car paid off."

Blue lights flashed behind them.

Cops. Just what she needed. She turned to get back into the cab, but Rick was in her way.

"You okay, Rosie?"

"Fine. I just want to go home."

The policeman flashed a light at them. "You folks okay?"

"Yes, officer. Just a fender bender, right?" The cabbie seemed anxious.

"Looks that way. What happened?"

Rosie told him about the photographers, and the cab driver turning right and hitting the woman's SUV. She omitted that Rick was slobbering all over her at the time.

Rick was talking to a knot of people who'd stopped to look at the accident. "You know who that is? That's Rosa Caballero. The chick who won the MegaBucks."

Rosie turned and stared at Rick. Was he crazy? The people stared back. One woman aimed her flipped-open cell phone at her and clicked a picture.

"*Madre de Dios,* not again."

The cop and the SUV driver had apparently overheard.

"No kidding? You're her?" The cop looked her up and down, then looked at the smashed-up taxi. "I imagined you riding a limo these days."

Rosie shrugged. "Not every day." She wished today had been one of them, with sturdy, unflappable Ted at the wheel.

The SUV's driver grabbed her neck, shrieked, and fell to the ground, writhing. "I think I broke my back," she cried.

The cabbie, who had been frowning at Rosie as if deep in thought, fell over in an unconvincing faint.

"Just dandy," the cop said, clearly disgusted. He tapped his shoulder radio and muttered a code, then leaned over the woman. "Just stay right there, ma'am. Don't move. I've called for an ambulance."

He straightened, then sighed and walked over to the cab-driver. The crowd had grown and moved in closer.

The officer crouched and took the cabbie's limp wrist. "Great pulse, buddy. But you're getting an ambulance, too."

And I'll pay for it. Her dinner with Rick was going to cost a fortune.

"Miss Caballero?"

She turned. An old lady had stepped off the curb and stood behind her.

"Please, if you have a moment?"

Rosie sighed. Maybe she could make some friends and lessen the tabloid impact. "Sure."

"My name is Vivian Holly. I wonder if you could help my grandson. He lost his job last Christmas and hasn't been able to find work since then. His wife and kids live in a shelter now, and they won't let him in because they don't allow men. Please, Ms. Caballero."

She saw the people behind Ms. Holly lean forward, trying to hear her answer.

"I'll do what I can, Ms. Holly. Give me your phone number and I'll call you in the morning."

Tears filled the woman's eyes as she scribbled on a receipt she'd pulled from her purse.

"I coach an after-school basketball program, and our funding's been cut." This from a craggy man with a paper fast-food sack in one hand.

"Give me your number, too."

The crowd closed in. It was like a grown-up, desperate version of a mall Santa Claus. Worse, because she could really grant wishes. She wanted to run, but they would chase her, and the police wouldn't like it, either.

Rick was in the middle of the group, talking earnestly.

More police cars arrived, and the people were pushed behind barricades. Rosie backed away. Those who hadn't had a chance to tell her their problems cried out and pushed to get back near her.

One of the cops grabbed her by the elbow. "You Miss Caballero?"

"Yes."

"Sergeant Banner. Get into my car and don't move. We'll have a riot here in a minute if you don't."

She crawled into the back of the police cruiser and he closed the door. It was quieter in the car, and she suddenly started to tremble. She wanted to get out of here. She called Leony's cell phone. She answered on the second ring.

"Leony? Help. There's been a car accident and I'm trapped by a crowd."

"Where? Are you hurt? Can you call 911?"

"I'm okay, and the cops are here. It wasn't serious, but my date told everyone who I am and there's a big crowd and—"

"Where are you?"

She told her the address.

"Don't move. Don't talk to anyone. I'm sending help."

"The police are here."

"Okay, that's good."

A bright light shone into the police car. She turned, shielding her eyes. It was a television camera. The reporter stood by, microphone in hand, eager to do his part.

She groaned and sank low in the seat. "Hurry up, Leony."

The passenger door on the other side of the cruiser opened. "Ms. Caballero? We rescued your date." The policeman smiled. Behind him stood Rick, who was grinning into the cameras pointed at him.

"Get him out of here," Rosie said. "I don't care what you do to him. I recommend charging him with inciting a riot."

The cop looked startled, then backed out and slammed the door shut before the TV newsman could zoom in. Rick looked confused, then frowned at her through the window. She gave him a little finger wave.

It was going to be a long night.

At the end of the week *The Atlanta Journal-Constitution* was still obsessing about her disastrous date. They'd run a picture on the front page and the story on the front of the Metro section the morning after the incident, headlined "Fender Bender Nets Prizes from Lottery Winner."

Today's were no better. Rosie threw the paper down, disgusted. Disgusted with herself, with scumbag journalists, and with Rick and the cab ride from hell.

Abuela had come to have breakfast with her. She held the paper at arm's length, trying to read without her glasses. "I don't understand. Why would you date a married man?"

"Because he said he was single again and I'm the idiot who

believed him. Because I wanted to prove to myself that I didn't want him anymore."

"Did it work?"

"Yes. I definitely don't want him anymore." *I want Brad.* She'd traded the problems of being poor for a whole different sort of misery. Abuela would just tell her that life was not fair.

"Hmm. That's a good thing." Abuela leafed through the paper. "There's a sale at Macy's. Want to go shopping?"

"Yes, but I'm afraid the photographers will be waiting. I'm being sued by the woman in the other car, by the driver of our cab, and by Nieves."

"Nieves? Rick's wife? Why would she sue you? She wasn't even there."

"Correspondent in her divorce."

"*Dios mío.*" Abuela's eyes widened. "What a witch. Settle it quickly."

"Leony hired a private investigator. He says that Nieves tipped off the photographers, who were hoping for a hotel-room shot, in flagrante. Her plan is to sue me as correspondent and make off big. Dump Rick and get rich at one time."

"Very clever," Abuela said. "She must have known her husband still liked you. What are you going to do?"

"I don't think she's that smart. Rick was probably in on it, too, but I don't care. I'm letting the lawyers handle it." She leaned back in her chair. "All the trouble to stay out of the news, and now this."

Abuela patted her hand. "It'll get better, *nena*. Wait and see."

It got worse. One of the tabloids hit the shelves with the headline, "Lottery Girl Home-Breaker Pics. Backseat Sex Leads to Injuries, Divorce."

Cheeto called, furious. "I'll kill him."

"Forget it. You'd only make things worse."

"You need to lay low, Rosie."

"Look on the bright side. At least you didn't have to bail *me* out of jail."

"I'm a man. It's different."

"Oh, thank you for that, Mr. Equality."

"I'm worried about you, Rosie. I hope you have a better lawyer than Mr. Pujol." He sounded sincere.

"Of course." She was lying. Leony had chosen several, and Rosie hadn't decided which one would represent her. Pathetic, that's what she was. And her luck seemed to be on temporary hold.

The phone rang again and she picked it up right away. "Cheeto?"

"It's Leony." Her assistant's voice seemed weary, as if she was exhausted by her controversial, accident-prone boss's big mouth. "I got a call from a Mrs. Holly about a promise to buy a house. Ring any bells?"

A house? "Never heard of her."

"That's what I thought. How are you holding up?"

"Pissed off."

"I can imagine. Don't give any interviews."

"I know it doesn't look like it, but I'm not stupid."

Leony laughed and hung up.

Later, as she soaked in a hot tub, trying to unwind the kinks in her back, she remembered Mrs. Holly. The old lady at the crash scene, the one whose kids needed a house.

She got out of the tub, wrapped herself in a thick terry robe, and dumped her purse out on her bed. A folded wad of receipts was in the inner pocket.

Rosie sat on the bed and unfolded the papers. Faces came back to her as she read the scribbled pleas. "Out of work for a year, family in a shelter." "Mother needs a decent nursing home." "Basketball team needs jerseys and a new practice hall for the winter." "A black Corvette." That last one made her laugh as she remembered the tall teenager who'd shoved the paper toward her.

She walked back to the tub with the phone, dialed Leony, and told her the plan.

"That sounds like a job for your foundation."

"Of course, why didn't I think of it?" Water splashed over the sides of the oversized tub as Rosie sat straight up.

She was going to make a lot of people happy.

CHAPTER FOURTEEN

* * * * * *

Cherish the moments when you see
your money put to good use.
—*The Instant Millionaire's Guide to Everything*

Diamond Rosie Hands Out Cash with Style,
But Where's Brad? Lani Prester Knows!
—*Star* magazine

Three weeks later, Rosie stood near the doors of the historic Crestmore Hotel's ballroom, watching elegantly dressed guests drift toward their dinner places. The annual Chamber of Commerce holiday party was hosted by the Caballero Foundation this year, and she was one of the hosts. She wished Brad could be here with her, but she hadn't asked him to come, even though the event planners had tried to get her to, saying that his presence would draw a lot of attention. Yeah, the wrong kind of attention. She didn't want the evening to turn into a "Brad and Rosie" circus. She wanted the guests and media to concentrate on the Caballero family's success, beyond the lottery win.

The room was filled with huge arrangements of exotic flowers, and the tables were beautifully decorated.

The room was filled with dignitaries eager to celebrate the

young foundation, and for once, the papers had been filled with praise for the Caballero family.

"Rosie?" Mrs. Everington, the head of the Junior League, stalked toward her, looking gorgeous. "Everything looks wonderful." She looked around as if assessing the cost of each floral arrangement and tablecloth.

"The decorators worked hard."

"You used the team that did your cousin's house?" Mrs. Everington looked her up and down. What was she doing, checking for a Wal-Mart tag?

"Hard to believe, isn't it?" Rosie touched a shell pink rose. "Not a steer hide or naked mermaid in sight. Plus, they volunteered their services."

The room was filling with beautifully dressed people. She thought she saw another familiar face, but then the crowd closed in. She hoped Mr. Pujol had come. She hadn't seen her attorney in weeks, and she wanted to publicly thank him for all he'd done for them as a family, and for the foundation, too.

She glanced at her reflection in a nearby mirror to make sure her smile was bright. As co-hostess of the banquet, along with Abuela and Cheeto, she had to greet each of her guests, five hundred of the southeast's richest and most influential residents, politicians, and community leaders.

After being wined and dined, they would witness the unveiling of the plan that the foundation staff had carefully crafted, based on Rosie's idea.

The foundation had already been hailed for its renovation plan for Rosie's old Chamblee apartment complex, which had been purchased by them and was going to be transformed, to the delight of its residents.

If a sneaky reporter came in tonight he'd score a different kind of picture of Rosie. She'd be captured in her glistening Givenchy gown, her hair in a sophisticated updo, a tasteful circle of diamonds glittering around her neck.

She was not the Rosie Caballero who had redeemed the winning lottery ticket. All she had to do tonight was to stay out of trouble and keep the broccoli out of her teeth.

Abuela looked stunning in beaded black, and Cheeto was unrecognizable in a tuxedo. He looked like one of the dignitaries.

Before dinner, the three of them stood on the podium at the head of the ballroom as the Chamber of Commerce president gave his speech.

"I am so proud," Abuela whispered to Rosie. "We've had so much help, and now we can help others."

She nodded, smiling for the watching crowd's benefit, but thought ungratefully that no one had helped them to get here. Everything they had was due to luck and hard work. The only thing that had gotten them here was dumb luck and a dollar bill.

The speech was done and the president stepped down and walked over to give Rosie his arm. Rosie smiled at the distinguished white-haired man. "I couldn't ask for a more handsome dinner partner, Mr. Morris."

Ben Morris, president of the Atlanta Chamber, winked and wrapped her hand around his elbow. "Lucky me."

After the salads were served, Mr. Morris stood. "And now we'll hear a few words from one of the Caballero Trust's founders, the very generous Rose Caballero."

The guests applauded and turned to her expectantly.

"A speech?" she muttered. She'd been promised that she wouldn't have to give one. And when had she become Rose instead of Rosie?

She stood, tripping on her skirt. She held on to the shoulder of the woman next to her. "Sorry."

She lifted her wineglass. No way was she walking to the podium. "I'm not a great speaker, so I promise I won't inflict you with a lame speech. I wish to thank you all for being here, and for allowing us to host this distinguished gathering, and I'd like to offer a toast, to all of you, my new friends, and the wonderful work we will do together."

Glasses were lifted and applause swelled, and then she sat down and someone else from the foundation spoke. Good thing she'd remembered Leony's advice to always be ready with a speech, and to make it very short.

Afterward, when Rosie was home at her new Atlantic Station loft, hanging up her gown and putting her shoes away, she wondered if the evening had been the best night of her life. It had certainly been a milestone, especially her conversation with Mrs. Everington. Maybe Atlanta society had accepted the Caballeros, for one night anyway.

She pulled her earrings off and put away the new diamond necklace, going over the next event. With the foundation's party over, now she could concentrate on Christmas.

It was just a few weeks away, and her plans had changed drastically from the day that Abuela and Cheeto had first talked about having it at her place.

Abuela had been invited to Argentina to spend Christmas

with her new beau and his family. The foundation's employees were going to spend the time with their own families. With the crowd diminished, she'd cancelled the cooking assistants.

She'd told Cheeto to bring a date and hoped that Brad would show up. She could handle dinner for four. Despite her cooking classes, she wasn't a brilliant cook, but she could handle the basic Cuban meal of *lechón asado,* black beans and rice, and *yucca con mojo.* What could go wrong?

Leony called the next day to congratulate her on the positive press coverage for the gala, and eager to share exciting news.

"We've had several offers for book deals," Leony said. "They want your life story, through your romance with Brad Merritt."

"Through? My life isn't over yet, as far as I know."

Leony laughed. "We'll call it Part One."

"Good. We can do Part Two when I'm old. I can't wait to tell Brad. He'll laugh."

Leony was silent.

"What?" Rosie felt her heart thump harder.

"I guess you haven't seen the tabloids. I keep telling you not to pay attention to them. They're full of lies, Rosie."

The thumping slowed, replaced with fear. "Now what?"

It probably had to do with Brad and her. Her heart sank farther. Abuela's call a minute later didn't help.

"Don't read tabloids," she said fiercely, before Rosie had even said hello.

She grabbed her wallet and headed for her private elevator. If there was bad news to be had, she didn't want to put off finding out, especially if it was bad enough for her grandmother to call to commiserate.

Half an hour later she was back in her loft, an icy glass in her hand and the pitcher at her side holding the world's largest rum and Coke. She'd filled the pitcher with Coke, added half a bottle of Bacardi Silver, then dumped half a jar of maraschino cherries into it, too. A lot of ice and a big straw, and she got down to anesthetizing herself while she read the bad news.

Around her were spread the three tabloids she found at the supermarket, as well as *The AJC,* all opened to the hot story of the week, Brad Merritt's romance with his costar, sexy starlet Lani Prester. Apparently the romance had heated up the set.

The photos were of Brad and Lani looking grim as they hustled through an airport, as well as Lani looking divine in a tiny bathing suit, and Brad looking cowboy hunky on the set of his film. And in every one, a sidebar photo of Rosie, pushing past the press, an angry look on her face.

She remembered that picture from when she flew back from California after her Mexican vacation. The press had been relentless, and she'd wished she'd stayed on the *MegaBucks* on its journey back through the Panama Canal to Miami.

"Jilted," the headlines read. "Angry Rosie Declares, 'I'll Ruin Him.'"

Untrue, all of it. Rosie Caballero was neither angry, nor vengeful. She was sitting high above the streets of Atlanta, tears dripping off her nose and onto Brad's newspaper photo.

Why was she weeping over a photo like some lovesick fan? She threw the newspaper across the room, where it smashed against the wall, knocking a print onto the tile floor.

Rosie sighed and went to pick up the papers. Her life was a big enough mess already.

CHAPTER FIFTEEN
✳ ✳ ✳ ✳ ✳ ✳

Don't forget that thoughtful gifts are the best.
—*The Instant Millionaire's Guide to Everything*

MegaBucks winner Enrique "Cheeto"
Caballero wining and dining a certain someone
at Pano's. Who is the luscious, and lucky, babe?
—*The Peach Buzz, The Atlanta Journal-Constitution*

On the twenty-third Rosie cut off a shopping trip after seeing a framed poster of Brad for sale at a shop in Atlantic Station. She'd been trying not to think about him, and wasn't surprised at the pang the sight of his face provoked, but she was surprised at how depressed she'd gotten afterward.

Brad had not called her, and she could not bring herself to dial his number, afraid of what he would say. She knew she was being juvenile. Where was the strong, empowered Rosie?

He probably hadn't called her because the tabloids were full of lies and he knew she wouldn't believe the stories. On the other hand, a warning phone call would have been nice, and the lack of one made her wonder if there wasn't some truth to the headlines.

They were too different. If she dated again, she was going to make some rules. No more movie stars. No celebrity musicians, either. They had weird schedules and work habits and she didn't want to cry over a man again.

Her dog was her best friend now. She called for Tootie when she got home, and the little dog looked up sleepily from her pillow, then perked up. Rosie's arrival sometimes meant a treat.

"Tootie, if you get any fatter I swear I'll think you're going into hibernation." Rosie wiped her eyes and blew her nose, mad at herself for shedding tears over Brad.

The elderly dog cocked her head, listening, then dropped her chin on her paws and closed her eyes.

Rosie had been dismissed. She gift-wrapped Cheeto's present and put it under the decorated tree that stood against the glass wall overlooking the shopping area.

It was almost three o'clock and Cheeto had promised to come by for a quick *merienda,* the Cuban version of afternoon tea. She hadn't seen him in a while, and he'd been evasive when she asked if he was seeing someone new.

She opened the fridge and pulled out the tray of little crustless sandwiches she'd fixed that morning. Her food-loving cousin would not be content with the usual coffee and crackers with sticky-sweet guava paste and cream cheese.

She pulled the plastic wrap from the tray, then brewed a pot of Bustelo. Minutes later the fabulous aroma of brewed *café cubano* filled the apartment.

She raced to the kitchen to turn down the burner and fix the *cortadito,* mixing the milk with equal parts coffee.

Take that, Starbucks, she thought, as she sipped her own. Cheeto wouldn't mind if she got a head start.

The doorbell rang and she walked toward it, enjoying the

light that streamed in through the wall of glass facing Atlanta's midtown area.

She flipped the door lock and pulled the door open, ready to kiss her cousin's cheek. Brad stood in the tiled hall, holding out a bouquet of tall flowers.

"Cheeto sent me in his place."

She stared as if she'd conjured him with her tears, then tried to close the door. He stepped in, catlike, before it moved.

"Come in then. What do you want?" She glanced around the outside hall. No cousin lurked there. "And where's Cheeto?"

"I called him and asked for your new address. He said to tell you that he was behind on his shopping and he'd see you Christmas Eve." He grinned at her, showing off his dimples.

Oh, God. She couldn't resist those dimples. "Did he tell you that I didn't want to see you again?" She debated running upstairs to hide, then gave herself a mental shake.

"Rosie, you didn't believe all that trash in the tabloids, did you?" He took a step toward her, then stopped when she stepped back.

"I don't know what to believe. You had to know that those pictures would upset me, and if you cared, if we really had something between us, then you would have called."

He ran his fingers through his hair. "You know I don't—"

"Bullshit." The word cut through his, cleanly, and apparently cauterizing the flow, because his smile vanished.

"I should have called. Rosie, I'm sorry. You scare me. I've never felt the way I feel for you."

Rosie wanted to hug him, but then realized that the hurt

little boy tone could be just good acting. She turned. "Come on, I fixed a snack for Cheeto. Hope you're hungry."

"I am. You cooked?" His tone had brightened, as if being offered food was a hopeful sign.

"Don't act so surprised. I won't poison you."

"You weren't expecting me."

Her cell phone started to play its little song somewhere in the kitchen. "Excuse me, that might be my grandmother."

And if it's Cheeto, she thought, I'm going to kill him.

The silvery phone's screen read "Cheeto." She flipped it open and put it to her ear, checking to be sure Brad couldn't see her.

"How dare you?" Her voice came out in a hiss.

"Rosita, I knew you'd gone to all that trouble, and I tried to call this morning, but you didn't answer any of your phones."

Rosie glanced at the kitchen phone on the wall by the fridge. Its little red message light was blinking, but so what? It was always blinking. She didn't answer unless it was Leony. "I meant giving Brad my address."

"Is he there?"

"Yes. You told him where I live."

"It was all lies, Rosie. You know how those tabloid slime are."

"Right. And it's your business how?"

"Face it, *prima,* you're lonely. Do you want to be an old maid?"

"I'm only twenty-four."

"Be nice to Brad. He's a good dude."

She hung up and returned to the living room, where Brad stood by the Christmas tree, enjoying the view below with a coffee cup in his hand. She took a couple of deep breaths to calm herself.

"This is a great space." He was watching her reflection in the glass.

"It was already sold when I originally wanted to buy it, but this guy's job moved him to London just as he was closing on the loan."

"Wow. Lucky."

"I've been called that." She tried to smile at him. "What do you think of the coffee? Is it as good as Jana's?"

"Jana's will put hair on your chest, but this is really good." He took an appreciative sip, as if he had to prove it to her.

"Sort of a turbo-charged latte."

"Yeah."

"So are you done working on location?"

He put the cup down on a nearby table. "It was long, miserable, and over. Let's talk about us."

"I thought there was no more us. I was planning on you coming for Christmas, but then this Lani Prester thing came up and you didn't call. Not even a text message. You could have told me that it wasn't true."

"Why should I have to tell you that a tabloid story is fake? After what they've printed about you? You know where Lani is now? Baltimore. At home with her parents, and her fiancé."

"Oh."

"Yeah, oh. The *Star* won't print that. Too boring. Too normal." He stared pointedly at her, eyebrows raised. "Not like wrecking an old boyfriend's marriage."

The spray of coffee caught Brad dead in the chest. He jumped back and hit the window, then leaped forward as he realized he'd smacked against glass ten stories in the air. He cracked his shin against the glass-topped stone coffee table and landed on the suede couch, rubbing his leg.

Rosie stared at him, aghast, then ran for the kitchen to get a towel. She swiped at his chest. "I'm sorry. Are you okay?"

"I'll live. Is this monster table from IKEA?"

"No. Cheeto gave it to me as a housewarming present."

He glared at it. "Figures." He pulled the towel out of her hands and dabbed at her chin. "You're dripping, too."

He swabbed her cashmere T-shirt with the damp, coffee-stained towel.

"Rick was never my boyfriend. He ditched me on our first date. The *Star* made all of that up."

"I know. That's why I didn't call."

"I wish you had." Her voice was choked with misery.

"Poor Rosie." He touched her cheek gently, then pulled back his hand, as if it had touched her of its own volition.

When she didn't respond, he picked up both coffee cups and took them to the kitchen. "Hey, sandwiches."

He came in with the tray and set it on the table. Tootie appeared, lured from her pillow by the combined aromas of shrimp salad and little sandwiches.

"Hi, old girl." He looked up at Rosie. "Is she allowed to nibble?"

"She's not allowed to eat people food, of course. But then, I'm not supposed to eat chocolate."

He grinned. "I'll remember that. Godiva okay?"

"Truffles are the best." She made a face. "No raspberry."

"Gotcha." He made the same face back at her.

He was still Brad. Still warm and fun. They still had stuff to talk about. She tried not to look upstairs, but the long sweep of stairs leading to the loft's master suite was hard to ignore.

He glanced up. "Is there a tour on the agenda?"

"There is no agenda. But grab some sandwiches and I'll show you around."

He scooped up a handful and followed her.

"This is the office. Not that I need it, but I don't need a bedroom downstairs, and I found all this cute office furniture. And that love seat opens up to a full-sized bed."

"It's not cute. It's beautiful." He looked around appreciatively.

"Thank you. You've seen the kitchen." She showed him around the downstairs, then sighed and started up the stairs. Why was she torturing herself?

"This is my bedroom." She blinked. The bed was made. Thank goodness for good habits, but she remembered that she'd left her underwear on the floor when she took a shower that morning. She rushed ahead and pulled the door closed.

"Secret room?" He tried to look inside before it shut.

"Messy bathroom."

"It can't be that bad. I want to see."

"It's just a bathroom. Toilet, sink, tub, shower, and underwear on the floor. Toothpaste in the sink. Maybe lipstick on the towels. Not sure."

"Sounds like you're human."

"Too human." She cringed inside. Why had she said that?

"Don't be so hard on yourself. I'll bet you look cute in the pink string bikini panties."

"You looked."

"I have socks on my bedroom floor at home, if it makes you feel any better."

She sniffed, trying to keep from crying. She wanted to cry. Actually, she wanted to break something. She looked around, but the IKEA look was kind of spare. No knickknacks to heave.

"What's wrong?" He sounded so patient, so kind, and up close he smelled wonderful. She remembered the smooth warmth of his shoulders and how safe she'd felt, cradled in his arms on the lanai.

She dropped onto the bed. "When you left on location, I thought, how cool, we'll see each other soon and meanwhile, I'll get a lot of stuff done. Then the tabloids started running all of these pictures of you and Lani Prester. I know we're not—" She paused, unsure of what to say. Not committed? Not in a long-term relationship?

She looked up at him and patted the spot next to her. "Sit, please. You're looming."

He sat next to her and put his hand over hers. "I'm not seeing anyone. The tabloids can't resist making up stories about love affairs between costars. I've been busy working." He looked at their joined hands. "You've been in the news, as well."

"And you didn't believe it, right?" Her tone said that she believed the opposite was true, or else why had he brought it up?

"I believe only what I hear from your lips." He flung a hand out dramatically and she laughed.

"So what have you heard from my lips?"

He shrugged. "An invitation to come tonight."

She smiled. "For Christmas Eve dinner?"

"That, too. Anything else?" He looked around, eyes lingering on the dresser, then the red leather reading chair, then slowly turning to examine her headboard. His voice softened. "Rosie, we're in bed."

Breathing went on manual override as his eyes locked onto hers. She licked her lips. "Yes, we are."

His eyes were on her mouth, then he lowered his lips to touch hers and his fingers tugged lightly at the bottom edge of her sweater.

A very merry Christmas indeed.

CHAPTER SIXTEEN
* * * * * *

Look beyond the stock market. Real estate,
precious gems, and art are fun investments.
But be careful!
—*The Instant Millionaire's Guide to Everything*

Brad's Atlanta Holiday—Lani Pouts in Vegas
—*Star* magazine

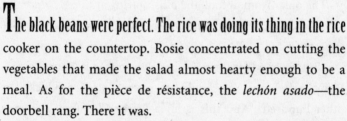

The black beans were perfect. The rice was doing its thing in the rice cooker on the countertop. Rosie concentrated on cutting the vegetables that made the salad almost hearty enough to be a meal. As for the pièce de résistance, the *lechón asado*—the doorbell rang. There it was.

She glanced at the retro wall clock next to the cabinets. Good. Cheeto and his girlfriend weren't due for half an hour.

She wiped her hands on her grandmother's old Christmas apron and opened the door.

It was Mirta Gonzales from the old neighborhood, cradling a roasting pan with a foil tent over a huge bulge in the middle. "Here's your *pernil*. Help me out, it gets heavier by the second."

The two women wrestled the baking pan onto the counter. "It just needs to stay in the oven another half an hour or so."

"Perfect." Rosie looked under the big pan's aluminum foil tent. "How big is it?"

"Ten pounds. I couldn't get a bigger one. It wouldn't fit in my oven."

"Mirta, *eres increíble*. Just incredible." Rosie put the heavy pan into her own preheated oven and closed the door. "No one will ever know I didn't cook it." She turned to her old neighbor. "You won't sell this story to the tabloids, will you?"

Mirta looked coy. Rosie slapped her forehead. "Of course. I almost forgot." She ran to the office, unlocked her desk drawer, and removed three bills.

"Here you go, *amiga*. One hundred dollars for cooking the *lechón* and another one for saving my backside."

The older woman took the bills, staring at them. "*Madre de Dios*. I didn't think you'd pay me this much. Twenty-five is all I expected."

"But you paid for the meat, and you cooked it. Expertly, too. It smells delicious. You should be a caterer." Rosie produced the other hundred. "And this is for a merry Christmas for your kids."

Mirta took the money and hugged her tight. "I hope this is another great year for you, *niña*. You deserve it."

Another great year? Her old neighbors were probably certain that she just sat around popping bonbons all day. She suddenly thought of the overzealous security guards. "Where did Armando park?"

"Not far. I'd better hurry back though." They kissed again, then Mirta hurried off, buttoning her cloth coat.

The heady aroma of cooking pork roast filled the loft. Dinner was going to be delicious. Rosie had just put a bottle of champagne on ice when Cheeto and his date arrived. Or rather, his dates.

Rosie stared, mouth open, as a girl walked in wearing a skintight sleeveless pantsuit that showed off her muscular arms. She pushed past Rosie and looked around as if she was house shopping. Cheeto grinned and gave Rosie a quick kiss.

"Merry Christmas," she said. She would have said more, but she heard a "Merry Christmas" from behind her and turned to see Nieves in the doorway. She was sure her eyes bugged out.

"Aren't you going to ask me in?" asked Rick's wife, tall and lean, long blond hair drifting over tanned shoulders, her top a tiny golden hanky thing tied at her neck with a chain.

Ask her in? Like a vampire? But the woman had stalked in and leaned close to kiss her before Rosie could step back.

Nieves had kissed her. She felt defiled. "Aren't you suing me?" She glared at Cheeto, who was unpacking two grocery sacks of his favorite cheese snack.

"It's nothing personal." Nieves smiled triumphantly and breezed into the living room, followed by Miriam, who was frowning. Rosie was speechless.

"What a beautiful home you have, Rosie." Nieves slinked around like a greyhound in gold lamé pants.

Nieves, in *her* home. Cheeto was so dead. The two women, who didn't seem to be on speaking terms, were examining everything as if they were taking inventory.

"Explain this, Cheeto," Rosie said when she finally cornered her cousin in the kitchen. "And here's a clue: Nieves has to go."

"She was all alone tonight. I know what a humanitarian you

are. You know, forgive and forget and all that?" Cheeto grabbed a fistful of fat orange wormy things and crunched happily. "Besides, I think it's my lucky night. I'm covering all the bases, you know?"

Rosie shuddered.

Miriam, who was smarter than her bimbo wrestler looks implied, had taken in the situation and tried to keep Nieves away from Rosie as she put the finishing touches on dinner. The evening was ruined. First Abuela couldn't come, then Cheeto announced he was bringing his strange new girlfriend, and now Nieves was joining them for dinner. What else could go wrong?

The doorbell chimed yet again, saving Nieves from a grisly death by paté spreader. Rosie dropped the would-be murder weapon to get the door. As if the guest list wasn't already awkward enough. Probably some of Cheeto's friends. Well, they'd soon discover that there were no bare-breasted mermaids in this house. Maybe they'd get bored and leave.

Thank goodness Mirta had gone overboard on the meat. At least there'd be enough food.

She opened the door. "What?"

Brad Merritt stood there, holding a bouquet of flowers and a bottle of wine. He smiled at her. "Merry Christmas, Rosie."

Rosie closed her mouth, which had fallen open. "M-merry Christmas. You came."

He waved the wine bottle in its cloth gift bag. "You invited me for Christmas Eve dinner, remember?"

"I thought—" What had she thought? That he'd leave town after he made love to her?

"Oh my God, it's Brad Merritt." Miriam's voice rose into a near squeal as she rushed the door.

Brad expertly sidestepped her hug and kissed Rosie's cheek. "You could at least say Merry Christmas."

"Merry Christmas." She looked over his shoulder. "Are you alone?"

He opened and closed his mouth, then muttered, "Quit being insecure."

Insecure? Her? Her perfect dinner had gone all wrong. Rosie wanted to throw Nieves through the window. Cheeto's other date was drooling over Brad and ignoring Cheeto, who was oblivious to everything but the food.

Nieves was drinking too much and flirting with Brad. She was making a total fool of herself. No wait, that was her normal state.

The night's one hit was the food. Everyone ate with gusto. When the plates were empty, Brad yawned and said he was too jetlagged to stay awake.

"Go upstairs, then. You can nap on my bed." Rosie noticed the two women look at each other, and Cheeto's frown.

"Thanks." Brad started up the stairs.

Rosie tried to erase the tabloid image of beautiful Lani Prester looking up at him adoringly. Cheeto was watching her. She blushed. Was she being obvious? She wondered if he would call Abuela to tell her about tonight. She couldn't wait for the night to be over.

During dessert Nieves and Miriam kept looking at the stairs. Afterward, when no one offered to help clear away the dishes, Rosie made three trips to the kitchen, thinking that maybe she should have had the whole event catered *and* served.

She'd wanted a homey *noche buena* dinner like the ones she'd shared with Cheeto and Abuela. Instead she'd worked all night to get ready and now she'd have to work to clean it up. She looked at the heaps of dirty plates and abandoned the kitchen. To heck with cleaning. She'd call a maid service in the morning.

She came out of the kitchen to see Nieves halfway up the stairs, her eyes on Rosie's bedroom door.

"Oh no you don't," she muttered. "Nieves," she called. "Come look at the view." The night sky was clear, and Atlanta's lights illuminated it like casually tossed jewels. Her Christmas tree's lights blinked in counterpoint. Nieves came back downstairs and joined Cheeto and Miriam at the window.

"Don't worry," Rosie joked. "We're too high up for the paparazzi." Cheeto glanced at her quickly. She winked at him then hurried up the stairs to check on Brad.

He was sprawled on her bed, asleep. He must have been exhausted. She picked up a bottle of pills on the nightstand and read the label. A prescription sleep aid. Had he taken some?

"I didn't think he'd come." Cheeto stood behind her, looking down at Brad.

"Me neither. I thought he had other things on his mind." She put the bottle back on the table.

Cheeto touched her shoulder. "I saw the way you looked at him."

"Pitiful, isn't it? I think all women look at him like that."

Cheeto shepherded her out of the room and closed the door behind them. "I think Rosie's in love." His face was serious for once.

She felt tears rise and swallowed them. "He's a friend, and a tired one, that's all."

The sound of a crash came from downstairs.

"What the hell?"

They leaned over the balcony. Miriam was staring at a stain on her silk tunic. Nieves stood by the sofa, an empty wineglass in her hand and a smirk on her face.

Miriam shrieked and jumped over the stone coffee table, upsetting the hors d'oeuvres dishes. She jumped onto Nieves, pushing them both onto the sofa, where they struggled until Miriam rolled over the sofa. Nieves dove after her, shrieking, scratching, and growling.

"If they get too near the windows, they might break through." Rosie bit her lip. She didn't want to call the police.

"That glass is tougher than you think," Cheeto said. "I checked on it when you moved in. Want to call the police?"

She gave him a look.

"Oh. Right. Bad press. Can't have that. Especially with Brad Merritt in your bed."

"Wait here."

She went back into the bedroom and filled her massaging footbath with cold water.

A crash and an "oh shit" came from below.

"Help me carry this out," she called. Brad stirred, then turned over, still asleep.

Rosie and Cheeto balanced the heavy water-filled bath onto the stair railing, stopping to stare at the mess the women had made.

The Christmas tree was overturned, and the floor glittered

with the shards of the shattered ornaments. Tootie came out of the bedroom, wagging her tail. She took one rheumy-eyed look at the mayhem downstairs and slid back into her basket.

"Smart girl. I'll bet you'd like to pull the covers over your head, too." Rosie tightened her grip on the footbath. "Ready?"

Cheeto nodded, eyes on the floor below, where Nieves and Miriam's fight had barreled under the balcony's overhang and out of sight.

Rosie and Cheeto waited until the fight made its way back toward their side of the room. At just the right moment, the two combatants were suddenly drenched in cold water.

"Merry Christmas," Rosie yelled. They quit fighting and stared at their dripping clothes, then up at Rosie and Cheeto.

"Thanks." Miriam wiped her face. "I was about to kill her. Don't want a homicide record."

"Yeah, right. They did you a favor, all right. They saved your life." Nieves attempted sneer didn't work too well through her rapidly swelling lips.

Rosie grabbed an armful of towels from the hall closet and tossed them over the railing.

A flurry of towels landed around the two women.

"Start mopping up that water. Spread the towels on the floor, then squeeze them out in the kitchen."

"No way." Nieves glared up at her. Miriam drew her fist back. Nieves backed away, picked up a towel, and started wiping the floor.

Cheeto watched them work. "What are you going to do about Brad?"

"Nothing. Let him sleep." She stared at her overturned sofa. Time to redecorate. "Should we help them?"

"Why? They trashed the place. Let them do it."

"You're all heart, Cheeto. Isn't Miriam your girlfriend?"

He shrugged. "No, we just hang out. Besides, she'd think it was weird if I went down there and helped. How about I open the champagne and we all have a toast?"

Rosie laughed. "Why not?" She went downstairs, picked her way through the holiday shrapnel and gathered the wet towels the women had used, then joined Cheeto in the dining room.

"Should I call them a cab?"

"Forget it. I'll take them home. Let's drink a Christmas toast before anything else goes wrong."

Cheeto was just about to pop open the champagne when Leony appeared, wide-eyed, in the doorway. She had the spare key to the loft in one hand and a shiny gift-wrapped box under her other arm.

"What happened here, and are the police on their way?"

"Leony!" Rosie hugged her assistant.

"This is for you." Leony extended the wrapped package, her eyes on the two women cleaning up the living room and occasionally stopping to swat at each other. "Friends of yours?"

"Cheeto's so-called dates. Miriam is the chick by what's left of the Christmas tree, and the other is Nieves. Oh, yes, *that* Nieves."

Nieves's shiny top was loose and she looked like she was going to have a black eye.

Leony glared at Cheeto. "What were you thinking?"

"Um, they were going to be lonely at Christmas?"

Leony rolled her eyes, muttered "moron" under her breath, and stomped into the kitchen.

"What's the matter with her?" Rosie looked at Cheeto, who shrugged. His gaze slid to the kitchen. "Okay, something is up, Cheeto. What is it?"

Cheeto popped open the champagne. "Time for a *noche buena* toast, that's all."

"Miriam, Nieves, want some champagne?"

Miriam and Nieves came in. Miriam's top was torn and she had a scratch on her arm, but was otherwise fine. Nieves held a raw steak over her eye. Leony followed her with a plastic bag full of chipped ice.

"Try this instead," she told the injured woman, and Nieves surrendered the steak. "I called a cab for you ladies." She gave the word "ladies" extra emphasis.

"To peace on earth," Rosie offered, lifting her champagne flute.

"Amen," Leony said forcefully.

The others raised their glasses. Bruised, angry, embarrassed, and—Rosie didn't know what to call the expression on Cheeto's face. It looked like guilt, and probably was, for exposing her to yet another lawsuit.

Rosie thought this was the strangest Christmas ever, and very different from the holiday she'd envisioned.

Rosie's intercom buzzed. The cab was here. Cheeto stood up, ready to walk Miriam and Nieves downstairs, but Leony jumped up, too.

"I'm going with you."

"Sure." Cheeto hugged Rosie. "This was the best Christmas Eve ever."

Rosie laughed. "You are such a fool." She followed them out to the elevators.

"Why don't you two let the cab take Nieves and Miriam home? We can visit longer."

"With the idol of millions snoring in your bed? Sorry, fish chick needs me. Besides, you'll be wanting alone time when he wakes up."

"Brad's here?" Leony grabbed Rosie's arm. "What about Lani—"

"We're not talking about her tonight." She lowered her voice. "I don't know how it will end, Leony. I should walk away, and I have, but I feel so good around him."

"You love him."

"Yes, I do." Rosie watched Cheeto maneuver to stay between Nieves and Miriam. "You'd better go or they'll start up again." Rosie hugged her. "Merry Christmas. Did you like your present?"

"I haven't opened it yet," Leony said. "It's under my tree, but I can't wait. Anything in a Tiffany blue box has got to be fabulous. Good luck with Brad. We'll leave you two alone."

Exactly what she was thinking. Alone time with Brad.

"Come on, Leony, my mermaid is calling to me."

"I don't want to hear about your unnatural relationship with your swimming pool statue." Leony's voice echoed in the foyer.

The elevator dinged and the doors slid open. Cheeto ran back to Rosie. "I'm glad Brad showed up, *prima*," he said in a low voice. "Shows he's a cool guy, and that he's got some feelings for you." He kissed her gently on the cheek. "I'll call you later. Merry Christmas."

"Don't leave yet. I have something for you." She ran to the tree and returned with a little square box wrapped in purple foil. "I got you a present. I'm amazed it's still in one piece."

He took it, laughing. "I didn't get you anything. I'd think it was something really expensive, but I know you. You have millions and you shop at IKEA. You're a weird chick, Rosie."

"I buy things that I like. Open it."

He unwrapped the gift and stared inside at the box marked ROLEX. He looked up at Rosie. "Is this for real? It's not really a box of pencils or socks, is it?"

"That would have been funny. Next year you get socks in a Rolex box."

He pried up the lid and pulled out a hinged green leather box with a silvery watch inside.

"It's called a—"

"A Presidential. I know. I love it."

"Pocket change, remember? And save the box. Next year you are so getting socks."

He laughed. "You've changed, Rosie. Remember when we won the lottery? What we wanted to buy?"

"Yeah. I went to Tiffany's and came back with about forty thousand dollars' worth of diamonds and pearls in Tootie's tote bag." She laughed.

He looked shocked. "For real?"

"Yeah. I ran back to the hotel to stash it." She patted his arm. "And then you showed up in your Hummer."

"Which is parked downstairs." He put his hands in his pockets. "Can I pick it up later? And hey, when I get back I'll have a present for you." He ruffled her hair, or tried to. His hands got caught in her updo and he yanked half of it down pulling himself free. "Oh God, I'm sorry."

She pushed back the hair hanging in her eyes. "I'll fix it. Merry Christmas, Cheeto."

"Cheeto, come on!" Leony stood in the elevator door.

"Merry Christmas." He stared at her for a moment, as if he wanted to say something else. Instead, he walked out to the elevators.

An hour later, as she was checking out a statuette that had lost an arm in the melee, the doorbell rang. She ran to get it, thinking Cheeto had forgotten something. Abuela stood outside, with a handsome older man behind her.

Rosie stared. "Aren't you supposed to be in Argentina?"

"Merry Christmas to you, too." Abuela lifted an eyebrow and turned to give the man behind her a look. "Bad weather cancelled the flight. We can't even buy a plane at this hour. Can we stay with you?" She hugged and kissed Rosie, smelling of Joy perfume and peppermint gum.

"Here?" Rosie looked around at the fallen Christmas tree, wet towels, and overturned furniture. "I guess." She could put them in the spare room.

The big good-looking guy had followed Abuela in. "Your party ended early." He looked around. "What happened?"

"Rosie, this is Marco Rio Seco, my *novio*." Abuela's voice changed as she saw the mess. "Oh, my. Were you playing *fútbol* in here?"

Rosie waved toward the disaster zone. "Cheeto's girlfriend did that. She was fighting Rick's wife, Nieves."

Abuela spun, a hand on her chest. She looked from Marco to Rosie. "Rick?" She mouthed the name as if it was a bad word. Not far from the truth.

"It's a long story. Why don't you two sit down? I'll tidy up a little. I'm expecting a work crew day after tomorrow. They thought they'd be cleaning up after a little dinner party. Won't they be surprised?"

"Why don't they come tomorrow?" Abuela poked the toe of her shoe at the shattered ornaments that Nieves and Miriam had swept into a pile.

"Because it's Christmas Day, Abuela."

It suddenly came to her that the two of them might not want to sleep together. If not, then Marco could sleep on the sofa and she could sleep with her grandmother. No way she'd crawl into bed with Brad with her grandmother in the house. Now she'd get points for being discreet.

"I'll make up the bed in the spare bedroom. Are you two . . ." She waggled two fingers at them, sure they'd get what she was driving at.

Abuela blushed. Marco looked down at her grandmother fondly. Why couldn't anyone look at *her* like that?

"We'll share," Abuela said, blushing again.

"Fabulous," Rosie muttered. The lovebirds got the spare bed, the movie star was in her bed, and with her grandmother here, she got stuck with the sofa. *Merry Christmas to me.*

*   *   *

"It's not true about Brad, you know," Leony said. "I've talked to insiders. The story was leaked by a publicity guy at the studio."

Leony had called to report that Miriam and Nieves had been safely delivered, and to wish her a Merry Christmas.

"Right. What about the pictures?" Rosie was stiff from sleeping on the stained and battered sofa. Why had she gone for the taut, contemporary look? Its replacement would have to be something big and overstuffed.

"You don't believe those rags, do you?" Leony sounded indignant.

Thank goodness for Leony. She felt better. She stared at her ruined Christmas tree. At least the presents weren't damaged.

Abuela emerged from the spare room. "*Felicidades,* Rosie. How about a little *cafecito*?" She was dressed in comfy-looking gray sweats trimmed in purple, and matching tennis shoes. "We can go for a walk afterward. What are you doing on the sofa?"

"Leony called to wish me a merry Christmas."

Abuela hadn't mentioned the mess in the living room, so Rosie played along. She kissed her grandmother. "It's not too cold outside, is it?"

"Chilly, that's all." Abuela pushed aside the blankets and sat on the sofa next to Rosie. "Why did you sleep down here?" She seemed to be trying not to look too closely at the tree. "Do you want to open your present?" She held out a slim box.

Rosie grinned, relieved that her grandmother had skipped right over her own question. Her wrecked living room temporarily forgotten, she took the box. "Should I shake it?"

"No," Abuela scolded. "Why do you kids always shake the box?"

"It's too little to be a glass clown."

Abuela leaned back against the sofa cushions. "I'm giving those to Cheeto. He's so fond of them."

"Hold on, let me get yours." She jumped up and picked her way through broken ornaments to free a flat rectangular package from the branches that had pushed it against the wall.

"Should we wait for Cheeto?" Abuela shot a quick sideways glance at the fallen tree. It looked somehow worse in the morning, like a debauched society matron, her jewels askew.

"Believe me, we'd wait hours for him." Rosie unwrapped her present and opened the flat gift box. Inside was a platinum charm bracelet with tiny enameled animals dangling from it. "So cute. *Gracias.*"

"A painting?" Abuela frowned at the large rectangle.

"Kind of obvious, isn't it? Close your eyes."

Her grandmother dutifully covered her eyes.

Rosie turned the picture around. "Okay, open them."

Abuela dropped her hands and opened her eyes, clearly savoring the moment. Then she gasped. "*Dios mío.* I love it." She leaped up and hugged Rosie. "I love it."

The painting was a vividly colored oil portrait of Rosie and Cheeto, sitting together on a bench, as if caught looking at a book of photographs. Rosie was glancing at Cheeto, who was looking out at the viewer.

Abuela crouched down to look at the photograph that the painted Rosie was holding. It was clearly the family photo of her parents, Abuela's daughter and son-in-law.

She hugged Rosie. "It's perfect, *mi amor.* Perfect. I'll put it in my condo in Miami, where I can always look at it."

Marco interrupted their teary embrace. "*Felicidades.* What a beautiful sight on a Christmas morning. Two lovely ladies."

He kissed each of them lightly on the cheek, then turned to look at the portrait. "What a beautiful painting. A very good likeness of you, Rosie. And Enrique, too."

"We met Enrique for dinner the other day," Abuela said. She whispered, "He thinks Marco is perfect for me."

Rosie made a mental note to kick Cheeto's ass for not filling her in.

A mighty yawn from upstairs made the three of them look up. Abuela gasped. On the landing above them stood a very naked Brad Merritt. He looked down, yelped, and ran back into the bedroom.

Abuela looked at Rosie. "This is why you slept here on the sofa."

Rosie thought she was making sure of her granddaughter's virtue, but it sounded a lot like "You're insane."

Marco was still looking up at the balcony. "He looks familiar. Like the actor in those spy movies I like. And the cowboy ones. What's his name?"

"He got tired during the dinner party. I let him sleep in my room."

"But why didn't you tell us your boyfriend was here, Rosie? I would have slept on the sofa and let you sleep on the bed with your grandmother." Marco was still frowning. "He really looks like that actor."

"That's because he *is* that actor. Brad Merritt," Abuela said.

Marco looked thoughtful. "He looks thinner in his movies."

"He looks thinner without any clothes," Abuela corrected.

Rosie fled to the kitchen to find breakfast for everyone.

When Brad came downstairs, dressed in yesterday's clothes, he found the three of them seated in a huddle at the end of the dining room table, where Rosie had cleared a spot.

Rosie introduced him to her grandmother and Marco, and the four of them drank *café con leche* and picked at the previous night's leftovers.

"So Brad, you are a real *vaquero*? Do you ride?" Marco broke off another piece of bread from the long *flauta* in front of him.

"I learned to ride the hard way. I lied my way into a part and then had to figure out how to manage the horse while I acted. How about you, Mr. Rio Seco? That means dry river, doesn't it?"

"That is correct. Not a common name, but not too unusual. I have a large cattle ranch in Argentina and enjoy fine horses. You must come with Rosie."

Rosie glanced at Abuela. So he wasn't a cruise gigolo; if he was telling the truth, that is. Rosie would get Leony to find out.

She cornered her grandmother in the kitchen. "Tell me all about him."

"I'm in love, *nena*. He's so handsome, and so smart and funny. I enjoy being with him. We play cards and laugh so much." She smiled, lost in thought.

Rosie nodded, thinking of Brad.

They sighed in unison, then looked at each other and laughed.

"Family money?"

"*Niña. Qué entrometida.*" Her grandmother looked offended.

"I'm not being nosy. You've got millions, and I want to make sure you're not going to be taken advantage of."

"I feel the same way about you. He's a widower. He has two grown sons, both lawyers, both married. He likes to spend time in Miami and New York."

"Sounds nice. And the money?"

"Family money. Not as much as we have, but enough. I haven't told him how much I'm worth, either, so don't ask."

"Like it wasn't in all the papers." She rolled her eyes. "What are his intentions?"

Abuela laughed. "I have no idea, and I don't care, either. I'm just grateful to feel again what I had not felt for many years."

"I'm happy for you," Rosie said. Loud masculine laughter erupted from the other room. If it weren't for her uncertainty about a certain starlet, Rosie might be just as happy as her grandmother.

She couldn't wait for her grandmother to continue on her trip so that she could have time alone with Brad. She wanted to tell him how much his visit had meant to her, and how sorry she was that the evening had turned out the way it had.

But when Abuela and Marco got ready to leave, Brad asked them for a ride to the airport. Rosie felt hollow inside. She busied herself picking up broken ornaments as the three of them discussed the logistics of the short trip to the airport.

He took Rosie aside while the others gathered their belongings. "I've got to go, but I want you to come out as soon as you can. We need to talk."

"We're here now."

He cupped her cheek. "We need more than a minute. Rosie, my life is complicated, but I want us to have a chance."

"And mine isn't? What are you trying to say?"

"You're looking for a way to make things normal. We are not normal. Whether you get used to your money or give it all away, you can never be the person you were. Quit trying so hard."

"I'm not trying too hard."

He kissed her, and she moaned, frustrated, when it came to an end. "Call me when you figure it out."

When he left with Abuela and Marco, Rosie watched the elevator doors close on them, and went back to the wreckage of her loft, wondering how closely it might resemble her love life.

Two weeks later, at midnight, Rosie celebrated the New Year by Cheeto's underground pool. Upstairs the house vibrated to the beat of a hot new band that Luny Tunes produced, and those nasty Solas sisters who had called her a cow in Miami were doing a live feed for RTV. Rosie had no idea why they adored Cheeto.

Rosie's date for the evening was Tootie. She poured the last of her bottle of Cristal into her glass and toasted Pamela the mermaid.

"Just us girls, Tootie. You, me, and Pam the fish chick." She straightened Tootie's party hat, which had tilted over one ear.

Wild giggles floated down the stairwell on the other side of the grotto.

"Uh-oh. Company." She picked up Tootie and made her way unsteadily to the other side of Pam, whose enormous tail flipped up to form a hiding place.

"Oh, Chucky, do you really know Cheeto Caballero?" The woman's voice was high and girly.

"I sure do. He's a friend of mine."

Rosie watched from under Pam's arm as the couple walked by. Cheeto was famous, all right. Everyone claimed him as a friend.

The giggly redhead was a reporter, the reason Rosie was hiding down here. She wasn't up to another tabloid photo standoff. After they went by she and Tootie went back upstairs. Time to grab another bottle of Cristal from the stacks of them in Cheeto's walk-in cooler.

The dancing crowd was clogging the hallway leading to the food and drinks. She'd hoped Christmas was as low as it would go. One minute into it, the New Year wasn't looking any better.

She should go home. Cheeto had enough friends to amuse him. He'd never miss her. She pushed her way through the dancers, shielding Tootie, who snapped and growled at the party-goers.

The main ballroom was full of dancers, and she saw Cheeto leap onto the stage with the DJ who'd replaced the earlier band. He reached down and pulled up a slim figure dressed in a tight red-sequined dress. The woman laughed and Rosie froze. It was Leony.

Her first thought was that if she'd known Leony was here she would have hung out with her, but then the sight sank in.

Cheeto's hand on her diminutive assistant's curvy backside. Leony laughing up at his face, the look that passed between them.

Leony should know better than to date Cheeto, and they probably hadn't told Rosie about it because they knew she'd disapprove. But then why invite her to the party? She felt really tired.

Outside, the noise seemed muffled, although the neighbors probably didn't think so. Cheeto was no fool, though. He didn't want the police to break up the party, so all the neighbors were probably inside dancing and drinking champagne. It was cold, and she'd left her coat and Tootie's Burberry tote inside.

"I'll get a new one. Let's call it a night, *viejita*."

The drivers of the fleet of cars Cheeto had hired for the night straightened when she approached. One of them came forward. Here she was walking out of party alone, just like on the night Rick had ditched her.

"Take you home, Miss?"

Was that pity in his eyes?

"Please." She gave him the address and slipped into the back of the car, grateful for the darkness and for Tootie's company. She didn't have a tissue, and the little dog licked the tears from her cheeks all the way home.

A few days later, Rosie had almost forgotten the wild party and was half-floating in a fragrant, steamy bath when the tub-side phone rang. She groaned, eyes still closed. She'd spent the day at the Caballero Foundation's Career Makeover Magic workshop, where a group of formerly homeless women received résumé help and interview suits, manicures and pantyhose and new shoes.

A team of hairdressers was on hand to make them look professional. For the ladies, it was a day of fun, regained dignity, and hope for a good-paying job. For Rosie it was a chance to see her money doing good. Everyone had left satisfied.

She felt she'd earned the right to relax a little. She almost let the phone ring unanswered, but finally groped for the receiver.

"Rosie? Are you okay?" It was Cheeto. Did the guy have radar, or what? He always knew the most inconvenient time to call. "You ducked out of my party without saying good-bye."

"And it took you a week to notice? Or were you too busy with Leony?"

"You saw us? Why didn't you say hello? We wanted to tell you, but it was crazy with all the people there. Have you seen the papers?"

"Nope. And whatever it is, I don't care. 'Bye, Enrique." She started to drop the receiver on its cradle.

"Wait, Rosie! Don't hang up." Cheeto's faraway little voice held a note of panic.

She sighed and held the phone to her ear again. "You aren't in jail, are you?"

"No."

"No need to sound offended, it's happened before. Why the anxiety?"

"Brad's hooked up with some *chiva loca* and the papers are full of his picture and yours."

She sat up, sloshing water on the floor. "Since when?" Her pulse had started racing, but then she snapped back to reality. "It's just the papers, Cheeto. Probably a slow news week."

"They also say that he's drying out somewhere. He didn't drink a lot at the beach, did he?"

"Not around me. He's probably just hiding from the press. Leave him alone. And me, too."

She picked up one of the tabloids at the supermarket the next day. Luckily the Publix was within walking distance. She wore a baseball cap and dark glasses and no one gave her a second glance.

"Brad in Rehab—Is His Career Over?" Cheeto was right. This was awful. The long article covered mostly invented details of their affair, and then alleged that he had taken to drinking after they broke up. When had they broken up? She shook her head, but didn't throw the paper away, because the photos of Brad were from earlier in the year and showed him tanned and fit.

She cut out the pictures that showed Brad alone and pinned them to her bedroom wall. It was a juvenile thing to do, but she slept better when he was the last thing she saw when she went to bed. She tried to call him but couldn't get through. She left two messages, then stopped, not wanting to appear needy.

She drove her Lexus to a park along the Chattahoochee River the next day, partly for the driving practice, but mostly because the riverside trails were so beautiful. She and Tootie took a long, peaceful walk through the woods, then returned to the car. Leony called as she was pulling out of the parking spot and she stopped to talk, not sure enough of her driving skills to talk behind the wheel of a moving vehicle.

"Rosie, can you get your family together and meet me at your place tonight?" Leony sounded odd.

"What's up? I've seen the papers, if it's about Brad. I'm okay."

"It's not about Brad. I need to tell you all something, and it has to be in private, and in person."

Rosie smiled. Leony and Cheeto were going to make an announcement. She was surprised that Cheeto had let Leony make the call, since he loved to be first to tell. "Sure. Should I chill the champagne?"

"No." Leony hung up.

Rosie stared at the silvery little phone. "Well, okay, Miss Touchy." She turned to Tootie, who was strapped into her doggie seat belt. "Girl, you'd better be glad you're fixed. Romance is hell."

Leony sat in the armchair opposite Rosie and Abuela, who occupied the comfy new sofa that had arrived that day. Cheeto slouched in the other armchair, his back to the glass wall that showed the vibrant Atlanta skyline against the night sky.

Rosy wondered why Leony hadn't chosen the sofa so that she and Cheeto could sit together.

Abuela glanced at her watch as Leony went through some papers from a file. "I hope this doesn't take long. I have a card game in an hour."

Leony glanced up, her face grim. She shot a look at Cheeto, who smiled at her. She didn't return the smile. Something was wrong if her ever-cheerful assistant didn't respond to Cheeto.

And if Cheeto was cheerful and she wasn't, maybe Rosie had gotten this all wrong. She sat up straight. "What's up, Leony?"

Leony bit her lip. "I don't know how to say this gently, and I don't want you to hear it from the cops." She looked at each of them. "You're broke. All the money is gone."

The three of them stared at the young woman.

"That's not funny," Cheeto said.

"Mr. Pujol's been gone for a while, right? And no one can find him?" Leony said. "Well, he's not on vacation. He's embezzled all of your money."

That got their attention.

"How do you know?" Rosie had to raise her voice to be heard over Cheeto's and Abuela's exclamations.

"The FBI called me," Leony said. "When was the last time any of you heard from Mr. Pujol?"

"I talked to him just before Christmas," Abuela said.

"Last time was when I had that run-in with the law." Cheeto sat up. "Is he really missing? Should we call the cops?"

"The police have been called." Leony met Rosie's eyes.

A dozen TV-inspired scenarios swirled through Rosie's mind. "Is he dead?"

Her assistant shook her head. "You're going to wish he was. He's gone. His apartment's empty, and so's his bank account." Leony took a deep breath. "So are yours."

It took a second for her words to sink in. "My bank account?" Rosie frowned. "He took my money?"

"He sacked all of your bank accounts, and your trust, too. Even the foundation. He filed phony papers." Leony glanced down at her papers. "One hundred and seventy-five million dollars so far."

"One hundred and seventy-five million . . ." Cheeto was on his feet. "Of my . . . of our money?"

"Yes. And maybe more. They're still investigating. I'm sorry," Leony said. "I wanted to tell you myself. I discovered it when I was doing Rosie's accounts. I got an insufficient funds notice from the bank, and I thought there was a mistake. The bank investigated, and then they called in the police."

"How come we weren't notified earlier?" Abuela asked.

"I'm the primary contact, after Mr. Pujol. He didn't foresee that Rosie would hire me." Leony handed each of them copies of the papers she'd pulled from the file. "Here are copies of the foundation's financials. And Rosie, here are your bank account and brokerage statements."

The three of them examined their papers silently. It was all gone. If Pujol took the money he was probably someplace far away. "Can you call the brokerage house to free up some cash? I wanted to go back to Playa Tierna in a couple of weeks."

Leony bowed her head, then looked up, lips pressed tightly together. "You can't, Rosie. You can't afford it."

"But the stocks—"

"He took everything. When he first set up the accounts he left himself a back door on every one of them. When you hired me I saw some strange transactions, and I've been trying to figure out what was going on. I guess I got too close and he ran."

"Why didn't you stop him?" Abuela leaned forward, brows together.

"I didn't have access to all of the accounts to see the details.

And the foundation was set up by Dr. Sloane. She's missing, too."

Rosie sat back, stunned. She'd trusted them, and they'd robbed her.

"There's more, Rosie," Leony said. "You have pending civil suits. You won't be able to afford the taxes on your condo and the yacht."

"But the *MegaBucks* is paid for. It's mine."

"The yacht is yours, but upkeep costs and taxes are high. You should consider selling it. Even then, I'm not sure how much will be left from the sale." Leony's honey-colored complexion had faded to a sallow paleness.

"Even if I only have a little bit left it'll still be more than a few million, right? I can live with that." Rosie was angry at the loss, but unafraid. "I still won't be poor."

Abuela shook her head. "I gave a lot of money to the church, and paid off my friends' medical bills. I know those transactions went through. You say that the foundation is in trouble?"

"The foundation has no money."

"Damn!" Cheeto smashed his fist into the wall, denting the wallboard. He turned to them. "I'm sorry." He shook his head, as if he was going to say something else, then raced out of the apartment.

Rosie jumped up. "Cheeto, wait. Where are you going?" The door crashed shut behind him.

In the living room, Abuela and Leony were on their feet.

"He's probably gone home," Abuela said, hugging her. "He'll be okay."

"I hope so." If reckless driving caused a wreck he'd be safe in his Hummer. And anyone who wanted to sue would be out of luck.

She pulled away from Abuela. "Leony, thanks for telling us. I know this was hard."

Leony glanced quickly at Abuela, then back at Rosie. "You know you can't afford me, either, but I'll see this through before I get another job."

Rosie nodded her thanks, not trusting her voice. She walked her former assistant to the door, then found Abuela on the phone with her own assistant.

She dialed Brad's number. She may as well break the news to him now. The phone rang several times, then went to voice mail. Rosie hung up without speaking.

Brad Merritt wanted to be in bed by nine o'clock, but the wrap party was still going strong at ten. He felt old after all the punishingly long days. To get the most out of the light he'd been in the makeup chair before dawn each day for three weeks, but tomorrow he'd be on a plane back home, and then he'd see if Rosie was up for receiving an early birthday present.

He'd wondered what to give the woman who could buy anything she wanted, and he'd hit on the perfect gift. When he finally got back to his trailer, he went to bed without turning his phone back on. He wanted to make sure he got a good night's rest, which wouldn't happen if the phone was on, especially since Lani Prester had gotten the number. His agent said the press was full of rumors that he'd gone into rehab, too. He hoped Rosie didn't believe all the crazy stories.

Leony's words echoed in the loft hours after she'd left. *Everything's gone.*

Every penny of the cash they'd had in the bank. The money for the foundation. Armando Pujol had fled with millions.

Outside, the jewel tones of the skyline lights seemed out of place. What would she do? The loft was paid for, but the taxes alone were more than she used to make.

Rosie needed a job. She pulled a notebook from a drawer of her desk and started to make a list, her automatic reaction to a new project, one that she'd learned from Leony.

Number one on the list became "sell the loft." Tears pricked her eyes as she wrote. She steeled herself, then added "sell the *MegaBucks*." A hot tear tickled its way down her cheek. She'd have to tell Manny. He'd worked so hard to learn how to captain the big yacht. Maybe his new skills would let him get a new position quickly.

She still had the diamonds, her Lexus, and the marina in Apalachicola. That's where she'd go, where no one knew her.

The phone on the wall sang and Abuela answered it and listened. "No," she whispered. Her hand flew up to cover her mouth.

Rosie was at her side in an instant. "What's wrong? Is it Cheeto?"

Abuela met her eyes and nodded. "I'm sorry, *niño.* Come back to Rosie's apartment. Let's plan what to do next."

She hung up and turned to Rosie, her face crumpled. "There was a letter waiting at his house. The bank is taking it back. That *diablo* Pujol promised your cousin that he would make all the payments, so Enrique foolishly gave him access to his accounts."

The Lotto Palace, foreclosed on. Rosie sat down hard on the armrest of her couch. "I think he might make the tabloids at last." The tabloids. Oh no. Rosie swiveled and slid off the armrest and onto the couch. The papers would be full of their humiliating fall. Imagination produced a likely headline, "Lotto Attorney Dupes Gullible Lottery Winners, Swindles Millions."

Abuela patted her shoulder. "Don't look so sad. We still have a lot of money."

"No we don't. Legal fees and taxes are going to eat up everything that's left. And don't forget the lawsuits still pending." She wanted to curl up in a ball until all the troubles went away.

"We'll figure it out, *nena*. We were poor before. If it's really bad, we can get jobs again." Her grandmother spoke lightly, but her tone was serious.

A job? Rosie sat up. "What can I do? I'm not trained to do anything. I spent my money on diamonds and trips and parties, and now that I have nothing, I'm going to have to go back to being a junior receptionist. I could have gone to college."

To her surprise, Abuela laughed. "You can still do that."

"I will, too. I'll get Leony to—" She stopped. She couldn't ask Leony to do anything. She couldn't afford her.

"Don't be so hard on yourself. We had enough money to

allow us to do what we wanted for the rest of our lives." Abuela read her face as easily as she read the *Financial Times*. "I'll make us a *cafecito*," she said gently.

Rosie remembered when Abuela had said those words in her apartment, after Rosie and Cheeto had just announced their lottery win.

Rosie didn't believe that Cuban coffee was the emotional cure-all her grandmother thought it was. The thought of losing Leony's help was painful, but another, deeper one loomed. Brad.

Would he still want her if she wasn't his financial equal? They had nothing in common except for their humble beginnings, and Rosie was headed toward a humble end. She wouldn't hide, though. She would confront him with the truth, and if he turned from her, she would know that what she felt for him was one-sided, and it wouldn't have worked out, not seriously. Maybe it was a good thing that she hadn't reached him.

Cheeto returned thirty minutes later, giving Abuela reason to brew more super-caffeinated coffee. At this rate Rosie would never sleep, not that she would have anyway.

They sat around Rosie's dinner table. No one spoke, their minds no doubt spinning, as hers was, in an endless list of lost joys, missed opportunities, and plain old shock.

Cheeto broke the silence. "If I ever find that *pendejo,* I'm going to kill him."

"Hush. You wouldn't do that," Abuela scolded. "And watch your language."

"Sorry." Cheeto poured himself another Cuban coffee and

doctored it with his usual pile of sugar, stirring it into black syrup. "So what are we going to do?"

"What Leony said to do. Nothing for now." Rosie sipped her own cooling coffee. It looked like *nothing* might be exactly what she'd have left.

CHAPTER SEVENTEEN

✶ ✶ ✶ ✶ ✶ ✶

Choose your advisors wisely, then trust
them to do what's right, but have a system
of checks and balances just in case.
—*The Instant Millionaire's Guide to Everything*

Diamond Rosie Broke! Assets Gone,
Suspect Attorney Flees
—*Star* magazine

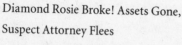

The three of them met with the FBI and the city and county police, their bankers, and their stockbrokers. The final tally was heartbreaking, and the news was too big to stay out of the media. Rosie's loft, the Ritz where Abuela still kept a suite, and the Lotto Palace were all staked out by TV trucks and photographers, and the headlines were more detailed every day.

"The foundation staff knows they're history. They're packing up," Cheeto announced the next week when the three of them met at the Ritz. "There's a company that will buy all the office equipment and resell it. They'll pay a fraction of its worth, of course, but it'll be done."

Abuela blew her nose, but Rosie was beyond tears. She was angry.

"That won't be necessary," she said. "I have a plan." She'd been thinking about their situation ever since they'd discovered what was left.

Cheeto had taken the hardest hit, since Pujol had the most access to his money, and the foundation was an unfunded fake. The Chamber of Commerce's holiday party funds had come straight from Cheeto's bank account. With the Lotto Palace repossessed, he had nothing.

Abuela had no cash left, but a small account she'd opened to help out a friend who was starting a career as a stockbroker had sheltered six hundred thousand dollars.

Rosie had the most. With the sale of the *MegaBucks*, which had a buyer within hours of the announcement of their predicament, she had almost thirty million dollars, plus the loft, which was worth almost two million.

"Let's hear your plan. I'm not looking forward to spreading pine straw for a living." Cheeto sipped an iced tea.

"You won't have to." Rosie consulted her notebook. "My plan is to give Cheeto enough money from what I got to start a landscaping business, a big one. You can buy your old boss's company and add to it, and I'll give you enough of a cushion to run it for five years, until you can be profitable. You'll have to hire Leony to do your company finances."

Cheeto grinned. "I like it. She can be my CFO."

"You don't have to give me money, *nena*," Abuela said. "I have my six hundred thousand, plus, Marco will take care of me."

"You'll move to Argentina?" Cheeto's brows rose in dismay.

"We'll live in Argentina several months of the year, but we both like to travel, and we love to cruise. We'll still visit. And you can come to stay with us whenever you want."

"Congratulations, Abuela." Rosie jumped up and hugged her grandmother. Cheeto did, too, but he moved more slowly.

"He'd better treat you right," he grumbled.

Abuela laughed and patted his cheeks. "He will. I'll see to it."

"Let me finish telling you my plans, then," Rosie said. "Leony helped me put this together, so I know it'll work."

"Shoot," Cheeto said, sitting down again.

Abuela leaned forward attentively.

"The rest of the money I have left I'm giving to the foundation, and we'll set it up properly this time."

The papers had gone on and on about the promise the foundation had held for the city, and how it had all fallen apart. The Caballero name had taken a beating.

Abuela frowned. "What will you do for money? You didn't mention what you get out of this."

"I get the old forty-foot yacht that came with the marina in Apalachicola when I bought the *MegaBucks*. Manny can run the marina, and we'll fix up the boat and rent it out for weekend cruises." She grinned at her grandmother. "I got the idea from you."

"What about your loft?"

"I'll sell it, too. With the *MegaBucks* sale and the loft, that should be just enough to get the foundation where it was before. And I'll keep enough to go to college and get a business degree."

Cheeto nodded thoughtfully. "College sounds good. Maybe I'll go, too."

"If you do, Marco will pay for it. For you too, Rosie." Abuela clapped her hands. "This is a good plan."

Rosie was glad that her family had approved, but she felt as if she was losing her freedom, item by item. Selling the *MegaBucks* had been painful, selling the diamonds had made her cry, but when real estate agents started bringing potential buyers through the loft, she moved to the Ritz.

All of them had read about the theft and knew why she was selling. She couldn't stand the curious eyes, or the idea that people were poking through her closets and touching her belongings.

Even the Ritz felt too public. Rosie's anxiety grew until finally she dialed the emergency number from the list that had been by the kitchen phone. She had to get away, and she knew just whom to ask for help.

The phone rang three times, before someone picked up.

"Hello? Abuela?" The woman didn't sound like her grandmother.

"Is this Josie Caballero's granddaughter?"

"You mean Josefa?"

"We call her Josie. Josefa is so clunky."

Rosie and Josie. They could have a Cuban talk show—like Dr. Phil, but with lots of hugs, recipes, and nagging.

"Is she there? I need to speak to her."

"Sure." The sound muted as if someone was loosely covering the receiver. "Hey, Josie! You aren't going to believe who's on the phone for you."

"Give me that, you old pirate." A loud squeal followed.

Rosie sat up straight. Her grandmother had never made a sound like that before.

"Hello? Who's there?" Abuela sounded like herself, but brighter.

"It's Rosie."

"*Querida,* I wondered when I'd hear your voice again."

"You heard my voice last week, when you left."

"Oh, that's right." Her grandmother giggled. "It's Tequila Tuesday and we've had two pitchers of margaritas already."

A voice in the background said, "Three."

"Was it three? No, we had one with breakfast, and we just finished this one. Oh, here comes another one. Three it is."

"Do they have a chapter of AA on board?" The old folks were out of it and it wasn't even noon.

"They probably do. They have everything on this ship. I keep telling you to come on one of these cruises, they're so much fun! Marco says he'll pay for your flight."

"I'm ready. I have to get away from Atlanta."

"*Ay, mi amor,* you're coming out now? That's wonderful." She turned her mouth away from the phone. "She's coming out now."

"With what, a rowboat?" Much geriatric laughter. Rosie rolled her eyes.

"Must be tough to travel with so many comedians. What should I pack?"

"All your nice things. Will it take you long to pack?"

"I'm good." Rosie glanced at the stack of suitcases that she'd filled when she emptied out the closets of her loft.

"See you soon then, *querida*."

"I love you, Abuela. See you soon." And thank God there weren't any tabloids on the cruise.

Marco's staff had arranged the flight and two days later she was on the plane to Guadeloupe, where she would board the *Island Princess* when it docked that night.

The airport in Guadeloupe was frighteningly small, but since it was dark beyond the runway lights, it didn't look so bad.

A car was waiting for her, thanks to Marco, and the driver, a dapper young guy, talked all the way to the ship, which was beautiful, sleek and brightly lit, and much smaller than the floating city blocks that docked in Miami.

A white-uniformed man took her luggage from the car trunk, or as the driver called it, the tronc.

She walked up the gangway; grateful for the darkness that masked how far up they were from the bay. Even with the covered sides, she could see scary glimpses of water glinting below.

A couple strolled by on the deck, the man in black tie, the woman in silvery sequins. Abuela had told her to pack all of her old glitz, and she had.

"Where's my grandmother's stateroom?"

The porter smiled. "Madam Caballero has a suite on the top deck."

"I hope there's an elevator. I thought this was the top deck."

"Oh, no, ma'am, there are two more levels above this one."

"But no mall, right?"

"That is correct. This ship is very exclusive. There are only two hundred passengers on board."

"I heard that." They'd stopped in front of a brass elevator. She heard applause from the other side of the lobby area.

The porter noticed her reaction. "There is a very good dance troupe performing onboard tonight."

Her grandmother was probably enjoying the performance.

The elevator doors whooshed open and she entered, followed by her luggage. She was glad that she had the opportunity to use the etiquette she'd learned a year ago. Now she didn't offer to carry it herself, and she knew just how much to tip.

She slipped her hand into her leather bag and felt for the individually folded bills she put there for tips. She teased out several to give to the porter.

The hallway was wide, with beautifully sculpted and colored carpeting. It was beautiful, and didn't look anything like she'd imagined.

The door opened, and Abuela was there, draped in flowing chiffon. "*Mi niña*, you're here."

She hadn't realized that she'd missed her grandmother so much. In a second her arms were around the older woman, enjoying her familiar scent, and warmth.

She had tears in her eyes when she stepped back. She sniffed. "I'm sorry, Abuela. I don't know what's gotten into me."

Abuela scrutinized her. "You're too thin, and you have circles under your eyes. You're not pregnant, are you?"

"Of course not. I just need a rest. Where do I sleep?"

"This way." Her grandmother moved with youthful grace

and Rosie followed, with the porter bringing up the rear, loaded with luggage.

Abuela had a huge suite with a private balcony, all done in earth tones, with hints of metallic gold and blue. The living room area had three small black lacquer tables set up with decks of cards on them.

"Ah, the scene of the crime. Were you playing cards tonight?"

"Earlier. I was headed to dinner, but I can wait for you to come with me." She stopped. "Unless you'd rather eat up here."

Rosie didn't want to dress for dinner, or even make conversation with strangers, but she didn't want to disappoint Abuela, who'd wanted her to join her on a cruise since they'd won the lottery. It was ironic that she was finally on board after they'd lost everything. Thank God for Marco.

"This is your bedroom, baby." Abuela pulled back a blue curtain to expose a contemporary bedroom as nice as the one she'd had at her loft in Atlanta.

A curved maple counter faced the bed, and above it hung a wide LCD TV screen. Rosie didn't try the mattress; afraid she'd sink into it and never come back up. She wanted to curl up and sleep for days.

She'd sleep later. She tipped the porter and found the suitcase that held her evening clothes, then showered, put a little eye makeup on, some spritz in her hair, and she was done. She chose a simple slip dress and high-heeled shoes that made her feel beautiful, and then pulled aside the blue curtain that separated her room from the rest of the suite.

Abuela was on the balcony, a slight breeze ruffling her golden hair. Rosie joined her, cautiously. She put a hand on the wood-and-brass railing and looked down.

It wasn't bad. The view was spectacular, but the balcony was only twenty feet above the next level.

"*No tengas miedo*. There's nothing to be afraid of." Abuela lifted her face to the moonlight. "Isn't it beautiful?"

"It is." A few feet away the palm fronds on the shore rattled in the salt-tinged breeze, reminding her of the beach in Mexico. Her chest hurt. She wondered what Brad was doing today. They'd have finished shooting by now. Maybe he'd be in the trailer he'd described to her. It had a queen-sized bed, and a commercial espresso machine.

"Let's go, before they start without us." Abuela took her arm, and they left the stateroom.

"When does the canasta begin?"

"You don't have to play, *querida*. I thought you'd enjoy the time off."

Rosie was relieved. Card games sounded like too much mental effort, especially playing against seasoned experts like Abuela's friends.

The restaurant, like the rest of the ship, was tastefully decorated. Only half of the tables were filled, and the guests were all dressed in the latest styles. Abuela's crowd was fashionable.

"Remember me, Rosie? Carlos from the *bodeguita* on North Druid Hills Road." A man of about Abuela's age leaned over his dinner companion's hand to take hers. He had salt-and-pepper hair and a small beard, and his teeth had been straightened and whitened. He looked pretty good.

She stared for a second, then her smile widened. "Of course. You look great. Having fun?"

He winked. "You bet. Your grandmother is a classy lady, and she takes good care of her friends."

The woman between them leaned back farther and Carlos leaned in. He was almost in her lap. His date, the leaned-upon woman, was a voluptuous redhead wearing a major boob top, sequined and dipped so low in front that her breasts seemed to hover in the air by themselves.

By midnight Rosie was ready for bed, though the oldsters were just getting their second wind. Abuela was dancing with her fiancé, and Carlos and his fiery redhead had run, giggling, out of the ballroom ten minutes earlier.

The dance floor was still choked with couples and the casino crowded with gamblers. She felt very alone, a familiar sensation.

Time for bed, she thought. Time to close my eyes and put this behind me.

A uniformed crewman stopped her to say that she had a call waiting. It was Cheeto.

"I looked everywhere for you," he said, peeved. "You didn't answer your cell phone."

"That's because we're out in the middle of the Caribbean." She hesitated. "I'm with Abuela, although you probably knew that."

Cheeto hooted. "Yeah, I heard you were with the *viejitos*. Girl, what made you do that? You must be desperate."

She held the phone at arm's length and took deep breaths so that he wouldn't hear her sob.

"You there, Rosie?"

"I'm here."

"Listen, I called because I want you to hear the news first, since I owe you. I totally did you wrong New Year's Eve."

"I agree."

"Sitting down?"

"Yes." She wasn't, but she wanted him to get on with it.

"Leony and I are getting married."

"Oh my God." She started jumping. "Can I tell Abuela? She's not going to believe it. Congratulations. Is Leony there? Can I talk to her?" She had a million questions.

Cheeto laughed. "No, you can't tell Abuela. I want to. And Leony went out. She didn't want to tell you yet."

"I'll make her pay for that. So when are you going to tell us, officially?"

"Soon. Play some canasta, take naps, whatever. But don't drink with the old guys. They're horny as hell and they all have hollow legs."

The mental picture made her cringe. "I don't want to learn how you know that."

"Just believe it. And after this, we're even. You fixed my money situation, I rescue you from the Denture Cream Cruise."

"They're not that bad, Cheeto. They're kind of cute."

"Stay away from alcohol."

"Right."

"So when are you going to touch land again?"

"The day after tomorrow we dock in St. Anges. It's this flea-speck of an island, but they have a pretty town and we're going bicycling." She waited for the laughter.

Cheeto didn't disappoint. "Girl, you need to get laid or something. Just don't do it on that ship."

"Now that's a promise I can make. Tell Leony I said hi. I'll keep your secret."

As she waited for the elevator to take her to her stateroom, she admired the view from the balcony. It was hard to tell where the sky ended, and the black ocean seemed to be filled with brilliant stars.

The elevator doors opened behind her and a crewman wheeled out a cart full of liquor bottles. Cheeto was right. This crowd liked to drink. Feeling older than Abuela's friends, she went upstairs and got ready for bed. She was used to sleeping alone, but tonight she found herself thinking of Brad as she punched her over-sized pillow into submission. If she ever saw him again, she'd tell him exactly what she thought of him.

She was done calling him. It was his turn. She gave the pillow one more smack, just because.

CHAPTER EIGHTEEN

Remember that, after all, it's only money.
—*The Instant Millionaire's Guide to Everything*

Lani Prester's Secret Baltimore Marriage to
Long-Time Dentist Boyfriend
—*Star* magazine

At breakfast the next morning, Rosie kept her word and didn't mention Cheeto's news, although she was dying to tell Abuela about the secret engagement.

Her grandmother wore a turban today, like an old-fashioned movie star. "I think this cruise is going very well. We've only had one incident."

Rosie's fork hovered over her fruit plate. "What kind of incident?" Probably something medical.

"Rosemarie Lipton slept with Maria Montenegro's husband. You met him the other night. We call him Monty."

"Little guy, bad rug?"

Abuela giggled. "That's him. I don't know what Rosemarie was thinking." She dropped her voice to a whisper. "Actually, the rumor is—"

Rosie dropped her fork and stuck her fingers in her ears. "Don't want to hear it, don't want to hear it."

Abuela sat back. "You are such a prude."

"I am not. But I want no stray and disgusting mental images of Monty floating in my brain."

"As you wish. Let's get our nails done. Then we'll look nice for the dancing tonight."

The "life is short" thought returned to her later, when the sun grew harsh and she withdrew under a crisp white awning with her book and a cold drink. Now that she had no money, this interlude seemed sweeter.

If this were all she ever did for the rest of her life, she'd be content. Too bad. She'd have to find work soon. Her old dead-end job had been easy compared to the endless meetings at the Caballero Foundation, which would now hum along without her. She'd sold everything but the marina and the old clunker boat to make the foundation strong again.

She couldn't part with the marina. Manny was fixing it up, making sure everything was ready, and Ted had quit driving and retired to Apalachicola to help run the business.

At least out here she was away from the photographers and reporters, and the afternoons were uneventful. The evenings made up for it, thanks to Abuela and her wacky friends.

She was asleep when the ship slipped into its berth on the deepwater piers of St. Anges Bay, and she awoke to a breeze that brought the unmistakable green scent of tropical vegetation.

The bustle of island life floated in through the stateroom windows, and light leaked through the slats of the wooden blinds. From shore, men's voices drifted up, the cries of vendors mixed with the noise of boat engines and cars.

Feeling much better, she took a quick shower, dressed in shorts and sandals, and went out to explore. One of the crew was at the end of the gangway, sorting out passengers and bicycles. Behind them the hills were covered in stucco houses with bright red roofs.

He smiled at her and waved her toward a gleaming yellow cruiser. "You want this one?"

"Sure." She had no intention of following the oldsters around. She wanted to explore on her own. A perky island guide set off with the bikers behind her. Some peddled smoothly, others wobbled until they gained speed and straightened out.

Rosie followed them for two blocks, then veered off down a side street working to keep the bike upright on the cobblestones. She passed shop windows full of colorful merchandise, and as she rode her muscles seemed to remember the skills needed to make quick moves, necessary as she approached a crowded market square.

She hopped off the bike when there were too many pedestrians to move forward easily. She glanced at her watch. Only half an hour had passed, but she needed to turn around soon or she wouldn't have time to make it back to the ship.

A table displaying beaded necklaces drew her eye and she admired a knotted, beaded choker. Brief haggling brought the price down a little, and she paid for it then turned her bright yellow bike around to face the other way. A man stepped off the curb across the street from her and she froze. It was Pujol, and he was climbing into a car.

For a second she stared, unmoving. It couldn't be. Pujol had fled the country, but why come here? She jumped onto the bike and followed the car, peddling in its pedestrian-free wake. At least here the cobblestones had given way to asphalt. She hoped Pujol didn't turn around and notice her, although the driver surely would.

They'd traveled another four blocks before the man behind the wheel glanced into his rearview mirror and locked eyes with her. She saw the reflection's mouth move, and then Pujol was on his knees looking back at her, eyes wide as a frightened rabbit's.

The car leaped ahead, gaining speed as they left the narrow lanes of the inner town and climbed to the countryside. Rosie pedaled furiously, but she was starting to lose ground. She should have brought a cell phone.

As if reading her mind, Pujol put a phone to his ear and spoke, mouth moving rapidly. She couldn't read lips. The car made a rapid right turn, and Rosie nearly laid the bike down as she followed suit.

A persistent grumbling behind her made her glance back. An open-air jeep followed, a man standing in the backseat, holding on to its single roll bar.

The jeep gained speed. They were going to hit her. She glanced back again. The standing man had a gun, and it was aimed at her. She turned back around to see Pujol on his knees once more, laughing at her.

He saluted her. A jolt pushed her bike forward, and then the front wheel slid sideways and she was falling.

The airport seemed to be deserted. Brad didn't expect luxury, but would a taxi stand be too much to ask? The runway ended in the blue water, and he could see a town on the other shore. Maybe he could swim across, or flag down one of the ski boats that were crisscrossing the little bay.

Leony was on her cell phone, as usual. Rosie's cousin was bent over next to the plane, hands on his knees.

"You okay, buddy?" Brad called out.

Cheeto waved a hand, head still down. "That. Was. Like. Riding. A. Corkscrew."

"It's a volcanic island. The runway's really short." Brad smacked Cheeto's back. "You'll be okay. We'll take the ferry back to St. Joe's after we find Rosie."

"Hey guys, come on." Leony stood next to a rusty Chevy Malibu. The keys dangled from her fingers and she held up a sheet of paper in her other hand. "I found this note under the windshield wiper. This is our car."

"This place is definitely far from the U.S, if you can leave cars with the keys on the hood." Brad looked at the tropical foliage that lined the landing field. "No coffee service, I guess."

"I'd settle for a glass of water and an aspirin." Cheeto straightened and got a good look at the sparkling inlet that opened out into the deeper blue of the Caribbean. "I hope we can get some fishing in."

Leony dumped her overnight bag into the backseat, where it fell with a solid thump. "Cheeto, I don't think Brad's after the fish on this trip."

Brad grinned at her. "I don't want to be obvious. Maybe I should do some fishing, for protective cover."

"You won't impress the girl that way." Leony put on her oversized sunglasses. "Let's go."

Brad climbed behind the wheel.

"Shotgun." Cheeto jumped in next to him, his duffel crackling oddly.

"What do you have in there?" Leony demanded. "Did you pack clothes?"

"Underwear," Cheeto said defensively. "And some snacks in case we get hungry." He turned to Brad. "I think this might turn out to be a good idea. Let's check out the beach."

"Right. The man wants to prove to Rosie that the stuff in the papers was all bullshit, and you want to go to the beach." Leony leaned forward. "Brad, you'd better aim this car to the docks of Plein Lune." She glanced at her watch. "We'll have just enough time to get there before the bike tour gathers."

"I don't think Rosie's ridden a bike since she was fourteen." Cheeto had his face against the window glass, staring despondently at the glimpses of water as they climbed the big greenery-covered hump of the dormant volcano.

Plein Lune, the deepwater harbor that was home base to the cruise ships, was on the other side.

They crested the mountain and then started down the other side, the weariness of the long, inconvenient trip forgotten as they neared their goal.

They drove around the winding road that hugged the coast and soon saw the sleek white ship that had to be the one Abuela and Rosie were on.

"It's not very big," Leony said. "Is it really a cruise ship? I thought those were all floating skyscrapers."

"This is an exclusive one. Abuela's fiancé owns part of the company that runs it." Cheeto seemed impressed.

Brad glanced at him. "Your grandmother's getting married?"

"Maybe. It's one reason our arrangement worked out so well. Marco's going to take care of Abuela, and she's still got a little something of her own. Watch out."

A horse stood in their lane. Brad swerved to avoid it, throwing Cheeto and Leony against their doors.

"That was a horse." Cheeto looked back through the rear window.

"They keep saddle horses up here for the tourists to ride on the beach. The locals ride in trucks or scooters." Leony grinned at him. "I read the brochure on the plane while you snoozed."

"I was snoozing in self-defense."

"So what are you going to tell Rosie when you see her?" Leony leaned forward, arms around the headrest so that she could hear Brad's answer.

"I'm going to apologize. Isn't that what all women want to hear?"

Cheeto laughed. "Man, you didn't do anything wrong. You were working."

"Yeah, I know."

"And Rosie knew, and she knows you don't call people up when you're doing movies. You like, bury yourself in the character."

Brad glanced at Cheeto. "How do you know that?"

"I read it in one of Rosie's magazines. She always buys them when they have your pic—Ow!" He turned on Leony. "What did you do that for?"

"What?" She was giving him big eyes.

Brad turned his eyes back to the road. So Rosie liked to read about him. This was very good news. He caught Leony's eyes in the rearview mirror and smiled.

She blushed and turned away. Oh, yeah. What Cheeto had said was true, or she wouldn't be embarrassed. He knew she liked him, maybe more than liked him, but his relationships didn't usually last after long separations. That's why he'd brought Cheeto and Leony along for reinforcement. He might not need them.

Leony's phone rang. Brad heard her snap it open. "Yes? What do you mean, gone? Calm down, Mrs. Caballero."

Cheeto turned around now, frowning.

"We're almost there," Leony continued. "Can you hold the boat? Okay, then. Don't worry, we'll find her."

Good thing he had the steering wheel in his grip. Brad wanted to break something. "What was it? Did she find out I was coming?"

"No." Leony bit her lip. "She joined a bike tour from the ship and got separated, then didn't return."

"Oh, she's okay, then. I thought there was an accident or something." Cheeto leaned back in his seat again. "She's probably worn out from pedaling in these hills and took a break. We just have to find her." He grinned at Brad. "Here's your chance to be a hero."

A jeep swerved from a side street and fishtailed into place in front of them. Brad stepped on the brake, making them all surge forward.

A woman seemed to be lying down in the backseat because he could see her leg come up, poised sexily. Someone should tell her that wearing sneakers was not sexy. The leg suddenly straightened and her foot connected with the knee of the man standing at the roll bar.

He screamed and fell out of the jeep, tumbling into the scrub at the side of the road. A flock of colorful birds erupted from the foliage and crossed over the old Malibu.

"Did you see that?" Cheeto clutched the dash.

The jeep's driver turned; head swiveling back and forth as he tried to see what had happened.

The woman sat up, then stood on the seat, balanced precariously.

"What's she doing? I'm trying to call 911." Leony was pressing buttons on her phone while watching the action.

The woman tried to grab the roll bar, failed, and fell to her knees, the wind pushing her hair into her face. The driver reached back and grabbed her by the neck and tugged her closer. The woman brought up her handcuffed wrists and her hair flew sideways.

Brad cursed as her pain-contorted face was revealed. It was Rosie.

CHAPTER NINETEEN
* * * * * *

When choosing vacation spots,
seek balance between excitement and
relaxation. And always make security a priority.
—*The Instant Millionaire's Guide to Everything*

Diamond Rosie's Caribbean Nightmare—Details Inside!
—*Star* magazine

St. Anges's Police Chief Denies the Island
Harbors Foreign Criminals
—*St. Anges–St. Pierre Gazette*

The jeep turned again, this time heading what seemed like straight up the mountainside, then sideways as it reached a dirt road.

The Malibu swerved after it, then skidded sideways as one of the tires hit the decorative stones that lined the road.

The car slammed into a metal fencepost and stopped. Brad pushed the door open and ran up the road after the jeep.

"Stop, Brad. The police are coming," Leony yelled. Brad couldn't stop. He'd worked out his entire adult life so that he could look good onscreen while pretending to be a hero.

The pain in his legs as he pumped his way up the hill was the real thing. Rosie's danger was real. He saw again the man's fingers pressing into Rosie's neck, the look on her face.

Glossy brown filled his peripheral vision and he realized that the pounding he'd heard was not his heart, but hooves. A young horse was playing with him, pacing him.

Ahead, a trio of horses galloped down the slope, spooked by the jeep that was gaining the junglelike growth at the other end of the pasture.

Brad reached sideways; arm stretched to its utmost, then dared a glance. He'd done this before. He threw himself at the horse, grabbing its mane in his fists, and pulled himself onto its back, praying that the animal wouldn't roll down the hill on top of him.

Rosie was going to die. She'd learned that Pujol was a thief, but now he'd have her death on his head, too. Abuela would avenge her. She'd figure it out.

The fingers in her throat dug deep, and she gasped for air, getting just enough to ensure that this would be a long, painful death.

Already, oxygen deprivation was making her hallucinate. She thought she'd seen Brad and Cheeto driving after them in an old beater.

The jeep swerved and the fingers released her, but then she was thrown to the hard, rough floorboards. Her cheek hit the handcuffs and she cried out at the sudden pain. She'd seen Brad because she loved him. Her brain had concocted him, pulling him up out of her memory cells so that she could see him one last time. She didn't know why she'd seen Cheeto.

She felt pushed against the base of the bench seat, so they were climbing. She opened her eyes and saw that the handcuffs were smeared thickly with blood. Great, now she'd have a scar.

Of course, she would be dead soon, so it wouldn't matter. She lifted her head to see grass flying by. They were in the country, somewhere, still climbing.

A hand grabbed her hair and shook her, smacking her head against the back of the front seat's armrest. That hurt, so much that suddenly she realized she was just lying here taking it. She'd go out fighting, and maybe she'd take one of Pujol's goons with her.

She braced herself with her joined hands, then pushed up so that she was kneeling. The driver glanced back at her and cursed in French and made another grab for her. She ducked and pushed away. She'd gotten a D in French in high school, the only bad grade she'd ever received.

"Let go, creep." Her movement had pushed her up to the seat, and she braced her legs against the jeep's little back door to push herself into the backseat.

The man pulled out a gun and pointed it at her. She could jump off the jeep. Jump and roll, like in the movies. She looked at the rocky pasture whizzing by. Who was she kidding? She wasn't a stuntwoman. She'd break every bone in her body.

So what did she have to lose? He'd shoot her. She'd seen people who'd been shot, back at the apartments. Guys who'd lain in what looked like a quart of blood, then had been back from the hospital three days later.

Before she could think about it too much, she launched herself at the man, fingers out, making the most of her best weapon, her manicure. He screamed and punched her, the gun apparently forgotten.

She finally got a good look at him. Tall and skinny, with bags under his reddened eyes, and long, bleeding stripes on his cheeks where she'd connected. He'd brushed her shoulder with his intended blow and punched the driver's arm instead. The jeep lurched and she fell against the roll bar. She threw her arms up and grabbed it, then stared, astonished, at the sight behind her.

Brad Merritt was galloping after her. Was she already dead? Brad didn't have that competent cowboy look. He looked grim, and very scared.

She remembered the gun and turned back. This asshole was not going to shoot her cowboy.

The horse was fast, and the jeep was hampered by the bad terrain. Rosie was up, face a bloody mess, but he'd seen her attack the man in the passenger seat. She'd seen him, too, and had stared at him with a curiously flat look before an unholy light had taken fire in her eyes.

By the time Brad had drawn close enough to jump, she had the handcuffs around the man's neck and was squeezing.

Brad made a leap for the roll bar and caught it, then swung his legs free from the horse. In the movies the horse would have peeled away to slow down and find a likely patch of grass to crop. This little fighter was keeping up with the jeep for the hell of it.

Rosie's attacker, now her victim, was leaning over the side of the jeep, trying to kick her free. One of his black oxfords connected solidly with the driver's head, and the car suddenly slowed, then veered toward a tree. Brad grabbed Rosie and pushed her down as they hit with an earsplitting crunch of wood and metal, followed by quiet and occasional pings and hisses from the dying jeep.

"Are we alive?" Rosie was horrified when her voice came out in a creaky whistle. Brad's heavy body had her pinned to the floorboards.

"I hope so." Brad pushed a tree branch out of the backseat and got up. The driver was facedown on the steering wheel. Brad put two fingers on his throat, checking for his pulse.

"Is he dead?"

"I don't think so." The other man was gone. Brad got out of the jeep gingerly and hobbled around to the other side. He looked down, then turned his face. "You'd better get out on the other side."

Rosie nodded, then stopped. "He's the one with the handcuff keys."

"Oh." Brad looked down again, shuddered, then bent over. They could hear sirens now, and someone calling their names.

"Cheeto?" She must have sounded as astonished as she felt.

"He came with me. And Leony," Brad said, sounding strained. "Are you sure this guy had the key?"

"I think so. I was knocked out a little when they ran me over."

"They did what?" He reappeared. "I thought you said you were all right."

"I am. I rolled over their hood and ended up on the street, and then ugly there put the cuffs on me and threw me in the backseat. They work for Mr. Pujol." She stopped as she realized that the man who'd stolen their millions had gotten away.

A small platoon of police and onlookers climbed the hill, led by a triumphant Cheeto, and an ambulance was carefully backed up as far as it would go so that the paramedics could carry Rosie down.

She'd wanted to say that she could make it on her own feet, but the sight of the hill they'd climbed changed her mind. Brad looked like he was going to throw up. He was sitting on the back of the open ambulance, waiting for the injured driver to be brought down. With only one emergency vehicle, victim and assailant had to share.

"It's the aftermath of adrenaline. I read that somewhere," Rosie told him. "You get all excited, then afterwards, when you don't need the rush, it makes you feel sick."

"I guess that's true." He was looking from the steep, rocky hill to the smashed jeep to the little brown horse that grazed nearby, peacefully tugging up grass as if he hadn't just chased a car with a crazy cowboy on his back.

"You saved my life," she said softly.

He looked at her, and she could tell that he was seeing the bruises and the blood. She wanted to be beautiful for him, and she hadn't even put on any mascara this morning. She'd lost one of her sneakers in the fight, too.

"You are not going to believe this," Leony said, phone to her ear. She was talking to them. "Your grandmother says that they caught Pujol trying to sneak onto the ship. He's under arrest."

Rosie wanted to ask about the money, but she almost didn't care. The money had only gotten in the way of what she wanted. It was all anyone could think about when she was around.

She met Brad's eyes. "I lost it all."

"Cheeto told me. And you didn't lose it. It was taken from you. He said you fixed him and your grandmother up."

"Pujol." She wanted to spit to get the taste of his name out of her mouth. "Do you think they'll send him back to the United States to stand trial?"

"No. It's probably why he's here." Brad shrugged. "But he's going to be charged with your kidnapping and assault, maybe attempted murder."

"Is that what the cops said, or did you lift that from a movie?"

His gaze never wavered from hers. "Sometimes the movies reflect real life."

"You chased me on a horse." She turned to look at the little brown horse. "Without a saddle or anything. Where's a paparazzo when you need one?"

The unconscious driver was loaded onto the ambulance, looking pitiful. Rosie had to remind herself of how dangerous he was.

She was released from the hospital after a checkup.

"Two stitches in my scalp and an ice bag for my knee," she told Leony, who came to see her in her stateroom on the ship.

The ship's purser had been overjoyed to see Brad Merritt come aboard, and after a heroic rescue, too.

"The dinner bell is ringing. Why don't you two go get something to eat? I'll be okay here," Rosie said. Abuela had not left Rosie's side since she'd arrived at the hospital with Marco.

Cheeto came in. "Hey, *prima*. You look like a special effect from a Tarantino movie."

"Thanks. It's so great to be loved." Rosie would have rolled her eyes, but everything hurt.

Her cousin went to stand behind Leony and put his hands on her shoulders. Her former assistant jumped at this touch. Rosie almost laughed, but Leony's expression was so serious.

"So, is there something you wanted to tell me?"

Leony reached up to touch one of Cheeto's hands. "Now that I'm not working for you, we can tell you our secret. We're getting married."

"Why did you wait? I wasn't standing in your way." And it stung a little that Leony thought she would.

"No, but it wouldn't have been ethical."

"You're going to be my sister." Rosie smiled, wincing a little.

"Cheeto's your cousin," Leony reminded her.

"Yeah, and cousin-in-law sounds weird. He's like a brother, right? I'm so happy for you both." She wondered how long her boisterous cousin and type A former assistant would last. Either five minutes, or forever.

Abuela beamed at them, the glint in her eyes probably the start of wedding plan giddiness, whether Cheeto wanted it or not. At least Leony knew how to defend herself from strong women like her grandmother. And she wouldn't have to worry about Brad. He'd probably be on the next plane back to Wyoming.

Her hero. Which reminded her . . .

"Guys, how did you and Brad figure out that I was in trouble?"

Cheeto glanced up at Leony, who looked away. "We didn't, exactly."

"You didn't?"

"No. Brad talked us into coming down. He wanted to talk to you, and he figured if you were mad at him you'd still talk to him if we came, too."

"Really." That was interesting. Brad had come looking for her, and he'd brought Cheeto and Leony, too? "So where is he?"

"He said he had to get something to show you. He'll be by." Cheeto kissed her forehead and her little family left for dinner.

Rosie closed her eyes and tried to ease the throb in her temples, a pain connected to every fiber of her aching body.

Disappointment gave the aches a sharper edge. She'd expected Brad to come at any moment, and had put on her poker face whenever she heard a noise at the door, and good thing, too. None of her visitors had been the one she'd hoped to see.

The ship's doctor had been a frequent visitor. He wasn't used to the kind of injuries she had, and he was fascinated. She heard him now. She kept her eyes closed, used to the familiar way he entered the room. Now he'd come stand by the bed. His footsteps approached, then stopped by her nightstand. Then he would clear his throat to let her know he was here, and he'd say, "How's our patient?" And she would say, "Better, thanks."

She waited, but he didn't make a sound. Was she looking worse? Maybe he was worried about her.

"Are you faking sleep?"

Her eyes shot open. Brad stood over her. "I thought you were the doctor."

"You fake being asleep for the doctor?"

"No, we just have a little routine. Why didn't you come earlier?"

"You had too many visitors." Brad sat on the edge of the mattress. "I wanted a little privacy."

"Everyone's at dinner." Her voice was husky, but it wasn't because of her injured neck.

"I know." He touched her cheek. "This looks painful."

She shrugged, and grimaced when her shoulder twinged.

"I heard you had some stitches."

"In my scalp." She pointed at her crown. "They shaved a little bit of hair off. I must look like a hippie monk."

He smiled, but it faded quickly. "You had such a close call. What made you follow Pujol by yourself?"

"I didn't know he'd be there. I just wanted to ride a bike by myself, then I saw him. But hey, speaking of 'why did you do that' moments, what made you chase the jeep on a horse?"

"It offered to help." He seemed to be checking her out, his eyes going over her carefully.

"Looking for something in particular?" She knew he was worried about her.

"I just want to know how hurt you are. Take your clothes off."

She grinned, then regretted it. "Okay, you're on. But I need help. And what's my reward?"

"Reward?"

"Yeah, you have to take your clothes off, too."

His troubled look smoothed, and his eyelids drooped. "I think you must feel better than you let on."

"I think maybe you're right."

He pulled his shirt over his head, revealing his toned chest and arms.

The view was stunning.

"I'm sorry I didn't call you." Brad stood over the bed, fingers hooked into the waistline of his jeans. "I owe you an apology."

"The papers said that you were off with some starlet. Why are we having this conversation now? Don't you want to make love?"

"In a bit." He undid the top button of his jeans. She could see the start of that little line of hair that headed straight down to her favorite vacation spot. It was not improving her concentration.

"You don't think we belong together, but I see it differently, Rosie. We're a lot alike."

"Uh-huh. As in, you're world famous and I'm richer than most? Bad news, Brad. I'm not rich anymore."

"It doesn't matter. It's you I love."

Love. Brad Merritt was talking seriously about love.

His hand closed gently around hers. "When I finished the shoot, I went to New York to talk to the stage director."

She lifted her head. "And?"

"And I told him that I wasn't cut out for serious theater."

She stopped to reach for a tissue and pat her eyes dry. The tissue came away smudged with black. Great. She probably looked like a raccoon.

"Are you sure? You won't regret it?"

He put an arm around her. "Sweet Rosie, you told me the absolute truth and I wasn't ready to hear it." He kissed the top of her head. "I've signed on for two more Jack Link films."

She threw her arms in the air and cheered. "I'm so glad. You know how much I love those movies."

He laughed. "Gotta love an enthusiastic fan. I thought of you when I signed. I almost called to tell you."

"Why didn't you?"

He leaned over and kissed her lightly. "Why do you think I'm here? I had to tell you in person.

"I don't want to mess up your life, Rosie. You know that with me, you'll always have the tabloids and the rumors. You have to accept it. The more you fight, the more they love it."

"So?"

"You hate that stuff." His eyes were on her face, trying to read her expression.

"I've learned to deal with it. If anyone recognizes me, I just wave and say hi. You taught me that, and it works."

"That's right, I did." He sat on the bed again, then flicked the straps of her nightie from her shoulders. His smile broadened at the effect. "I think I have some other things to teach you."

"Yeah?" She sounded breathless, but she didn't care. She wanted to see how this movie played out. She was cheering for the heroine.

He touched her breasts with a fingertip, running it lightly over the rounded tops, then around each center.

She closed her eyes. "Don't stop."

"Wasn't planning to." He kissed her again. "Let me know if any of this hurts."

"I'm okay. What's the plan, cowboy?" She closed her eyes, awaiting the next touch.

"Do you have protection?"

Rosie opened her eyes, disappointed. "With one hundred and eight old guys on board and one hundred twenty women vying for them, why would I need any?"

"Don't worry. I brought some." He reached into his pocket.

"Pretty sure of yourself." Rosie held her hand out. "Let me."

"No, I'll put it on you."

"On me?" Her puzzled frown vanished when she saw the ring box in his hand. He opened it, revealing a solitaire with a stone big enough to rate its own tabloid page.

"Gaudy, but real. I want folks to know you're mine, even from across the street." He grinned at the look on her face. "Will you marry me, Rosie?"

She'd sold all of her diamonds. Now she was getting one back. Still, she didn't want to seem too eager over mere jewels. "I'm not sure."

"Not sure?" He pulled an envelope from the back pocket of his jeans. "I wasn't sure you'd say yes, so I have a backup present, without diamonds." He handed her the envelope. "Actually, I bought this for your birthday."

It looked as if it had spent some time in that pocket. She slit it open with her finger and pulled out a sheet of paper. "I hope this is a gift certificate for a massage, because I could really use one." She glanced at the writing, then looked again. It was an official-looking document, all in Spanish.

"What's this?"

He smiled, eyes twinkling. "Try to read it. You'll get it."

She examined it. "It looks almost like a deed." She ran a finger down the typed text until she hit some familiar words. Casa Maravilla, Playa Tierna. "You bought it?"

"I thought we needed to go whenever we want. Efraim and Jana said they'd stay on."

She threw herself into his arms, laughing, then kissed his face all over.

"Rosie, you are definitely the woman for me. The old beach shack thrills you more than the diamond." He laughed and held her tight. "So how about it, Rosie? Will you marry me?"

She looked up at the face that she'd worshiped for so long. The man behind those cerulean eyes was so much more wonderful than she'd ever suspected back when she avidly read every mention of his name in *People* magazine. And now he would be all hers.

She touched his chest, just above his heart. "Cowboy, I thought you'd never ask."

"I think we can leave now, Abuela. It's creepy eavesdropping under their window."

"One moment more, Cheeto. This is so romantic." His grandmother had tears in her eyes. "Rosie's going to get married."

"Yeah? Well, I give them six months."

"Enrique, that is bad luck. You're cursing their good fortune."

"I'm being practical."

"If you were practical, you'd get married, too."

He flipped his sunglasses down and stared at her. "I'm a kid, Abue. I ain't getting married yet." He hugged her. "Don't worry, *viejita*. You'll get your great-grandchildren." He wondered if Leony wanted children. They hadn't discussed it.

He hustled the damp-eyed woman from under the balcony before she noticed that they could hear Rosie and Brad working on the first great-grandchild already. A glance at his watch told him he would just make the deadline for his phone call.

Good thing he had the number programmed into his speed dial. He pulled out his cell phone and checked the signal strength. Perfect. Two buttons pushed and he was connected.

"Hey, Cal, it's Cheeto. How's life at the *Star*? Listen, have I got a story for you. . . ."